KATE RHODES

Crossbones Yard

MULHOLLAND
BOOKS
HODDER

First published in Great Britain in 2012 by Mulholland Books
An imprint of Hodder & Stoughton
An Hachette UK company

1

A CIP catalogue record for this title is available from the British Library

Hardback ISBN 978 1 444 73874 2
Trade Paperback ISBN 978 1 444 73875 9
eBook ISBN 978 1 444 73877 3

Typeset by Hewer Text UK Ltd, Edinburgh
Printed and bound by Clays Ltd, St Ives plc

Hodder & Stoughton policy is to use papers that are natural, renewable
and recyclable products and made from wood grown in sustainable
forests. The logging and manufacturing processes are expected to
conform to the environmental regulations of the country of origin.

Hodder & Stoughton Ltd
338 Euston Road
London NW1 3BH

www.hodder.co.uk

For all the women who lie buried at Crossbones Graveyard

PROLOGUE

Your mother is holding your hand too tightly. You whimper and cling to her dress, because you know what will happen next. She stares at you, as if she's forgotten how to blink. There's one last glimpse of her face before she bundles you into the cupboard under the stairs. 'Don't make a sound,' she hisses, 'don't even breathe.' Darkness smothers you as the key twists in the lock. There's a chance that he won't find you, cowering on the floor, between the broom and floor mops, a stack of wellington boots.

Your father is closer now. Even his footsteps are angry, thudding too hard on the worn lino, while he looks for someone to hurt. He's so close, you can smell him. Whisky mixed with the sickliness of the sherry he hides in the garage, and something else, bitter and hard to identify. Splinters of light needle you through cracks in the door. There's dust everywhere. When you stand up the black skirt of your school uniform will be grey with dirt. Tomorrow he will shout at you when you come down to breakfast. You already know what he'll say. He will tell you you're filthy, you should be ashamed.

The footsteps move further away and you let yourself exhale. Through a knothole in the door you can see into the living room. Your mother is keeping her mouth shut while your father waits for her to move or argue, looking for his excuse. Your mouth is full of dust. You close your eyes and try to swallow. When you open them again your mother is trapped. He's caught her by the tops of her arms, hands flapping against her sides. Your brother is trying to melt into the flowered wallpaper. It's hard to tell what he's thinking, his face frozen in a grimace or a smile. Your father lands punch after punch on your mother's arms and ribs and belly. Tomorrow she will put on lipstick, go to work as usual, the neighbours will never know. But one day, he might go too far. An ambulance will take your mother away and no one will remember to set you free.

Your brother's expression is the thing that frightens you most. Relaxed, as if he's watching his favourite programme on TV. The cupboard is shrinking, in a few seconds the air will have been used up. You want to run into the light, but you must stay there, for as long as it takes. You listen to the dull beat of your father's fists. Your mother is trying not to cry, but sometimes she can't help herself and a breathless moan escapes her. Your brother leans back, making himself comfortable, storing your father's actions in his memory.

The beating sound has stopped, and you know what will happen next. Your father's footsteps are returning. There's no point in crying, because he knows every hiding place. He has stolen the key from your mother's pocket and he won't care how hard you beg. Tears are for cry-babies he says, and when he hits you, it will be harder than before.

I

I peered into the metal box without stepping inside. It had the familiar smell of all hospital lifts, handwash and anti-septic, an undertone of urine and fear. I had only managed the twenty-four-storey journey to the psychology department once, with my eyes closed, holding my breath. It wasn't the speed that got me, just the space itself. Tiny and airless, no windows to escape through. I forced myself over the threshold, keeping the door open with my hand, but panic kicked in immediately, a surge of adrenalin just under my ribcage. My reflection stared at me from the mirrored back wall. My face was white and pinched, eyes glittering with anxiety. I looked like a small blonde child dressed up in her mother's smartest clothes. I backed out of the lift and the doors snapped shut, almost catching my fingers. My only option was to take the stairs, all two hundred and seventy-eight of them. By now the signs on every landing were imprinted on my memory: oncol-ogy, urology, orthopaedics, X-ray. But at least the daily climb was keeping me fit – at a steady pace the ascent took less than six minutes.

I was out of breath by the time I arrived at my consult-ing room, with just a few minutes to spare before the first appointment of the day. I changed out of my running shoes into a smart pair of heels. One of the unwritten rules is that psychologists must be well dressed, to convince their patients that the world is safe and orderly. But I needn't have bothered.

There was a handwritten note on my computer, informing me that my morning appointments had been cancelled, and a police officer would collect me in an hour's time. For a second my legs felt weak. I pictured my brother locked in a holding cell, just like last time, swearing his head off at anyone who tried to question him or bring him a cup of tea. Then I remembered that my name was on the rota for Met duty that week, and my heart rate slowed again.

My inbox was crammed with new emails: an invitation to speak to the British Psychological Society in April, eight GP referrals, dozens of circulars from drug companies offering extravagant bribes. I should have worked on my case notes, but my eyes kept drifting towards the window. The sky was a dull January white, threatening to snow, but the view was still staggering. London Bridge Station laid out like a train set, with half a dozen miniature engines arriving or leaving, and to the east the Thames curving past Tower Bridge to Canary Wharf. Red lights were blinking on the roofs of banks, while the money men cheated at sums. In the opposite direction office buildings lined the river, almost as tall as St Paul's. To a girl from the suburbs it was still the most glamorous view in the world.

Switchboard called just after ten to say that a visitor was waiting for me in reception. When I reached the ground floor an enormous man was standing by the entrance. He was wearing a pale grey suit, and from a distance he looked almost completely round.

'Dr Quentin?' He walked towards me with surprising grace for a man carrying at least twenty stone. 'DCI Don Burns, from Southwark police. Thanks for giving me your time.'

His accent was an odd hybrid of raw south London and genteel Edinburgh. Behind his thick black-rimmed glasses, his eyes were small and inquisitive in the pale moon of his face.

I offered a polite smile in reply, but felt like reminding him that I had no choice. The department was obliged to carry out assessments for the Met whenever a request came in. Any other work, no matter how important, was put on hold.

When we reached the car park, DCI Burns took several minutes to squeeze behind the steering wheel of his drab blue Mondeo. The car smelled of stale coffee, cooking fat and smoke. He must have stopped at McDonald's on his way to work, followed his breakfast with a quick fag.

'I could have walked to the station,' I commented, 'saved you a trip.'

'We're not going there. I'll fill you in on the way.'

He drove south, swearing under his breath at the traffic on Borough High Street. He seemed to have forgotten he had a passenger, completely absorbed in the journey, until we reached the embankment.

'Detective Chief Inspector. That's top rank, isn't it?' I asked.

He kept his eyes fixed on the road. 'Not far off. I look after most of the borough.'

'Quite a responsibility. Couldn't one of your underlings take me?'

'I didn't want them to.' We drove past Battersea Power Station. It looked like a massive table lying on its back, concrete legs pointing at the sky. 'We're going to see Morris Cley. Have you heard of him?'

'Vaguely. He killed someone, didn't he?'

'That's him,' he frowned. 'A prostitute called Jeannie Anderson in Bermondsey four years ago. He gets out of Wandsworth tomorrow because some hotshot lawyer got his sentence cut in half.'

'How come?'

'Unsafe evidence,' Burns sighed, 'which is total bollocks. He managed to con the judge into thinking Cley's got learning difficulties.'

'And he hasn't?'

'No way.' He scowled at the traffic jam ahead. 'Slippery little bastard pretends to be simple, but he kept us running round for weeks. I want to know how closely to watch him when he's out.'

'Sounds like he's not your favourite client.'

'Not exactly. The bloke's as dodgy as they get.' Burns gave the indicator an angry flick, like he would have preferred to snap it off and hurl it through the window. 'Guess who his mum's best mates were?'

'Who?'

'Ray and Marie Benson.'

I couldn't think of a reply. I knew plenty about the Bensons because a friend from the Maudsley had been consultant psychologist during the court case, and Ray and Marie had kept the tabloids happy for months. Pictures of the girls they killed appeared on every front cover, as if they were movie stars. Some of them were found under the patio of the hostel the Bensons ran off Southwark Bridge Road. One in the garden, another sealed inside a disused chimney, and a few more dumped on waste ground. Anyone who could read or owned a TV knew more than they wanted to about the couple's grisly recreational activities.

Wandsworth Common appeared in the car window. Women were pushing prams along the footpaths, joggers running slow laps round the perimeter, like there was all the time in the world.

'Ever visited Wandsworth before?' Burns asked.

'I haven't had the pleasure.'

'Paradise,' he muttered. 'Sixteen hundred blokes, high as kites on every drug under the sun.'

The prison looked like a cross between a Gothic castle and a Victorian workhouse, with filthy windows and a gate big enough to drive a juggernaut through. It was so vast it blotted out most of the sky.

'Welcome to England's biggest clink.' Burns flashed his ID at the entrance and we were waved inside.

The interview room was miles along a corridor that must have been white once upon a time. I was beginning to regret the clothes I'd chosen that morning. My skirt was too tight to take a proper stride, and my high heels clattered on the tiled floor like a pair of castanets. Rivulets of sweat were pouring down Burns's face.

'He's in the Onslow Centre,' he puffed, 'for his own protection. The bloke won't be getting many bon voyage cards tomorrow.'

'How did he kill the girl?' I asked.

'There's no nice way to put it.' Burns wiped his face with a large white handkerchief. 'Basically, he shagged her, then smothered her with a pillow.'

'They were in a relationship?'

'Christ, no.' He looked appalled. 'He says they were, but you'll see why not when you clap eyes on him.'

'I can hardly wait.'

Burns pushed his glasses up the bridge of his nose with a stubby index finger. 'She looked a bit like you, actually.' His gaze rested on me. 'Petite, green eyes, shoulder-length blonde hair.'

'You mean, I'm his type?'

'I'm afraid so, yeah.'

Footsteps grew louder in the corridor. I've always hated prisons. Everything about them makes me want to run for the door, especially the way sounds carry. You can hear keys twisting in locks half a mile away. When Morris Cley was shown into the interview room I could see why he had to pay for sex. Grey hair jutted from his skull in awkward tufts, and everything about his face was slightly wrong. Heavy eyebrows lowered above eyes that had sunk so deep into their sockets that I couldn't tell what colour they were. From the dullness of his skin I guessed that he hadn't been outside for weeks. When we shook hands he held my fingers for a few seconds too long. His touch was clammy, and it made me desperate to run outside, find somewhere to scrub my hands.

'Afternoon, Morris,' Burns barked from his seat in the corner of the room.

Cley's thin shoulders were hunched around his ears, his eyes flitting from the floor to the window and back again. He lowered himself on to the plastic chair cautiously, as if it might be booby-trapped.

'I hear you're going home tomorrow,' I said.

'No home to go to.' His voice was high-pitched and breathless.

'Rubbish,' Burns snapped. 'You're going to your mum's.'

'She's dead,' Cley frowned.

'How long ago did you lose your mum?' I asked.

Cley looked confused for a minute, then did a slow calculation on his fingers before answering. 'Five months, one week, two days.'

'I'm sorry to hear that,' I told him.

He studied the backs of his hands, thin fingers twisting into knots.

'What about you, Morris?' Burns's voice was cold enough to freeze anyone in listening distance. 'Are you sorry for what you did?'

The question had an immediate impact. Cley's head slumped over his knees, as if someone had cut the string that held him upright. 'It wasn't me,' he whispered. 'I never touched her.'

'Shut up,' Burns hissed in disgust. 'I'm sick of your rubbish.'

I kept my peace. It was easier to learn about Cley from watching his reactions than asking questions. His whole body was trembling, face still turned to the ground. A tear splashed on to the dirty lino.

'Don't give us any more play-acting, Morris,' Burns groaned. 'I had a bellyful the first time.'

When Cley eventually lifted his head his expression was a mixture of fear and resentment. He looked like a child who would rather run away than face another beating.

'Tell me what happened to you, Morris,' I said quietly.

'Jeannie was my friend, I gave her money sometimes. I wanted her to have nice things.' Cley's falsetto relaxed to a lower pitch as he remembered her.

'How long did you know Jeannie for?'

Cley considered the question carefully before answering. 'A long time. I saw her every week. I asked her to be my girlfriend.'

'And what did she say?'

His head lolled forward again and another fat tear landed on the knee of his grey prison-issue tracksuit. 'She said she wasn't good enough for me.' Cley struggled to regain control, rubbing his eyes with his balled fists.

'But you didn't agree?'

He shook his head violently. 'She loved me. I know she did, because she let me sleep in her bed sometimes.'

Burns gave a loud sigh and Cley's mouth sealed itself. There was a rime of dirt around the collar of his grey top, and I wondered how often he risked using the communal showers. No wonder he was being kept in the secure wing. There might as well have been a neon sign over his head spelling out the word victim. When we got up to leave, his eyes lingered on my face.

'Alice Quentin.' He repeated my name slowly, as if he was doing everything in his power to commit it to memory.

On the way back Burns stopped at a greasy spoon on Wandsworth Road.

'He took a serious shine to you,' he commented. 'You handled him well though. Some of my girls wouldn't stay in the same room, said he gave them the heebie-jeebies.'

He was slugging down a large black coffee and I fought the urge to tell him to lay off the caffeine. The last thing his heart needed was a chemically induced workout. Beads of sweat had gathered on his forehead, as though sitting down was just as exhausting as standing up. The exchange at the prison had taught me more about his personality than about Cley's. Obsessive, struggling to empathise, stress levels hitting the roof.

I stirred sugar into my cappuccino. 'What's Cley's IQ?'

'Less than fifty, but that means bugger all. Playing dumb's his party trick.'

'You told me he didn't have learning difficulties.'

Burns shrugged. 'The little shit probably cheated in the test.'

'But you're positive it was him who killed the girl?'

Burns nodded vigorously, double chins rippling. 'Open and shut: his semen inside her, and bob's your uncle, unanimous guilty verdict.'

'Was there any other proof?'

'He was her last punter.' Burns gave me the long unblinking stare that liars always favour. 'Trust me, it's all there.'

'Right.' I watched him drop his gaze.

'Okay, the case was a bit light on forensics but Cley had no alibi, nothing to defend himself with.'

'So that meant he was guilty?'

'With respect, Dr Quentin, that's water under the bridge. All I need to know is how closely to watch him when he gets out tomorrow.'

'So you can blame me if he kills someone else.'

Burns's small mouth twitched with irritation or amusement.

'Based on a thirty-minute observation I'd say he's got learning difficulties, with the mental ability of a seven- or eight-year-old. Possibly he's clinically depressed, and he's still grieving for his mother, but no, I don't think he's an immediate threat to anyone.'

'You're positive about that?'

'Except to himself, when he realises no one's going to take care of him.'

'My heart bleeds.' Burns took a deep breath then slowly levered himself to his feet.

It was twelve thirty by the time we arrived back at the hospital car park. Burns's beady eyes observed me as I undid my seat belt.

'I'll ask for you again, Dr Quentin.'

'And why's that?'

'Because you don't fuck about.'

'I assume that's a compliment, Inspector.'

'It is. We had some bigwig from the Maudsley last year, for ever reeling out jargon, dazzling us with his intelligence.' His mouth puckered, like he had swallowed something sour.

I watched as Burns's Mondeo wove through the parked cars nimbly. The man behind the wheel could have been an athlete at the top of his game.

I saw three patients that afternoon. One for anger management, an agoraphobic and a girl called Laura with such advanced anorexia that I wanted to admit her immediately, but there were no beds. Six different wards refused to help before a staff nurse finally buckled and agreed to keep one free the following day. After my last appointment, I checked my email. One hundred and thirty-six messages with red flags, screaming for an answer. I could have stayed there until midnight and still not emptied my inbox.

At seven I changed into my running gear and headed for the best part of the day. Soon I was running down the stairs so fast that it felt like flight, vaulting three steps at a time. When I reached the street the freezing air made me gasp. Commuters traipsed by, hands in their pockets, bracing themselves against the dark. As soon as I got to the river path the stress of the day evaporated. By HMS *Belfast* I was picking up speed, wondering why anyone ever bothered to go on board. The posters gave too much away, revealing the cramped living quarters where sailors slept in bunks as narrow as their bodies, stacked in alcoves like dinner plates. It would take ten seconds in one of those cabins for my claustrophobia to kick in.

I made myself run at intervals, jogging for a hundred metres then sprinting until my lungs burned, passing huge Victorian warehouses converted into expensive restaurants. By the time I reached China Wharf I'd been going for twenty minutes. I stopped by the railings to let my breathing steady. The water was oily and black, lights from the bus boats catching its dirty surface. God knows how many secrets were hidden underneath. I made my way home at a slow trot, enjoying the rush of endorphins – nature's reward for nearly killing yourself.

There was no sign of my brother Will's ancient VW camper van when I got home. Usually it was sitting in my parking space on Providence Square. Maybe he'd decided to move on, park his troubles outside someone else's flat. The security door to the building had been left open as usual. A woman on the second floor worked from home as a reflexologist and her clients never remembered to pull it shut behind them. I took the stairs to the third floor and let myself in. The red light on my answer-machine blinked at me.

'I wondered if you'd seen your brother.' My mother's voice petered out, but soon regained its emotionless Home Counties calm. 'I'll have to ring tomorrow, I'm going to the Phillipses' for dinner.'

The second and third messages were from Sean.

'All I can see is you in my bed, wearing red silk stockings,' he sighed. 'Call me, Alice, as soon as you get this.'

I deleted the messages then investigated the contents of the fridge. One ciabatta roll, past its sell-by date, a piece of mozzarella and half a family-sized bar of chocolate. I chopped up a few sun-dried tomatoes and smeared a dollop of pesto on the dried-out bread, covered it with slices of cheese and stuck it under the grill.

Curled up on the sofa, I planned my evening. I would turn off my mobile, eat chocolate in the bath, and for once go to sleep alone.

2

When I woke up my uneaten meal was still on the coffee table, and someone was tapping on the front door. The sound was quiet but insistent, unlikely to go away. When I finally opened the door, Sean was standing there, clutching a bunch of sunflowers and a carrier of takeaway food. He gave me a long kiss, then pushed past me into the kitchen. It was impossible not to fancy him. Tall, blue eyes, clean-cut, and thirty-two years old, exactly my own age. I don't know why I always resented the jolt of lust I felt whenever I saw him.

'You were meant to ring me, Alice.' Sean dumped the flowers on the table.

'I fancied a night in. What time is it anyway?'

'Eight thirty.' He gave a narrow smile. 'God, you're hard work. If I didn't know better I'd think you couldn't stand me.'

I looked at the sunflowers' ragged yellow faces. 'Where on earth grows these in January?'

'Somewhere an obscene, guilt-inducing number of air miles away.'

'You villain. Let me have a shower, then I'll try and be nice to you.'

The hot water put things back in perspective and afterwards I felt almost human again. When I slipped out of my bathrobe Sean was leaning against the doorframe, ogling me.

'Don't get dressed on my account.'

I ignored him, pulling on a silk jumper, then wriggling into a pair of jeans.

In the kitchen he unloaded the takeaway.

'Vietnamese, my favourite.' I rubbed my hands together.

'Clear soup, sticky rice, duck in ginger sauce.'

'Yum.'

The duck was perfect, with small, fiery chillies that sizzled on my tongue. Sean watched me plough through a mountain of food.

'How do you stay so tiny, Alice?'

'Lucky genes.' I put down my chopsticks and looked at him. 'What did you get up to today anyway?'

He shrugged. 'Same old, same old. I cut people up, stitched them together again, listened to Marvin Gaye.'

'A bit of Motown encourages you to chop people to pieces, does it?'

'I don't need encouragement, Dr Quentin.' He pushed his plate away and grinned at me. 'You fix sick minds and I cut people up. It's what we do.'

'You seem a bit preoccupied, that's all.'

He glanced at his watch. 'I am. And it's a serious problem, actually.'

'Yeah?'

'The thing is, I'm on duty soon. I haven't got long to ravish you.'

I rolled my eyes. 'I don't need ravishing, thanks all the same.'

'But that wouldn't be fair, would it? I've raised your hopes.'

He was on his feet, hand in the small of my back steering me into the bedroom. It crossed my mind to say no, and I realise now that I should have done.

'It's going to take three seconds to undress you,' he muttered.

'It won't.' I pulled my jumper over my head. 'Because I always undress myself.'

The first time was too quick. But the second was slower and more considered. Sean was a natural show-off, and he had done his research, taught himself every fail-safe trick to make a woman come. Afterwards my lips burned; a combination of red-hot chillies and his stubble grazing my face.

'How long have I been seeing you?' Sean lay on his side, staring at me.

'A few weeks.'

'Longer, Alice. At least three months.'

A ripple of panic stirred under my breastbone. Before long he'd want me to go on holiday with him, or meet his parents.

'Look, Sean, this is all getting a bit out of control, isn't it?'

He kissed me again. 'Absolutely. Deliciously out of control.'

And then he was up, gathering the clothes he'd scattered across the floor. It was impossible not to admire the taut muscles spanning his back as he pulled on his jeans. He slammed the door shut behind him at ten o'clock and I stared at the ceiling. My body felt smug and satisfied, but my thoughts were struggling to get comfortable.

At 6 a.m. I sat up in bed, heart racing. Someone was banging on the front door. It crossed my mind that Sean had come back for another helping of low-commitment sex, but only one person would dream of making such a racket at the crack of dawn. My brother was wearing a thin cotton shirt, teeth chattering, pupils so dilated his eyes looked black instead of green.

'You locked the door,' he muttered.

'Come in, Will.'

'You shouldn't do that, Alice. Not ever.'

'It's okay, sweetheart, come inside.'

'People will think you don't like them.'

'Of course I like you. Come on, you'll get cold.'

It took ages to coax him into the hall, but I knew better than to touch him. Under the overhead light in the kitchen he looked even worse than he had the week before – unshaven, with hollows under his cheekbones, a deep sore on his upper lip. The muscles in his face kept twitching, his mouth stretched into a rictus like the Joker's grin in the Batman films. God knows what he'd taken this time; ketamine maybe. Enough to send every nerve ending in his body into overdrive. He ran the tap and dipped his mouth to the stream of water, slurping greedily. I rummaged in the food cupboard. It was almost empty except for a bag of rice and a packet of tortilla chips. I handed him the chips and he tore open the packet, crammed a handful into his mouth.

'Where are your keys, Will?'

He was too busy eating to reply, so I approached cautiously, dipped my hand into the pocket of his shirt and held them in front of him.

'Look, they're here. You could have let yourself in. I'd never lock you out.'

I must have gone too close, or maybe my tone of voice frightened him. He flinched, and then he came at me with both fists, crisps scattering across the floor. I ran out of the kitchen and along the hall, slamming the front door behind me. I got my key into the lock just in time, then leaned against the door to catch my breath. His feet pounded against the small of my back through the wood. I waited for him to exhaust himself, and when the noise finally stopped I ran downstairs to check his van. It was unlocked and a torn sleeping bag was lying on the fold-out bed, newspapers strewn across the slatted floor. Filthy shirts, underwear and towels were piled everywhere. I grabbed the clothes then forced myself to go back.

At the bottom of the stairs I weighed up the risks. There was an outside chance he'd beat me black and blue, but if I called an ambulance he'd leg it as soon as he heard the siren. I could have knocked on someone's door and asked for help, but after a few deep breaths I let myself into the flat, legs shaky with adrenalin. Will was in the lounge, chattering peacefully to himself, rummaging in a cupboard. He had already forgotten whatever had triggered his rage. I piled his clothes into the washing machine and poured a liberal amount of detergent into the dispenser. He had found a shoebox full of papers to flick through. I hovered a safe distance away.

'Found something interesting?' I took care to make my voice as calm as possible.

'Pictures,' he murmured.

He was laying photos on the wooden floor like a game of solitaire. One was of a family holiday. My father's arms were wrapped tight round my mother and me, and Will was standing outside the circle, already several inches taller than me. Another was of his graduation day at Cambridge; he looked invincible, hair almost white in the sun. He pulled another from the box. This time he was holding hands with one of the dark-haired beauties he went out with. She was gazing at him, determined not to let him go. I bit my lip. Normally it was easier to ignore the gap between then and now.

'Is there anything you need, Will?'

He was too busy with his new game to reply, so I left him to it and got ready for work. By the time I had taken a shower and put on my make-up, Will had disappeared, leaving the front door hanging wide open. But he had been busy before he left: the lounge floor was covered with rows of photos, as evenly spaced as kitchen tiles. They ran in chronological order, starting with us as babies, a few in school uniform, then the pair of us in our twenties on a beach with Lola, right through to one of him outside the Stock Exchange when he started his job as a trader. He was beaming, as if someone had handed him the keys to the City. I dropped the picture face down into the box. Part of me wanted to burn the lot, train myself to accept that he would never look like that again – triumphant, like everything he wanted was easily in reach.

I cycled to work along Tooley Street. It was startlingly cold, frost glittering on the pavement. For a second I imagined making a getaway, pedalling until my legs failed me, forgetting about the sick people and the worried well, queuing for their appointments. A crowd had already collected outside the London Dungeon, hungry for waxwork murder and artificial gore. At Great Maze Pond I chained my bike to the railings and gazed up at the hospital: a thirty-four-storey shaft of grey concrete studded with minute windows. No wonder Guy's had won prizes for being London's ugliest building. If there had been time it would have been easy to calculate which pane of glass belonged to my room, twenty-four floors up, fifth from the left. Climbing the stairs was harder than normal. By the tenth landing my stomach was churning, and I was regretting skipping breakfast. Fourteen flights later my head was spinning, lungs heaving in more oxygen than they could hold.

A steady procession of out-patients filed through my door at forty-five-minute intervals, and the day went by on autopilot. There was one victory though. The girl with advanced anorexia had been safely admitted to Ruskin Ward. I found her hooked to a drip, feeding saline and minerals into her starving body. The chart at the bottom of her bed reminded me that she was Laura Wallis, fifteen years old, five stone and two pounds on admittance. Her mother was perched on an armchair beside her pillow, her face grey under the overhead lights. She looked like she hadn't slept for days.

'How's Laura doing today?' I asked.

'I've never seen her this bad. She can't even stay awake.' The woman's eyes had the hollow look of trauma victims, as if she was reliving the moments before a bomb exploded. 'Why's she doing this to herself?' she whispered.

I could have reeled off all the clinical factors: depression, body dysmorphia, low self-esteem; but it wouldn't have helped.

'Laura's got a good chance of beating this, believe me.'

Even in sleep the girl's face looked tense, every bone visible under transparent skin. Her chances of survival were still stacked eighty–twenty in her favour, if she could be persuaded to eat.

'I'll see you both tomorrow.'

Mrs Wallis nodded, without taking her eyes off her daughter. Maybe she was afraid the girl would complete her vanishing act if she glanced away.

On the way home I stopped at the supermarket on Tower Bridge Road and bought fresh bread, milk, muesli, bananas, Camembert – two carrier bags heaving with food. At least if Will came back tonight the fridge would be full.

I went into the kitchen, dropped a lump of butter into a frying pan, two eggs, three rashers of bacon. I ate them with a huge doorstep of bread, standing in the kitchen, without taking off my coat.

The phone rang just as I finished the last bite.

'Hello?'

'It's your turn to pay me a visit.' Sean sounded relaxed. He must have finished his shift in the operating theatre then played a game of squash, like he always did.

'I can't, sorry. My brother might be coming round.'

'Fine, I'll come to you then. I'll get to meet him at last.'

I glanced around the kitchen. Evidence of Sean's presence was everywhere. His scarf hanging from the back of a chair, an overnight bag huddled by the door, containers from last night's takeaway still stacked by the sink. I took a deep breath.

'Look, I'm sorry, but I think we should take a break.'

When he finally replied his tone was icy. Another man seemed to have picked up the receiver. 'What's your definition of a break?'

'I mean, we've been seeing so much of each other.'

'Sounds like you're trying to end it.' Sean's voice was rising with anger.

'I'm sorry. I feel a bit suffocated, that's all.'

'Jesus, Alice. We've just spent the last three months in bed. You never complained.'

I tried to explain, but he had stopped listening. I held the phone away from my ear while he ranted. Eventually I agreed to meet him the following day to talk.

Afterwards I sat on the settee in the stupor that follows a huge meal or a hard decision. It was half past eight when the moon appeared: a fragile white crescent in the corner of the window, outlined by a fuzz of yellow. For some reason it made me desperate to be outside.

I felt better as soon as my feet hit the pavement. Running is the best form of therapy. It's impossible to fret or feel guilty when you're struggling to breathe. I jogged until a rhythm set in, gradually picking up speed. Smokers were loitering outside the Anchor Tavern at Butler's Wharf, watching a dredger haul itself upstream, like an old man crawling on his hands and knees. I stopped to stretch my hamstrings by the *Golden Hinde*. The replica ship was lit up to please the tourists, dripping with gold paint, new windows gleaming. Francis Drake would have laughed himself sick. By now the endorphins were working their magic, my brain pulsing with a sublime belief that everything could be fixed. I looped back down Marshalsea

Road, and for some reason I turned again at Redcross Way, searching for the river and the quickest way home.

That's when something caught my eye. Two ironwork gates I'd never noticed before, with dozens of ribbons and tags of paper hanging from the railings. Then I glanced down and my endorphin glow evaporated instantly. A second look confirmed that my eyes were telling the truth. A hand was lying on the pavement beside my foot. It was even smaller than mine, holding out its palm, as if it was waiting to be filled with coins.

3

The hand was connected to a fragile wrist, and the fingertips looked raw, as if they had been burned. I forced myself to press two fingers against the freezing skin, but there was no pulse. When I peered under the ironwork gate the body was less than a foot away, swaddled in black cloth, too dark to tell whether it was a boy or a girl. My thoughts raced away from me. The killer could be anywhere, watching me panic. The street was deserted: a row of vacant office buildings, an abandoned warehouse, no one in sight. The nearest building with lit windows was a hundred metres away, or I could run to the Marshalsea pub in a couple of minutes. Scanning the road warily, I pulled my phone out of my pocket and dialled 999. A woman with a calm voice promised to send an ambulance immediately.

'You can stay on the line if you like, until it arrives.' She sounded like a concerned grandmother, plump and middle-aged, a cup of tea at her elbow.

But my thoughts were taking too long to translate into statements, so I thanked her and zipped my phone back into my pocket. Chill from the pavement was travelling up through my legs into my vertebrae. For some reason I didn't want to leave the body alone, even though it was too late to matter who kept it company.

It felt like hours until the police arrived. By then I had been through every reason why a body would be lying on an abandoned lot in Southwark. Maybe someone had got on the wrong side of a gang, or a teenage runaway had fallen asleep and given in to hypothermia? My hands had stopped tingling, fingers completely numb. When the ambulance and two police vans finally pulled up on the opposite side of the road, everything swung into motion, like an episode from *Casualty*. A man in a long overcoat seemed to be in charge. Police officers buzzed around him, following his instructions, then moving away again, lifting boxes of equipment from the van. When he came towards me it was too dark to make out the details of his face, apart from the contrasts: dark eyes and eyebrows against pale skin. He seemed to have forgotten how to smile.

'Alice Quentin?'

'That's me.' My teeth chattered as he peered down at me.

Men spilled out of a van behind him. Lights were being set up; someone else was working on the gates, using bolt cutters on the chain.

'How long have you been here?' he asked.

'Twenty minutes or so.'

A bright light flicked on. The man was standing too close, as if the rules about personal space had ceased to apply. He was as thickset as a boxer, black hair spilling across his face.

'What were you doing by yourself, on a street like this?' He scowled at me like I might be the perpetrator.

'Running. I do it all the time.'

'Then you're mad.' He shook his head in disbelief. 'Certifiable.'

'Arrogant shit,' I muttered under my breath as he strutted away.

The gates were open now, arc lights cutting through the dark. A woman in white overalls was tying black and yellow tape to the telegraph pole I was leaning against. She unwound the reel, stranding me inside the circle, like I was another piece of evidence to be bagged up and taken to the lab. I edged closer to the gates. People were rushing in and out, collecting things, taking things away. Someone paused to scribble down my witness statement. Over the policeman's shoulder I caught a glimpse of the naked body. It belonged to a young woman, her small bare feet sticking out under a tarpaulin. Another white-suited drone leaned over her and released a searing flashlight, inches from her face. The detective in the expensive coat marched by again.

'Can I go home now?' I asked.

'Exactly how do you plan to get there?' he sneered.

'On foot.'

'You're joking,' he shook his head. 'Come with me.'

I was too tired to argue when he opened the passenger door of his car, or to protest when he fastened my seat belt, his forearm skimming my thighs. He sat back and studied me.

'Why in God's name go running at night, in an area notorious for knife attacks and gun crime?'

I returned his stare. 'I run pretty fast. If anyone bothered me I'd leave them standing.' When he started the car his jaw was set, face immobile. 'I bet you're great at poker, aren't you?'

'What do you mean?'

'Your expression never changes. You look angry all the time.'

He frowned. 'Most days I'm the calmest man in the world, but people like you taking unnecessary risks, that annoys me.'

'I'd gathered that. I bet you'd like to change the law, wouldn't you? Keep women indoors, doing needlepoint.'

His jaw clenched even more tightly, fists gripping the steering wheel. He was a perfect candidate for the anger management group I ran on Friday afternoons. At least by the time he parked on Providence Square he was beginning to simmer instead of boil.

'Anyone home to look after you?' he asked.

'I'm fine, honestly.'

He laughed. 'You're kidding, take a look at your hands.'

They were twitching in my lap, refusing to obey instructions.

'Come on, I'll help you in.'

He leaned over me to release the door, so close that his hair brushed against my mouth. His hand gripped the top of my arm as he helped me out of the car.

'I can manage, thanks.'

'You can hardly stand up.' His fingers were still locked round my arm.

'Really, I'm okay,' I said firmly. 'Believe it or not, I can climb stairs all by myself.'

'Have it your own way.'

As his car sped away I realised that he hadn't even bothered to introduce himself. My brother's van was back in my parking space on the opposite side of the street, but his light was switched off. Either he was sleeping, or keeping warm in a shelter somewhere. The security door to my block was unlocked again. I made a mental note to put up a sign the next day, reminding everyone to keep it shut.

Will must have been in the flat recently. He had helped himself to the remains of the bread and a block of cheese, and emptied his clothes from the dryer. I poured an inch of brandy into a tumbler, and held it to my mouth, the glass clattering against my teeth. My thoughts ran in circles when I finally got into bed, looking for a safe place to rest. Eventually they settled on the stocky dark-haired man with the permanent scowl, and I fell asleep.

The phone rang at quarter to eight. Somehow I'd managed to sleep through the alarm. The voice was familiar and insistent, a toned-down version of refined public school.

'Alice, it's me.'

I rubbed my eyes and tried to think straight.

'Sean,' I mumbled.

'I can't stop thinking about you. You know you'd be mad to end this, don't you?'

'Look, I can't talk now, sorry. You wouldn't believe what's been happening, it's too crazy to explain.'

'Tonight then, after work,' he insisted. 'Jesus, Alice. Are all shrinks this unpredictable?'

'Statistically unlikely, I think.'

There was a choking sound at the end of the line. 'Just as bloody well.'

I made a detour on my way to work, cycling back along Redcross Way. By daylight there was nothing scary about it. It was just a drab Southwark street with no trees, a cluster of ugly office blocks dominating the view. The area was still cordoned off with black and yellow tape, but there was no one around so I ducked underneath. Ribbons and artificial flowers fluttered from the railings, glittering in the winter sun, and a brass plaque caught my eye:

CROSSBONES YARD

THIS IS THE SITE OF CROSSBONES CEMETERY. OVER A THOU-SAND PROSTITUTES WERE BURIED HERE, BETWEEN THE MIDDLE AGES AND THE 1850S. IN 1994 THE GRAVEYARD WAS PARTIALLY CLEARED TO MAKE WAY FOR A POWER STATION TO SERVE THE LONDON UNDERGROUND, BUT LOCAL RESIDENTS FOUGHT THE DECISION AND CONTINUE TO PETITION SOUTH-WARK COUNCIL TO ESTABLISH A MEMORIAL GARDEN, TO COMMEMORATE THE LIVES OF THE WOMEN WHO LIE HERE.

I stood on my toes and peered over the gate, but there was nothing to see; just an expanse of black tarmac with nettles and buddleia forcing their way through the cracks. The site was as featureless as an ice rink, except for a few crisp packets and Tesco bags the wind had carried in, and some shattered bottles bored teenagers had lobbed over the wall. I half closed my eyes and tried to imagine a thousand women standing together, staring back at me. Someone tapped me hard on the shoulder.

'Can't you read?' It was a policewoman, her voice an outraged squawk. 'This is a crime scene.'

'I wanted to see the graveyard.'

'There's nothing to see.' Her face was rigid with cold and disapproval. She flapped her hands at me, like I was an unwelcome cat. 'Go on, get on your way.'

It was a relief to spend the morning buried in other people's worries, with no time to think about anything except treatments and referrals, therapeutic cures. When the phone rang at one o'clock I was just about to eat the sandwich I had grabbed from the staff canteen. It was DCI Burns, his voice a mixture of cigarettes, Bermondsey and the Scottish Lowlands.

'Too many coincidences,' he muttered. 'You said Morris Cley wasn't a threat, but, hey presto, this happens the minute he's out.'

I thought about Cley's expression when I interviewed him, puzzled as a child dealing with the mysteries of the adult world. 'There's no way it was him.'

'We can't rule him out,' Burns sighed into the receiver. 'The girl he killed lived a stone's throw from Redcross Way. It's his patch.'

'Have you interviewed him?'

'He's nowhere to be seen.' There was a long pause. 'The thing is, Dr Quentin . . .'

'Alice.'

'I'd appreciate your help.'

'To do what?'

'The whole thing's too close to the Southwark murders. This has got Ray and Marie's fingerprints all over it.'

'But the Bensons are in prison, aren't they?'

'Marie's been in Rampton for six years. Ray died last year at Broadmoor.'

'So it's a copycat?'

'Worse than that. He knows stuff the press never got hold of, like the way they carved crosses all over the girls' skin.'

'And where do I come in?'

'The thing is, Cley's got to be involved. He must be working with someone else. But whoever it is, they know their stuff. They've done their research and they'll want to use it again.'

'I can't help, Inspector. I'm not a forensic psychologist. It's not my job to work out why people are dead, I help them stay alive.'

'That's why I need you, Alice. I want you to take a look at the girl's body, see what you think.'

'What good would that do?'

He scrabbled around for an explanation. 'You might spot something. Something we've missed.'

By the time the conversation ended he had worn me down. I kept picturing the dead girl's hand lying on the pavement, reaching out to me, like I was her only hope. Somehow Burns had persuaded me to get involved, and I had a pain in my upper back, right between my shoulder blades.

I left work just after seven and cycled towards London Bridge, chaining my bike to a lamppost beside Southwark Cathedral. I stopped to admire the building. It had been restored a few years earlier, when public cash was still available to beautify historic buildings. Every stone gleamed. If I'd been a believer

I'd have ducked inside, said a quick prayer for the Crossbones girl, and for Will, but nothing ever happened when I closed my eyes. The marketplace was deserted, discarded fruit and vegetables the traders hadn't bothered to sweep away still littering the ground.

Sean's flat was above a shop on Winchester Walk. His living room smelled of coffee and spices, drifting from the store-room downstairs. I glanced around while he fetched me a drink. His flat was the opposite of mine: shelves loaded with CDs and books, his piano crammed in the corner, jazz maga-zines and newspapers heaped on the coffee table. For some reason when he put a glass of red wine in my hand, I told him everything – from finding the girl's body to meeting the world's most arrogant policeman.

'Stay here,' Sean said. 'You shouldn't be on your own. I'll sleep on the settee, if you like.'

'You wouldn't last five minutes.'

'Give me some credit,' he smiled. 'I'm sure I could manage ten.'

'I'd better go.'

His hand settled on my waist, and it was suddenly much harder to stick to my plan. Instinct kept telling me to shut up and let myself be persuaded.

His dark blue eyes pinpointed me, and the smile had disap-peared from his face. 'Two things to consider, Alice, before you make up your mind.'

'And they are?'

'The first is that I'm great in bed.'

'You've proved that already. That's not what this is about.'

'And I've fallen for you, hook, line and sinker.'

I didn't know how to reply, so I dropped my gaze and started to head for the door.

'You're not getting away that easily.'

For the first time, I noticed something odd in his expression, the clench-jawed determination of obsessives, or maybe he was just a bad loser. He stood in front of me, and for a minute I thought he might not let me go.

'Change your mind, Alice. This is crazy.'

'I need to leave, Sean. You're blocking my way.'

A muscle flickered in his cheek. 'I could keep you here, if I wanted to.'

'Don't be ridiculous.'

'This is what you always do.' An ugly sneer spread across his face. 'First you say no, then you say yes, like I'm not worthy of you.'

'That's not true.' I pulled in a deep breath. 'It's over, Sean. I'm sorry, but it is.'

The finality in my tone forced him to snap back into reality. He dropped his gaze and stepped to one side. On the doorstep he bundled a carrier bag into my hands, which contained everything I had left at his flat.

It was a huge relief to get outside. My breathing felt easy and relaxed for the first time in months. I stood on the pavement and peered into the bag. There wasn't much to show for three months' worth of visits: a silver bracelet with a broken clasp, a packet of contraceptive pills, a white camisole and a birthday card from Sean promising to take me to Paris. I dropped the bag in the nearest rubbish bin and jumped on my bike.

The ride home took less than ten minutes, but for some reason it exhausted me. All I wanted to do was stumble through the door and into the bath, but when I reached my floor I heard a noise. The light on the landing wasn't working, and someone was hovering by my front door. I held my breath and got ready to sprint back down the stairs.

4

'Al, is that you?'

It was Lola. I would have known her voice anywhere. It hadn't changed since we were at school, still husky and excitable, like she'd spent a weekend in bed with the most attractive man in the world. I gave her a hug then helped her wheel an enormous red suitcase into the hall. The backpack she was carrying was bursting at the seams.

'God, Lola. What's happened?'

'I'll give you the whole tragic saga when we've drunk these.' She thrust two bottles of wine into my hands. It was the same pattern as always. Months went by, then Lola would arrive out of the blue bearing gifts, and things carried on just as they always had. Two glasses of Beaujolais later, she was still haranguing her landlord.

'Scum of the bloody earth.' She twisted a long auburn curl around her finger. 'One month in arrears, and what does he say?'

'I can guess.'

'Be nice to me, and we'll skip the rent. Like a fucking pantomime villain.' She shook her head in disgust. 'All he needed was a black cloak and a fake moustache.'

'And what did you say?'

'Nothing, I was too busy running away. God knows, I wish he'd been shaggable, then I could have stayed in my lovely flat.' Lola was revelling in the drama, freckles scattered across the bridge of her nose, hands buried in her gorgeous hair. 'And I've been to loads of auditions this month. Not a single call back.'

'You can have the spare room as long as you like,' I said.

Her pale green eyes lit up. 'Can I? Just till I find somewhere.'

'Of course. But you know that Will's in and out, almost every day.'

Lola's expression softened. 'How's he doing?'

'Not brilliant.'

'Still in his van?'

I nodded. 'I keep hoping he'll move in, but it never happens.'

'I'd love to see him,' she beamed. 'It'll be like the old days.'

'No, it won't, Lola.' I caught her hand and forced her to look me in the eye. 'You need to understand. Will's different these days, he can be scary.'

'Scary?' She looked disbelieving. 'In what way?'

'Jittery, bouncing off the walls most of the time. You really don't want to be around if he loses it.'

Lola shook her head in disbelief. 'Do you remember when we went to Crete? Girls queued up to dance with him. He was always the golden boy. I can't get my head round it.'

'I can. It's been like this for eight years.'

'Jeez. Is it that long?' Something in my expression must have warned her to change the topic. 'So, tell me, how are things with the surgeon?'

'Gone the way of all things.'

'You're kidding. He sounded like the most eligible man in London.'

'He was,' I smiled ruefully.

'So what was it this time?' Lola glanced at me. 'Or are you just sticking to your policy of ditching them the second they get keen?'

'I don't know.' I took a swig of wine. 'Maybe I'm just an evil man-hating bitch.'

'Nah,' she laughed. 'You want my theory?'

'Go on, Dr Tremaine, psychoanalyse me.'

'You work too hard. And you only go out with serious, professional men.' She waved her empty wine glass in the air. 'You need more fun.'

'That's your diagnosis, is it?'

'More parties. I prescribe dancing and more alcohol.' She filled both of our glasses to the brim. 'Did I tell you about the director?' She launched into an elaborate story about an American film director who kept bombarding her with phone calls since she had done a screen test for him. 'Dinner, week-ends away, photo shoots, you name it. He won't give me a part in his fucking film though.'

'You'll have to stop being irresistible, Lo.'

'Impossible, darling.' Lola's grin widened. 'It's in my DNA.'

She entertained me for the rest of the evening with a string of anecdotes, complete with foreign accents and a huge cast of characters. By the time I checked my watch it was 2 a.m. and we'd polished off both bottles of wine.

'That's enough fun for me tonight,' I smiled. 'Bedtime.'

'Can you wake me? I've got an audition in Hammersmith at ten.'

'Great. What's the part?'

'Ophelia's maid.' She wrinkled her nose. 'Still, beggars can't be choosers.'

Lola wouldn't wake up in the morning. She was out for the count, curled up in the middle of the bed like an exotic cat. She had already colonised the spare room. A rainbow of high heels lined the walls, and a bright green leather jacket was draped across the chair. I set the alarm clock for eight and left it beside her pillow. My head was still throbbing from last night's booze, so I knocked back a breakfast of Nurofen and orange juice, then dragged my bike downstairs to the street.

I took a different route into Guy's that morning, crossing the quadrangle of Georgian buildings, through the centre of the old hospital site. I was cursing DCI Burns for making me do something so horrible it was bound to linger with me all day. The mortuary was hidden behind Pathology, blinds lowered, keeping itself to itself. I ran my pass card through the reader and let myself in. There are two mortuaries at Guy's. The first is for people who die under normal circumstances. Their bodies are kept cool, between 2°C and 4°C for a week or two, before being taken away for burial or cremation. The second is the cold room, where the temperature stays below freezing point, between -15°C and -25°C. Bodies spend months or even years there, while forensic work is done, or the unidentified wait to be claimed. Roman Catholics would describe it as a particularly chilly version of limbo.

I let myself into the cold room, scanning the wall for yesterday's date, then forced myself to pull out the drawer. Dead bodies unsettle me. It was one of the reasons why I chose psychology over general practice. I didn't fancy being called out in the middle of the night to comfort relatives and rubber-stamp death certificates.

Taking a deep breath, I unzipped the silver body bag, releasing a cloud of freezing condensation and the bitter smell of formaldehyde. The girl looked about seventeen, maybe even younger. Her face was completely unlined, brown roots growing through her bottle-blonde hair. She was so thin I could count every rib. It didn't take a degree in pathology to see how she had died. Her throat had been cut, the wound so deep that her severed windpipe and larynx were exposed. I stared at the grey rubber floor of the mortuary for a second, fighting to hang on to my chemical breakfast. Hundreds of small, deep crosses had been carved into her skin, across her breasts and torso, the insides of her thighs. Hopefully the cuts had been made after she died. I looked at her hand and remembered how small it had seemed, lying on the pavement. The ends of her fingers were bloody, fingernails torn, as if she had spent days trying to claw her way through a brick wall. A tattooed butterfly hovered on the girl's shoulder, simple as a child's drawing, with a tiny pink heart at the centre of each wing.

After a minute I let the drawer slide back into place. A mortuary assistant had written 'Crossbones Girl' on her label. There was nothing I could do for her. For the time being she would have to stay in the freezer by herself, nursing her wounds.

The rest of my morning was quiet: a team meeting, phone calls, an hour to catch up on case notes. But the afternoon was busier. Eleven out-patients attended my anger management group. It was easy to tell who wanted to be there, and who had no choice, because their social worker or probation officer insisted. We went through the usual steps: confide in people before the problem escalates, monitor your breathing, count to ten, walk away. One middle-aged man jumped to his feet halfway through the first exercise, his face brick-red.

'Fucking bollocks, the lot of it,' he spluttered. 'I don't need this shit.'

He slammed the door so hard on his way out that the door-frame shook. I glanced around at the group's startled faces. All of them were so used to yelling at people or using their fists, they had forgotten how it felt to be on the receiving end.

'Christ, it's not pretty, is it?' one of the women muttered. She looked surprised, as if she had glimpsed herself unexpectedly in a mirror, without make-up.

*　　*　　*

At five o'clock I cycled south, following the rush-hour traffic out of the city to neighbourhoods where you could still afford to buy, the drivers kidding themselves that Wandsworth was almost as desirable as Hampstead. I arrived at Southwark Police Station to find DCI Burns wedged so tightly between the wall and his desk it was a wonder he could still breathe. He motioned for me to sit opposite him on a battered plastic chair.

'Not looking her best, is she?' Burns peered at me. 'I wanted you to see what we're up against.'

'Someone who isn't crazy about women, that's for sure.'

'You can say that again.'

'Did the Bensons do that to all their victims? Cut their skin to shreds?'

'Put it this way, the girls wouldn't have won any beauty contests by the time we found them.' Burns grimaced. 'We haven't identified this one yet, no one's reported her missing. Looks like the poor kid was kept locked away somewhere for a week or two, with no food.'

'And you've got some suspects?'

'Cley's still on my list. He's only been back to his mother's place once since he got out. We're searching for him.'

I blinked at him. 'There's no way he could do something that elaborate. And how could it be him? You're saying the girl was held somewhere for days before he was released.'

'I never said he was acting on his own.' The phone on Burns's desk jangled. 'Ben, can you join us for a minute?'

'Is that your deputy?'

Burns nodded. 'He's keen to get you involved. He looked you up on the Internet, says you're the best around.'

The bad-tempered detective who had given me a lift home appeared in the doorway. He was wearing black trousers and a white shirt with the top button undone, grey tie loose around his neck, as if he was afraid it might strangle him. He looked different by daylight. His black hair and pale skin made him look exotic, Middle Eastern maybe, starved of sunshine for much too long. There was still no indication that he knew how to smile.

'You two have met, haven't you?' Burns asked.

'But I didn't get your name.'

'DS Alvarez,' he snapped. He wasn't acting like he had asked for my help on the case. Meeting me again seemed to be a spectacular waste of his time. His broad shoulders were tense with stored energy.

'Can you give us an update, Ben?'

'What do you want to know?' Alvarez lowered himself reluctantly onto the chair beside me. 'With respect, boss, this isn't the best time. We've got dozens of interviews to do. We just need to get on with it.'

'You'll get back to it soon enough.' Burns drew in a deep breath. 'And you said yourself, Alice can help us build a better profile.'

Alvarez sighed. 'It's pretty close to the Southwark killings. The Bensons locked their victims away for weeks, raped them, then slit their throats and dumped them on waste ground. One was buried in the garden and others under the patio.'

'But this girl wasn't raped?' I asked.

'Apparently not.'

'That's the only difference?'

'Looks like it,' he nodded. 'She was skin and bone by the time he killed her. Then he brought her to Crossbones and got into the site through a broken fence. He dragged her body over to the gate, so she'd be found.'

Burns caught my eye. 'The thing is, Alice, Morris Cley was in and out of the Bensons' hostel like a yo-yo. He never admitted anything, but maybe he heard all about how they mutilated the victims' bodies. No one else would have known.'

'Apart from everyone on the original investigation,' I commented.

'So it's one of us now, is it?' Alvarez snarled.

'Just thinking aloud. Information must get leaked sometimes.'

A muscle twitched in Alvarez's jaw, as if he was struggling not to call me every name under the sun.

'All right, Ben,' Burns said abruptly. 'We'd better let you get back to it.' He sounded tense, like a teacher trying to prevent another fight breaking out in the playground.

Alvarez vanished without saying goodbye.

'Don't mind him,' Burns muttered. 'He's been working like a dog since this kicked off.'

'Not exactly the friendly type, is he?'

'He's had a hell of a year, poor sod. You'll get used to him.'

I left Burns to deal with his deputy's attitude problem and cycled home. Lola was there already, weeping into a cup of coffee. There was no need to ask whether or not she'd got the part. She was looking ridiculously glamorous, in a bright red silk top and short black skirt. When I told her that the only reason they couldn't cast her was because she was too gorgeous and poor Ophelia would be upstaged, she began to brighten. After a few minutes she had rallied enough to go and wash her face.

'I'm a blubbering wreck, Al. Sorry.'

'I've seen worse.'

A casserole was bubbling on the hob; when I lifted the lid an aroma of herbs, garlic and red wine wafted out.

'I made dinner for you.' Lola was almost back to her normal self. Even when we were at school her depressions never lasted more than ten minutes.

We ate the stew with chunks of warm French bread, but she turned down a glass of wine.

'I'm on the wagon, until I get to the pub.'

'Where are you going?'

'Soho, to see Craig and his mates. You're coming too.'

'Too knackered, sorry.'

'You're meant to be having fun, Al.' She shook her head at me. 'Come and meet some new people, let your hair down.'

'Next time, I promise.'

'Your loss. One of them's just your type, a blond Adonis.'

'No thanks.' I held up my hands. 'I'm off men for the time being.'

Lola threw on a dark red coat, then dashed out of the door. The kitchen seemed to have been hit by a whirlwind. Every saucepan had been used, potato peelings were clogging the sink, and there was a coffee stain on my pristine wooden worktop. I loaded the dishwasher and cleared everything away. Afterwards I stepped out on to the balcony for some fresh air. It was incredibly cold. Under the orange streetlights a thick frost was already sparkling on the roofs of cars. Across the street Will's van was still in my parking space; the interior light was on and the curtains drawn.

I pulled on my shoes and ran downstairs. Will didn't answer my taps on the window, so I put my hand on the freezing door handle and slid it open. He was lying on the narrow bunk, propped up on a filthy pillow. The air inside the van was only slightly warmer than outdoors, beads of condensation forming on the windows. When I touched his shoulder he startled awake. His hand lashed out, but his movements were so uncontrolled, he didn't make contact.

'Don't touch me.' His words slurred, as if he was talking in his sleep. 'Leave me alone.'

'It's freezing, Will. Come inside.'

'Let me sleep.' He shifted away, turning his back on me.

'Jesus. You're fucking impossible to help.'

I slammed the door and headed inside, fists clenched so tightly that my nails dug into my palms. Ever since his breakdown he'd been impossible to reach, and the problem was exaggerated by the drugs he took. Whatever he could get his hands on: ketamine, heroin, cocaine. He refused to see a doctor since he was diagnosed bipolar, but he self-medicated all the time. Anything to keep the demons at bay.

I rooted in a chest of drawers for a blanket, then ladled a large portion of stew into a bowl. Five minutes later I was back in the van.

'Lola made this for you.'

He stirred on the bed. 'Lola?'

'She's staying for a bit. You can come in and see her.'

I spread the blanket across his legs. By now he was sitting up, spooning down huge, greedy mouthfuls of stew from the bowl I had given him.

'It's good,' he mumbled.

'I know. She's still the comfort food queen, isn't she?'

It was a relief to see him eat something substantial for once. I wanted to reach out and brush his matted hair back from his forehead; it had faded from gold to the colour of wet straw, greying prematurely round his temples. When he finally put down the empty bowl his eyes had come back into focus.

'Why do you bother, Alice?' He sounded so calm and like his old self that I couldn't reply. 'After everything I've done to you, everything I've seen. Why waste your time?'

I rested my hand on his foot. 'You're my big brother, that's why.'

His eyes closed again. Whatever he'd taken was making it impossible for him to stay awake. Pulling the blanket up to his shoulders, I dropped a kiss on his cheek.

'Come indoors when you wake up, Will, or you'll freeze.'

I don't know what made me so angry when I walked away from the van. The exact reason was hard to pinpoint. On my way into the building I gave the rubbish bin a vicious kick, but it didn't help.

When I got back inside I turned on the TV. Normally I don't bother with it. I'd rather spend my evenings running, or reading, or listening to the radio in the bath, but I was too tired to think. Flicking through the channels, I settled on a romantic comedy with Tom Hanks and Meg Ryan, which was like every film they starred in, slushy and comforting. It must have sent me to sleep because something woke me with a start. It was Will's familiar loud knocking on the front door. He must have seen sense at last, and decided to come in and keep warm.

But the man standing in the doorway wasn't my brother. Afterwards I realised I should have slammed the door in his face and called the police, but my reactions were too slow. By then there was nothing I could do.

5

Morris Cley was standing in front of the door, blocking my escape route. My heart battered against my ribcage.

'What are you doing here, Morris?'

He looked exactly as he had at Wandsworth: frizzy grey hair, misshapen features, unable to look me in the eye.

'You were nice to me,' he stammered. 'A lady in the library helped me find where you work on the computer. I followed you home afterwards, to see where you live.'

My tongue kept sticking to the roof of my mouth. Cley must have walked out of the huge gates of the prison, intent on tracking me down immediately. 'You shouldn't have done that, Morris. The police could put you straight back inside.' I tried to steady my breathing. 'But now that you're here, would you like a drink or something to eat before you go home?'

He shook his head. He was growing more agitated, shifting his weight from foot to foot, clenching his fists. I glanced behind me, trying to remember where I'd left my phone.

'I like you, you see,' he said. 'I thought you'd let me stay here.'

'There's no room, I'm afraid, Morris. My friend lives here too.' I looked at my watch. It was nearly midnight. Lola must be drowning her sorrows. Or maybe she was already asleep on someone else's settee.

Cley's face contorted. It was hard to tell if he was angry or afraid. 'I can't go back there. My mum's stuff's in every room.'

'And you can't bear to look at it.'

'She left her slippers by the door, all her bits and bobs.' His eyes were brimming.

'Where have you been staying then?'

'In the park last night. There's nowhere else to go.'

'You can't have had much rest.'

'Jeannie let me sleep in her bed.' He smiled and took a step towards me. 'You look just like her.'

When I looked into his eyes I could see abject loneliness, but no hint of violence. Then common sense kicked in and my heart rate doubled. It dawned on me that a convicted murderer was telling me I was the spitting image of his victim.

'No, Morris. You have to go home. Right now.'

I reached for the handle of the front door, but he caught my arm.

'Please, just for tonight.' His fingers locked round my wrist. 'I'll leave in the morning, I promise.'

He grabbed my other hand before I could free myself. Instinct told me that my best chance was to fight my way past him, get out into the corridor. But he was determined, and twice as strong as me. I tried to wrench myself free, then there was a burst of pain as my skull hit the doorframe.

God knows how long I was out for, but the next thing I remember was lying on my back in the hall, with Lola peering down at me.

'Hell,' she said, 'that looks nasty.'

There was an odd, metallic taste in my mouth, black spots appearing and disappearing in front of my eyes. Drops of blood were falling on to the floor.

I sat up cautiously. 'What happened?'

'I bashed him with the lamp.' Lola sounded as if she expected a medal for conspicuous bravery. 'Then I called the police.'

Pieces of the china lamp base were scattered across the floor.

'But he got away?'

She nodded. 'He had you against the wall, trying to hang on to you.'

The raw skin on my cheek burned when I touched my face.

'Stay there,' she said. 'I'll get some ice.'

I was still sitting on the floor with a bag of frozen peas against my eye when DS Alvarez arrived. I gritted my teeth. He seemed determined to give me another dose of industrial-strength arrogance when he crouched in front of me.

'You don't have much luck, do you, Dr Quentin?'

'That's not true, actually. This is the exception.'

'And you got me out of bed. The station called me because Cley's at the top of our wanted list.' He leaned towards me. 'Let's see your face.' There was a vertical frown line between his eyebrows, as if he spent all his spare time worrying about things he couldn't fix. He winced when I looked up at him. 'I'd better run you to the hospital.'

'For a split lip and a few bruises? Don't be ridiculous. If it's bad in the morning I'll get it checked out.'

He reached forward and pressed the compress to my cheek. 'Look, I don't want to give you another lecture about personal safety.'

'Praise the lord.'

'But why put a spy-hole in your door if you don't intend to use it?'

'I do normally. I was expecting someone.'

'Your boyfriend?'

'No.'

'She was expecting me.' Lola emerged from the living room.

Alvarez reacted the way men always do when they see Lola for the first time. She hovered in the doorway, tall and pale-skinned as a lily, red curls flowing across her shoulders, the original Pre-Raphaelite stunner. Eventually he dragged his gaze back to me. Maybe it was the effect of concussion but his face was too close. I could read the dark smudges under his eyes, judge the exact length of his five o'clock shadow. I edged away, pressing my spine to the wall.

'Cley didn't mean any harm,' I muttered.

'You're defending him now?' Alvarez shook his head in amazement.

'He's afraid, that's all. He wanted somewhere to hide.'

'It's crazy. You don't seem to realise when you're in danger.' He rose to his feet. Maybe he had decided I was a lost cause. 'Use both locks on that door in future.'

The heavy soles of Alvarez's shoes thundered along the corridor as he made his escape.

'Jesus,' I muttered. 'He talks to me like I'm five years old.'

'At least he talks to you.' Lola's eyes were misty and out of focus. 'Why are the gorgeous ones always married?'

'You thinks he's attractive?'

'God, yeah. But did you clock his wedding ring? It's half an inch thick.'

The next morning I stayed in the shower for a long time, soaping away the remains of the day before. My encounter with Cley hadn't left any ill-effects, apart from a slight throbbing behind my right eye. When I confronted myself in the mirror the damage looked worse than it felt. There was swelling across my cheekbone, with a streak of dark blue bruises, but my vision was fine. The split in the middle of my lip was already beginning to heal. I dabbed on some make-up, pulled on my black wool skirt and white silk shirt.

Lola was in the kitchen in a bright blue tracksuit, drinking coffee. She stared at me in amazement.

'You're not seriously intending to go to work.'

'Course I am.'

'Al, some madman attacked you last night. He knocked you out cold. Lie on the sofa all day eating chocolate like a normal person.'

'I can't. I'd be bored rigid.'

'Jesus wept.' She threw her hands in the air. 'You're an android, aren't you? No human feelings at all.'

'You finally rumbled me. Where are you off to, anyway?'

'Dance class. I'm trying to get back in shape.'

She peered down at her mile-long legs anxiously, as if they might have lost a few inches overnight.

Fortunately people at work were too polite to mention my injuries. Psychologists are famous for it. Years of training makes it impossible to ask a direct question, or say exactly what you mean.

My boss Hari drifted up to me in the corridor. He's been a friend for years and I've never seen him look less than immaculate, with his saffron turban, expensive suit and well-groomed beard. He'd been circling all morning, trying to find the right time for a meaningful conversation. They're his speciality because he's an expert on counselling skills, impossible to offend, upset or surprise.

'Just ask me how I got the shiner, Hari. Go on, you're dying to know.'

He gave his usual peaceful smile. 'By saying that, I assume you're dying to tell me.'

'Reverse psychology, Hari. My favourite technique.'

Hari's dark brown eyes studied my face thoughtfully, and I could see why my friend Tejo had married him. If it had been the sixties he could have grown his beard and become a guru. Pop stars would have paid fortunes to sit at his feet cross-legged, absorbing his advice.

'I'm not going to ask how you hurt yourself, Alice, but I do think you're working too hard, and that concerns me. You're my star player. Don't run yourself into the ground.' He rested his hand on my shoulder for a second before turning away.

After my last appointment I walked down to Ruskin Ward to see the anorexic girl I'd admitted. Her mother was still sitting motionless by her daughter's bed, like she had been there since the dawn of time. She nodded a greeting, but seemed too exhausted to speak. A piece of apple pie was balanced on Laura's tray, swimming in bright yellow custard. She was conscious, but her skin was white and papery. When I stood at the end of her bed she stared at me, eyes so deeply shadowed she could have been fifty, instead of fifteen. There was a fuzz of downy hair on her cheeks. A sign that her hormones were running riot, while her starving body consumed the last of her fat reserves. Her anger flared up out of nowhere.

'You can't make me eat that shit.' She shoved the pudding bowl away with surprising energy, custard slopping across the table.

'I know I can't.' I held her gaze. 'I can help you, but you'll have to do the hard work for yourself.'

I felt relieved as I walked away, because I knew she'd recover. Her rage showed that she was still fighting to stay alive. The ones you have to worry about have already shut down. They lie under the covers without moving, willing themselves to disappear.

★   ★   ★

There was no sign of Lola when I got home. It was dark outside and a pile of mail was waiting on the doormat, which I scooped up and dumped on the kitchen table. I looked out of the window. Will's van had gone, but a police car was parked across the road, two officers inside, eating sandwiches. I didn't know whether to be grateful or afraid that Ben Alvarez was keeping an eye on me, in case any more ex-cons decided to pay a call.

I stepped into my trainers and ran down the stairs two at a time. One of the policeman gawped at me in amazement. Obviously I was failing to display appropriate victim behaviour. It was a relief to get moving, heading west, towards Tower Bridge. It's always been my favourite, delicate as a cat's cradle, but robust enough to carry a million cars each year. And it can open its jaw wide enough to allow the largest battleship in the naval fleet to sail through.

Reaching St Katharine's Dock, I tried to imagine what it had been like before the property developers got hold of it, and it still belonged to the East India Company. Tall ships must have docked there every day, loaded to the portholes with spices and silk. I sprinted along Capital Wharf, keeping the river to my right. The tide was almost out, sluggish water drifting slowly east. By Wapping Old Stairs the backs of my legs were burning. I sat on the top step and watched a River Police boat dart up the central channel. Yards of dark brown silt gaped in front of me. It smelled of sewage and brine, everything the river had been forced to swallow.

It was after nine by the time I got home and the police car had disappeared. Sean had left two messages on my answermachine. The first one was calm and reasonable, but the second sounded like a different man.

'You're a coward, Alice,' his words slurred. 'You ran off because you were starting to feel something, weren't you? It's too fucking weird. I know you're the shrink, but you need some help, you really do.'

The message rambled on for several minutes, explaining that I was afraid of my own feelings and listing reasons why we should be together. His tone veered between tenderness and rage. At times he sounded completely unhinged. He must have got back from work and sunk a bottle of wine. I pressed the delete button and went into the kitchen and boiled water for spaghetti, rooted in the fridge for ragu sauce and the last crumbs of parmesan.

When the meal was ready I browsed through the post. An animal welfare charity had written to me, enclosing a photo of a golden Labrador gazing longingly at the camera, like I was his last hope. My bank statement showed that my mortgage was consuming two-thirds of my wage. Stuffing it back in the envelope, I tried not to calculate how many years of debt were hanging round my neck. I gulped down another mouthful of spaghetti and moved on to the next envelope. It had been posted in central London. The writing was unfamiliar, tiny black letters leaning backwards, like a strong wind was blowing them in the wrong direction. The letter had been written on good quality white paper, no address or date, unsigned.

Dear Alice,

I feel I know you already. You're the kind of person who works late because you imagine you can help people. Then you go running, almost every day. You look different when you run. Relaxed, as if no one could catch you, and there's nothing to fear. One thing you don't know yet is that pain is a kind of intimacy. It's fulfilling. When someone's in pain they can't hide anything. You can see right inside them.

I am looking forward to seeing inside you, Alice.

My fork dropped out of my hand. Suddenly the heap of spaghetti looked disgusting, a splatter of red sauce congealing on the pale strands. I scraped my plate into the bin, then walked out on to the balcony. I couldn't decide whether to shred the letter or accept that it was like the worst kind of toothache, unlikely to go away.

6

I chose my clothes carefully the next morning. Normally the weekends are an opportunity to be scruffy, and slouch around in jeans and battered trainers. But that Saturday I picked black, slim-legged trousers, a cashmere cardigan, high-heeled boots, then combed my hair into a ponytail and slipped on my best coat.

Outside there was no sign of Will's van, but the police car was back, with a new pair of coppers inside. A young woman was sitting in the passenger seat, flirting with the man at the wheel. They were so busy enjoying the chemistry that they didn't even notice me leave. My walk took me down Tooley Street with my hands buried in my pockets, wishing I had worn gloves. At London Bridge I waited by platform eight for my train, watching people on the concourse. The station changed its identity completely at the weekend. For once you could wander at your own pace, without an army of sharp-suited executives barging you out of the way.

The journey south took less than half an hour, the train skimming across familiar territory: Camberwell's high-rise flats; the grubby roof of Lewisham shopping precinct; mile upon mile of Victorian redbrick terraces that had seen better days. I arrived in Blackheath just after ten. The grey pound was out in force, walking their well-groomed dogs and window-shopping outside designer kitchen shops. I caught sight of my mother before she spotted me. She was sitting at the table she always reserved, by the window in her favourite coffee shop. She looked the same as always: immaculate grey hair, elegant, understated clothes.

'Darling.' She kissed the air beside my cheek.

'I hope I'm not late, Mum.'

'Your poor face,' she murmured. 'Whatever happened?'

'Nothing. Just a slip on an icy pavement.'

She studied my black eye in horror.

'What are you having?' I asked.

'The usual, I think.'

I scanned the menu. 'Eggs Benedict for me, and granary toast.'

'At least you're eating, darling. That's a good sign.'

'What do you mean?'

'You mustn't lose any more weight, Alice. You're quite thin enough.'

'I haven't lost an ounce, Mum. I'm a ten, like I've always been.'

'It was meant as a compliment.' She raised both hands, like she was calming a dangerous animal. 'My goodness, you're snappy. Is work stressful at the moment?'

I counted to ten before answering. 'It's great, thanks. In March I get my very own trainee.'

My mother's pale grey eyes studied me intently. She was wearing the same make-up as always, so subtle you could hardly detect it, blending away every shadow and blemish. She nibbled the corner from her almond croissant.

'Have you seen your brother?'

'A couple of times this week. He's pretty much the same.'

She watched me devour my breakfast. 'Is he still going to that group of his?'

'I'm not sure,' I shrugged. 'He never tells me anything.'

My mother frowned. Suddenly she looked her age, a network of deep lines appearing around her eyes.

'Couldn't he stay with you for a while, Alice?'

'I've told you, it's not that simple.'

'He can't go on for ever in that wretched van. And you're settled now, in your own flat.' Her voice was increasingly strident, as if she had forgotten we were in a public place.

'Or he could live with you, Mum, couldn't he?' I kept my voice level. 'You've got a spare room.'

'That's below the belt,' she scowled. 'You know he doesn't even return my calls.'

I put down my fork. 'Let's drop this, please, before we argue.'

'All right, subject closed.' Her pale eyes bored into me. 'But remember that he's your brother, Alice. You should be helping him.'

I returned her stare. 'We should both be helping him, Mum.'

There was no point in explaining how many times I had begged Will to move in. There would only be something else to criticise. The pattern of blame hadn't shifted much since Dad died. And it was easy to understand why she always deflected any hint of blame. Denial had become a way of life. It was how she held herself together. The house could be falling down around her ears, my father staggering drunk, looking for his next victim. But none of it was ever her fault. So long as the outside world thought we were getting along fine, just like any other respectable middle-class family, she had fulfilled her duty. Maybe it had broken her heart that she couldn't keep Will and me safe when we were kids, but it was unlikely she would ever talk about it, because that would involve removing her ice queen mask for a minute.

We struggled through our brunch in the usual way. She told me about a party she had attended for fellow retirees from the library, her friend Sheila's insufferable husband, a sculpture exhibition she had seen at the Hayward Gallery. And I told her nothing whatsoever.

'Surely there are some nice men at that hospital of yours, Alice?'

'I'm not looking.'

'Maybe you should, darling.'

Her hand hovered above my shoulder when she said good-bye, like she wanted to make contact but didn't know how. 'Same time, two weeks today?'

'Okay, Mum. I'll call you.'

She belted her charcoal trench-coat and pulled on a pair of suede gloves, which were either perfectly preserved or brand-new. I ordered another espresso and watched her stroll away, jaunty and straight-backed, as if her life had always been trouble-free.

There was time for a walk on the heath before catching the train home. As a child I crossed it every day on the way to school, the sky so empty and blameless that it was comforting. The horizon was more complicated now, tower blocks hover-ing in the distance. Without them the view from the heath would have been unchanged since the nineteenth century: grand terraces of four-storey Georgian buildings, the open land in front of them criss-crossed by paths so the genteel families could promenade.

The wind cut through me on the way to Morden Road. It was the first time I had gone back to the house since it was sold. But when I got to the junction I nearly chickened out. My heart was pounding, but I forced myself to stand in front of the big Edwardian semi. It looked completely differ-ent. The sash windows had been ripped out and replaced by double-glazing, and the tatty picket fence had given way to expensive silver railings. I tried to talk myself through the exercise that works best for patients with phobias. Stay close to the object you fear, until you learn it can't hurt you, let the anxiety run its course. The instinct to run was overwhelming, but I made myself wait on the pavement for five minutes, eyes flitting from the gabled roof, over the pale bricks, to the cherry tree my mother planted when I was five years old. Maybe I was expecting someone to run out and drag me back into the past, and hold me prisoner there against my will.

Lola was lounging on the sofa when I got back, watching a black and white film. I flopped down next to her.

'Perfect, isn't she?' Lola sighed. Katharine Hepburn drifted across the screen in a black cocktail dress and opera gloves. 'It's the cheekbones.'

I watched the characters argue and make friends again for fifteen minutes, without taking anything in.

'Where've you been, anyway?' Lola glanced at me.

'Blackheath.'

'The old stamping ground.' Her eyes widened. 'Do you need a drink?'

'Gin, please. Don't worry about the tonic.'

She giggled. 'As bad as that? Never mind, there's a party later.'

'What's it in aid of?'

'It's a party, Al. It doesn't have to be in aid of anything.'

'I'm not really in the mood.'

'You will be. Come on, let's check out that enormous walk-in wardrobe of yours.'

Lola went through my clothes like a whirlwind.

'God, Al, you should be an undertaker. You've got six black suits.'

'Maybe I could retrain.'

Lola pulled out a silver mini dress and held it against me.

'No way,' I protested. 'I haven't worn that for ten years.'

'Great for dancing.'

'I probably couldn't even get into it.'

'Bollocks.' Lola gave me her fiercest look. 'You're coming out, Al, and that's that. I'll perk you up a bit before we go.'

Lola's idea of perking involved heated rollers, eyelash curlers and half a ton of foundation. When we were ready to get in the taxi, she made me look in the mirror again. The silver dress shimmered in all the right places. Lola towered over me in a short green dress and skin-tight leggings.

'We look amazing,' she purred. 'They'll be fighting over us.'

Lola's friends lived near Waterloo in a flat with a tiny living room. The party was well under way by the time we arrived. The air reeked of dope, and the guests must have been actors, because the volume of conversation was twice as loud as normal, a sea of hands gesticulating wildly. Lola did her usual vanishing act as soon as we got through the door.

'I'd better schmooze, Al. This place is full of casting agents.'

Soon she was leaning against the wall, listening to a short, unattractive man pontificate, like he was the most riveting conversationalist in the world, and I was remembering why I had stopped going to parties. The room was so crammed it was hard to breathe. A blond man with abnormally white teeth grinned at me.

'I've seen you in something,' he said. 'Chekhov, wasn't it, at the Donmar?'

I shook my head.

'Come on. I'll get your life story later.'

He grabbed my hand and pulled me through some French doors on to a roof terrace. People were dancing to a mix of Motown and trance, as if two different generations were fighting over every track. The man told me his name, but the music was too loud to hear. Once we started to dance, I didn't care. It always took a few drinks to get me on the floor, but once I started, there was no stopping me. It had the same effect as running, a mixture of booze and feel-good chemicals flooding my system. After a few songs everyone looked more attractive and the trip to Blackheath slipped to the back of my mind.

'Want another drink?' the blond man yelled in my ear.

When I shook my head he disappeared. He was replaced immediately by a man with beautiful North African features, then a woman with red lipstick and incredibly short hair. And then I was dancing alone, oblivious to the cold, the music carrying me. When the music slowed down I finally gave up and went inside, edging through the crowded kitchen for a glass of water. The man with the immaculate teeth looked straight through me. By now his arm was locked around a girl in gold hot pants, as if he was terrified she might escape. Lola was still listening to the short man holding forth; luckily he hadn't noticed how despairing she looked. I blew her a kiss on my way out.

Two hours of dancing had done the trick. My body was completely relaxed, sweat still warm between my shoulder blades. Rather than catch cold waiting for a taxi or a night bus, I began to walk down Stamford Street, but within half a mile my shoes were crucifying me. People were still milling around on the South Bank, coming out of a party on the ground floor of the Oxo Tower. By City Hall the booze had almost worn off. Every step hurt, and I was questioning the sanity of women who only wear high heels. Maybe they had discovered a technique for long-distance walking without injuring yourself.

The streets were growing quieter. A handful of tourists lingered by Tower Bridge, waiting for taxis, but after that there was no one. The boardwalk by China Wharf was deserted. I crossed the wooden bridge between the warehouses that towered above me, at least eight or ten storeys high.

For some reason I felt jittery. I could hear footsteps, but there was no one in sight. Alcohol-induced paranoia probably. When the footsteps drummed closer it was a struggle to stay calm. Maybe it was my heartbeat, or the echo of my ridiculous heels clattering on the walkway. It was a relief to arrive at Providence Square. There was no sign of either the police car or Will's van.

'You're out late,' a voice came from behind me.

'Jesus.' My heart lurched against my ribcage. 'What are you doing here?'

DS Alvarez stepped out from the alleyway between the flats. 'I drew the short straw.'

'Sorry?'

'It's my turn to keep an eye on you.'

I didn't know how to reply. As usual he was standing too close, wearing his trademark black coat. My eyes were level with his mouth.

'Where have you been?'

'A party,' I snapped. 'Not that it's any of your business.'

'Is this how you always react to GBH?' He shook his head disapprovingly. 'Put your glad rags on and hit the town?'

'Better than moping at home.'

'Does anything actually bother you, Dr Quentin?'

'What do you mean?'

'Or is all that emotional stuff just for your patients?'

'You know fuck all about me. You've got no right to make judgements.'

I started to walk away, but his hand closed around my wrist and then he leaned down to kiss me. It crossed my mind to let him, but I turned away just in time. His warm breath touched my cheek. An odd tingling feeling ran across the back of my neck.

'Sorry,' he muttered. 'That was completely out of order.'

'It certainly was.' He was still standing too close, my hand resting on his shoulder where I'd pushed him away. His face hovered above me. It looked like he was weighing his chances, wondering whether to try again.

'I could report you, you know,' I whispered.

'Who to?' He studied my face carefully. 'Burns wouldn't do a thing.'

'To your wife, then.'

He looked shocked. 'I can explain.'

'That you're planning to separate?' I sneered.

This time he didn't try to stop me walking away. My legs felt weak as I climbed the stairs, as if they couldn't be relied on. The kitchen clock said that it was nearly 2 a.m., but there was no point in going to bed. My thoughts would only keep dancing around in my head, refusing to slow down.

7

It took a long time to get to sleep. I was too angry, with Alvarez for trying to kiss me and with myself for wanting to kiss him back. Maybe he made a habit of approaching women he met at work, then sneaking home to his long-suffering wife, complaining about the demands of his job. It unsettled me that I could still remember the pressure of his hand on my wrist, and his stare, as if he was determined to read my thoughts.

When sleep finally came I dreamed of Crossbones Yard. I was looking through the ironwork gate into the darkness. The tarmac had been replaced by a garden, and a huge crowd of women were holding a party. Lanterns swung from the trees, young girls dancing, while others chatted beside a bonfire. For a time none of them noticed me spying on them, then one by one they turned in my direction. The chatter stopped and so did the music. The dead girl had come back to life, but the crosses on her skin were still there, chains of them circling her wrists like bracelets. She was standing alone at the edge of the crowd. The women's faces swam in front of me, their expressions neither friendly nor hostile. They were expectant, waiting for me to make the next move. They carried on watching me as I surfaced from the dream.

My head was spinning. Lola's diet of gin and late nights definitely didn't agree with me. In the kitchen I knocked back half a litre of orange juice, straight from the carton. My feet still ached from the marathon walk home. I was checking the fridge to see if I could face eating anything when someone banged on the door. Will was standing on the doormat, twitching from head to foot. For the first time in weeks he came in without having to be coaxed. There were black, greasy stains on his jeans and his hair looked matted, as if it hadn't been washed in weeks.

'Do you want some breakfast, Will?'

'He came back.' His eyes were so wide open that the dull whites were exposed.

'Who's he?'

'In the night,' he insisted. 'I've seen him before, but I don't know what side he's on.'

'Ssh.' I pressed a finger to my lips. 'Lola's asleep.'

'He wanted me to go with him.'

'Calm down, Will. Come in here and tell me about it.'

He stood in the middle of the kitchen, legs moving compulsively, like a sprinter warming up for a race. My heart was thudding too hard inside my chest. It always upset me when Will described his apparitions. Most of the time I kidded myself that he was on the mend, ignoring his delusions and paranoia. I piled cheese on two slices of bread, and stuck them under the grill. When I handed him a glass of juice the tremor in his hands sent half the liquid slopping on to the floor. It was hard to tell if it was the effect of drugs, or another night sleeping in the freezing cold. He ate his food too fast, melted cheese smearing around his mouth.

'He knocked on my window.' Will crammed another chunk of toast into his mouth. 'I recognised him.'

'Was it the police?'

Will shook his head. 'He said he'd give me food and money and a bed for the night.'

'But you can have all those things here.'

'He didn't want anything back, he wasn't trying to control me.' The bitterness in Will's voice ignited then fizzled out. When he spoke again he sounded like a little boy. 'I said I'd go with him, Al, but he ran off. I must have said something wrong.' He looked ready to burst into tears.

'You don't need to go off with strangers, Will. Come here if you need anything. You know you can do that, don't you?'

He perched on a stool, chattering quietly to himself, as if an invisible friend was sitting beside him. It was hard to know whether the man he had seen the night before had been real or imaginary, but at least the food was settling him. Maybe later he could be persuaded to take a bath. His smell lingered in the kitchen: damp clothes and sweat with a sour, chemical edge. By the time I had showered and eaten breakfast, Will was asleep on the settee in the lounge, breathing deeply, like he hadn't shut his eyes for weeks. Just as I was about to go and buy a Sunday paper Lola emerged from her room, wrapped in my favourite blue kimono.

'Morning, disco queen.' She gave me a bleary smile. 'How are you feeling?'

'A bit frazzled. Will's flaked out in there.'

Lola's face lit up. She had always had a soft spot for Will, but the smile slipped from her face when she pushed open the living room door. His thin form was stretched out on the settee, like a living scarecrow.

'Jesus,' she whispered. 'How long's he been like that?'

'About six months, but the last few weeks have been the worst. He won't see a doctor, because he thinks his GP wants to slam him back in hospital. And he's using every fucking drug he can lay his hands on, except the lithium he needs.'

Lola sat beside me and pressed her hand on top of mine. 'Why didn't you tell me, Al?'

'What could you do? I've taken him to specialists, but he always runs away.'

'God, you poor thing.' Lola's green eyes fixed on me. 'When's the last time you had a good cry?'

'On my thirtieth birthday. Too much vodka.'

'You worry me, Al. You really do. I cry if the bus is late, but you've forgotten how. You're so bloody controlled.'

'So everyone keeps telling me.'

'Because it's true.'

'Someone's got to be, in my family,' I said sharply.

'You don't have to do it all by yourself.'

'I do, Lola.' I stared at her. 'I'm all he's got.'

She wrapped an arm round my shoulder. 'Do you know what you need to do?'

'I dread to think.'

'Watch *Love Story*. Do you the world of good to bawl your eyes out for a few hours.'

Lola retreated back to bed with a plate of toast, and I carried on racking my brains. I'd already rung Narcotics Anonymous, and researched rehab centres in the UK and abroad, but none of it was any use unless Will agreed to be treated. He was still fast asleep, hands balled into fists, fighting monsters in his dreams. I tiptoed into the hall and peered under the flap of his rucksack. It was crammed with dirty clothes: socks, shirts and jeans that hadn't seen a washing machine in weeks. Underneath them there was a copy of *Zen and the Art of Motorcycle Maintenance*, a scrap of paper with phone numbers scrawled all over it and a silver foil package, no bigger than my thumb. I held it to my nose: it was a lump of cannabis resin, giving off its odd smell of treacle and musk. God knows what other drugs he kept hidden under the seats in his van.

I was just about to put everything back when something else caught my eye, glinting against the canvas. I fished it out and let it rest in my hand, cold and compact. Our teacher showed us flick-knives once at school. He warned us that they were lethal, so all the boys wanted one. A gang of them disappeared behind the science block at lunch break to show off their weapons. I released the safety catch and a six-inch blade flicked out, sharp enough to slice my fingers to the bone.

A picture of my brother as a boy appeared out of nowhere. I remembered the way he used to stand there, completely passive, when my father lashed out at my mother or me. For some reason it was never his turn. All he had to do was watch, and I'd never questioned why. I'd always assumed that he took the path of least resistance, too scared to run or call for help. But the expression on his face had been more complicated than pure fear. There was a mix of emotions there: excitement, voyeurism, maybe even envy of my father's power.

I stared down at the blade in my hand, then folded it back into its sheath. By now Will was shifting in his sleep, beginning to wake up, so I dropped the knife back into his bag.

By the evening he was less agitated. Lola ran him a bath, and he didn't even flinch when she teased him about his beard.

'Going for the beatnik look, are you, William?'

'I ran out of razors, that's all.'

'Use one of mine. Go on, liberate that handsome face of yours.'

Sitting in my room I listened to Lola trying to flirt with Will, as if nothing had changed. It was months since he'd sounded so relaxed. He could string whole sentences together if he chose to. There was no more talk of strangers arriving in the night. Maybe he was fine with everybody else, and it was only me he struggled with.

It was just after nine. No doubt Alvarez would say I was criminally insane if I went for a run, but my trainers were tempting me, sitting patiently beside the wardrobe. When I got outside there was still no sign of a police car. Maybe they were bored of waiting in the cold, or they had found Morris Cley and slammed him back in his cell. It took a long time to hit my stride. I ran west along the river for a while, trying to pace myself, the backs of my legs aching. But by the Tate Modern I felt like I could run for ever, follow the river through Chelsea and Putney, until it flowed through fields instead of streets. At Lambeth Palace I forced myself to stop. A security guard glared at me through the railings. Maybe he expected me to hop over the wall and throw stones at the stained-glass windows.

After five deep breaths I started the run home, taking a short cut past a line of men queuing for burgers outside Waterloo Station. These were the kind of streets Alvarez wanted women to avoid, full of neglected council blocks and boarded-up shops. For some reason I ended up by Southwark Cathedral, less than a hundred yards from Sean's flat, with a stitch in my side. It hurt every time I breathed. Sean's lights were on above the shop, and it was tempting to knock on his front door. At that moment all I wanted was for him to run me a bath, soap my back, then fall into his bed. But it would only be a matter of time before the pressure and the expectations started up again.

The stitch got the better of me as soon as I began to run again. I slumped on a wall outside a run-down pub and tried to catch my breath. The pub sign showed an angel, with a sly smirk on her face and a lopsided halo. I leaned forward and waited for the pain to go.

'Are you all right, love?'

A dark-haired woman in heavy make-up and a breathtakingly short skirt perched on the wall beside me.

'Fine, thanks, just a bit out of breath.'

'Overdone it, have you?'

'Looks like it, yeah.'

She must have been about my age, but there were deep lines carved around her mouth, as if she had been born with a cigarette between her lips. Her eyes were a soft, out-of-focus blue. She gave an exaggerated shiver.

'Fucking freezing tonight, isn't it?' Her teeth chattered when she spoke.

'Go back in, don't worry about me.'

She looked at me as if I was simple. 'I can't, love. I'm working.'

'Working?'

She nodded at the cars crawling past. 'I might miss one of my regulars.'

I glanced at her outfit: sheer black tights, stilettos, crimson lipstick, Cleopatra lines circling her eyes.

'Sorry,' I muttered. 'Not enough oxygen getting to my brain.'

A car pulled up on the opposite side of the street and the driver's window lowered a few inches before he sped away.

'Fucking charming.' She made a V sign at the departing car.

'How long have you been doing this?' I asked.

'Longer than I want,' she said, her smile wavering. 'Did you hear about the girl at Crossbones?'

I thought about confessing that I had been the one who found her, but decided against it. 'Did you know her?'

The woman shook her head. She fumbled in her bag and brought out a pack of Silk Cut. 'I stayed at home a few nights after that, I can tell you.'

I thought about the girl, lying in the hospital freezer, eyes wide open, staring at the lining of her silver body bag.

'I'm stopping in September.' Her milky eyes kept shifting in and out of focus. 'I've got a place at college to do hairdressing.'

'That's great,' I nodded. 'What are you called, anyway?'

'Michelle.'

73

There was no time to tell her my name, because a black car pulled up and flashed its headlights. It was too dark to make out the driver's face.

'That's one of mine.' Michelle's expression hardened. She ground her cigarette into the pavement with the toe of her stiletto.

'Thanks for the company,' I said.

'Best give up the jogging, love.' She grinned at me. 'You're not fit enough.' She strutted towards the car and leaned down to negotiate with the slimeball behind the wheel.

I thought about calling her back, paying her to go home, but she would only be out again tomorrow, working her patch. I bent over to stretch my hamstrings, and by the time I looked up again the black car had vanished.

Will was still at home, watching TV with Lola, wearing a clean pair of jeans. He looked like a changed man. Even his ragged beard had disappeared.

Lola dragged her eyes from the screen. 'We saved you some pizza, Al.'

In the kitchen I helped myself to a slice loaded with ham and pepperoni from the takeaway box. The front door slammed before I had taken two bites.

'Jesus.' Lola peered out of the window. 'He was out of here like a bat out of hell.'

'That's how it goes,' I nodded. 'You think he's doing okay, then you don't see him for weeks.'

We watched Will's van speeding away around the corner.

'He was just beginning to relax.' Lola's eyes were brimming.

'You did well.' I put my arm round her shoulders. 'You even got him to take a bath. He never does that for me. You must have special powers.'

'I just want to help him, that's all.'

'I looked in his bag today, while he was asleep.'

'Did you find what he's been taking?'

'He's got a knife, Lo. A nasty one, with a horrible long blade.'

'Jesus, the poor soul.' Lola covered her mouth with her hand.

'What do you mean?'

'He's terrified. He thinks the whole world wants to hurt him.'

I drew in a deep breath. 'Do you think he'd ever use it?'

'Course not, Al.' Lola's eyes were round with shock. 'He's still our Will, isn't he? He wouldn't harm a fly.'

She rested her head on my shoulder for a moment then went into the bathroom. Before long the flat filled with the scent of bath oil and her voice singing operatic scales, a fraction off-key.

8

The lift took several minutes to arrive the next morning. The interior looked the same as always, slick metal, big enough for six people to pack themselves shoulder to shoulder, like sardines. The whirr of the air-conditioning reminded me that you don't die if you step inside. Lifts may look like coffins, but they rarely are, if you can hold your nerve. I jumped in before there was time to change my mind, and the floor lurched upwards as panic bubbled in my chest. The advice I gave my patients seemed ridiculous: distract yourself, control your breathing, imagine yourself somewhere safe. None of it worked. By the eighth floor I felt like an astronaut stuck in a capsule, oxygen supply almost exhausted. The walls played tricks on me, expanding and contracting like a concertina. And then I was back in the cupboard under the stairs, with no chance of escape, my father's footsteps pounding on the floor above, bringing the ceiling down around my ears. The emergency button was no use. Pressing it would only make the lift stop immediately, and I would be trapped between floors. The idea made me want to claw through the metal walls. Luckily the lift juddered to a halt at the sixteenth floor. A student nurse watched me stagger into the fresh air.

'Are you okay?' she asked anxiously. 'Do you need to sit down?'

I tried to smile, but my legs were buckling. I made it to the toilets before the shaking kicked in, and the anger. Gradually my breathing slowed down. It was a syndrome, that was all. Fear of confinement, a terror of losing control. People conquered claustrophobia all the time. After six cognitive behavioural therapy sessions they could use the Underground again, sit on a packed bus, walk through a busy shopping centre. But I still couldn't do any of those things. My avoidance was getting worse. I had stopped travelling at rush hour, steered clear of shopping centres, anywhere where there would be crowds. My reflection stared back at me. I gave myself a forced smile, tried to make myself look like a normal person, rather than a neurotic idiot crippled by irrational fears.

Laura Wallis was already dressed and waiting for me on Ruskin Ward, eyes huge in her emaciated face. She observed me closely, like I might be dangerous, while I scanned her chart.

'It's looking good, Laura. At this rate you'll be home in a few weeks.'

'You're not going to ask me loads of questions, are you?' Her voice was a mixture of resentment and fear.

I smiled. 'Not today. We're just going for a walk.'

'Where are we going?' Laura shuffled along the ward like an old woman, skin stretched tight across the hollows of her face.

'Not far. How about going round this floor, just once?'

She said nothing to start with, pausing every few metres to catch her breath. And then she began to explain, which is what always happens. Something about motion frees people to say what's on their minds. The story ebbed out of her, a few sentences at a time. Bullying at school, her mother's suffocating kindness, and the magazines she bought, populated by models who kept themselves child-sized. I don't know why I took a liking to Laura. I think it was her determination to resist instructions, and the way she was trying so hard not to be afraid. She leaned on my arm as we dawdled back through the ward, an odd combination of a geriatric and a child. I laid a blanket across her legs and sat down on the edge of her bed.

'You'll come back tomorrow, won't you?' Her eyes glistened.

'Course I will.' I touched her hand for a second and was surprised that she didn't try to draw away.

Someone was waiting outside my consulting room when I got back. I could see who it was immediately. In his pale grey suit he looked like a huge boulder, dumped in the middle of the corridor. DCI Burns raised himself slowly to his feet and held out his hand.

'Sorry to bother you at work, Alice.'

'Don't worry. I've got a few minutes before my next appointment.'

'I thought you'd like an update.'

Burns sat opposite me. His shrewd eyes took in the details of my room. I wondered what he made of the abstract landscape an ex-patient had given me, and the cheese plant in its tiny pot, struggling to stay alive.

'How's the investigation going?' I asked.

'Not great,' he sighed. 'The official position is that we are following all available lines of enquiry.'

'But having no luck?'

'Fuck all, to be honest. The post-mortem told us what we already knew. The kid was starving by the time she died. The pressure sores on her back mean she was kept somewhere too small to stand up in, like the Benson girls.'

My eyes closed for a second. 'He kept her in a box.'

'Or a very small room.' Burns flicked through his notebook as if he had lost interest in the topic. 'No news on Morris Cley either, except he was spotted at London Bridge Station two days ago. He hasn't been to his mum's place since he attacked you.'

'So long as he keeps his distance, I'm happy.'

'I bet.' Burns peered over the top of his glasses. 'How's the face?'

'Fine. I haven't exactly been maimed.'

Burns's smile was a tiny pink crescent against the pallor of his face. 'You don't believe in making a fuss, do you, Alice?'

For a second I thought about shopping Alvarez. No doubt Burns would take a dim view of coppers flirting with the women they were meant to protect. 'There's something I meant to tell you,' I said. 'I got a letter.'

'Fan mail?'

'Not exactly. It's pretty nasty actually, posted to my flat.'

'I'd better take a look. Bring it in if you like, or I'll send someone round.'

'It's probably nothing,' I said. 'If a patient's delusional, you can work your guts out and they still think you're the enemy. And it can't be that hard to figure out my address, if Morris Cley managed it.'

Burns looked aghast. 'God almighty, there's no way on earth I could do your job.'

'No?'

'Wouldn't have the patience. That's the good thing about my work. Someone does something wrong' – he clapped his hands together as if he was closing a book – 'and that's it. End of story.'

'Except it's not always that simple, is it?'

'Not this time.' Burns passed a large white handkerchief across his forehead. 'That's why I came to see you.'

'I thought there'd be an ulterior motive.'

'The thing is, Alice, I need you to go and see Marie Benson. She's in London for some hospital treatment.'

I stared at him open-mouthed. The idea of going to see the woman the tabloids billed as the most evil in Britain didn't appeal at all. It sounded like the worst imaginable way to spend an evening, and it was bound to leave me processing the experience for days. If our memories were like hard-drives I wouldn't have minded so much. That way I would be able to delete the experience as soon as I'd given Burns the information he needed.

'I can't do that. Sorry.'

Burns rested his heavy jaw on his hands. 'Please, Alice.'

'It's not my specialism. I've told you, I don't do forensic work. I'd be out of my depth.'

'But you've been involved from the start.'

I leaned back in my chair. 'More involved than I want to be.'

'If you do it, I won't ask for any more favours. I promise.'

Burns's eyes bored into me. He was oddly hard to resist. There was something dogged about him, a pathological commitment to his work, no matter how tough it got. God knows how his wife would keep him occupied when she finally forced him to retire. Somehow he coaxed an agreement out of me, then levered himself out of his chair with unusual speed. Evidently his strategy was to escape before I had time to change my mind.

My next patient was a woman I had just begun working with. Her face was already swollen with anger because the start of her session had been delayed. As soon as she sat down she launched into a description of the rage she felt when she woke up each morning, the way it stuck to her like a dress she couldn't take off, even when she went to bed. Another person inhabited her body. It made her yell at her kids. Yesterday she had punched her husband, for no reason she could identify. A torrent of words flooded out of her and I waited for a gap, so

I could explain that anger is often a symptom of depression. No gap came. She was so busy venting her spleen that she didn't notice me staring out of the window, worrying about the devil's bargain Burns had squeezed out of me.

9

Running downstairs gave me no pleasure that evening. Normally it's a crazy four-minute dash past every landing, desperate to fly through the exit doors into air that hasn't been filtered. But knowing what I had to do made me want to hide under my desk. I considered turning up my collar and sneaking away, but by now Burns would be waiting, and I couldn't let him down.

A black car crawled past, lights flashing. Alvarez was in the driver's seat, wearing his smart coat and his usual unreadable expression.

'Where's Burns?' I snapped.

'Stuck in a meeting. He sends his apologies.' Alvarez parked in an empty space and turned to face me as I got in.

'Can we just go, please? Let's get this over with.'

'Okay.' He held up his hands. 'But I should apologise first, shouldn't I?'

'You should,' I agreed, 'but the question is, do you know how?'

'It's not easy for me.' He ran his hand over the back of his neck. 'I'm Spanish, you see. My family are from Valencia.'

'Is that meant to be some kind of excuse?'

'Spanish men don't apologise.' His face was grave, but his tone suggested that he might be joking. 'That would be a sign of weakness. It would be *una pérdida de honor.*'

'What does *una pérdida de honor* mean?'

'A loss of honour.'

'Maybe you could do with losing some. We can start over, if you say sorry.'

He took a deep breath. '*Le ruego que me disculpe.*'

'How do I know that's an apology?'

'Trust me, it was hard to say.'

I expected him to turn away, but he carried on studying me, beyond the point of comfort. His gaze passed across my face. He seemed to be memorising the colour of my eyes, the exact set of my mouth.

'Shouldn't we get moving?'

'If you insist.' Eventually he put his hands back on the wheel. The car eased into the traffic on Newcomen Street and I glanced at him. His hair was too long, flopping across his forehead, dark stubble turning into a beard. Apart from his expensive clothes, he had forgotten how to take care of himself. I wondered what his wife felt about him coming home late every night. Maybe they had one of those marriages where no questions got asked, each doing exactly what they pleased.

'I bet Burns had to twist your arm to do this,' he said.

'Too right. I wish I'd said no.' I stared out of the window. We were crawling down the Walworth Road at walking pace. A group of women in hijabs were standing outside a halal supermarket. It was hard to tell whether they were talking or silent, black veils obscuring their mouths. 'It's not my idea of fun.'

'I thought psychologists were fascinated by the workings of sick minds.'

'I am, but there's no point in working with psychopaths. Most of them are untreatable. If you have a personality disorder, no one exists except you. You'll march over the dying bodies of your children to get what you want, without any guilt at all.'

Alvarez glanced at me. 'Sounds like you're scared.'

'Not scared, just a bit apprehensive.'

'Same thing, isn't it?'

I was about to correct him, but we were already pulling into the car park of the Maudsley, on Denmark Hill. I've always had a soft spot for the place. I did my training there and lived with Tejo for five years in a flat in Camberwell that shook every time a train went by. We got used to it after a while. Every fifteen minutes the jam jars rattled in the cupboard like teeth chattering.

I followed Alvarez through the colonnaded entrance of the hospital. I've always loved the grandeur of the building, with its pillars and chequered marble floors. The Maudsley was built on a wave of Victorian scientific optimism, when they believed that even madness would find a cure.

Alvarez trotted ahead of me up the stairs. By the fourth floor he wasn't even out of breath. I felt like challenging him to race me to my office at Guy's, to see if he'd survive.

I couldn't predict what kind of woman would be waiting for us in the consulting room. When I was a girl I was convinced that our faces held a record of our lives. If you studied someone's expression for long enough, you would find an inventory of their deeds. Marie Benson had changed since her picture was splattered across the tabloids six years earlier. Back then she was the archetypal barmaid with a gap-toothed smile, bottle-blonde hair, a penchant for low-cut tops. She was unrecognisable now.

When she turned in our direction her face was expressionless. There was no evidence of the murders she had carried out, all the lies she'd told. It could have been exhaustion, or maybe she had been in solitary confinement so long that she had forgotten how to interact. Her grey hair was badly cut, a ragged frizz that almost reached her shoulders. She couldn't have been more than fifty, but already she looked like one of those old women you see in the lounge of OAPs' homes, washed up on a tide of daytime TV.

Her gaze flickered in my direction when I introduced myself. 'And who's that with you?'

'DS Alvarez, Marie. You remember me, don't you?'

'How could I forget?' She primped her hair for a second, then folded her hands neatly in her lap, like gloves waiting to be put away.

When I sat down I noticed that her eyes were fixed on the middle distance, never anchoring on anything. It dawned on me that she must be almost completely blind.

'What's this about then?' Benson's voice was roughened by years of smoking. She angled her face to catch my reply, using her ears instead of her eyes to pick up nuances.

'The police asked me to visit you, Marie. It's nothing to worry about.'

She gave a loud, nasal laugh. For a moment I caught a glimpse of the woman who kept the journalists intrigued for all those months. She must have used that odd, leering smile of hers as a magnet to draw people into her orbit.

'Nothing worries me these days, Doctor.' She touched the small gold crucifix around her neck. 'I've got everything I need.'

'How's Rampton treating you?'

Benson held the cross between her fingertips, like I was an evil spirit that only her faith could keep at bay.

'Could be worse. They let me go to church, and I've got a radio, so I know what's going on in the world. A woman reads to me now and then.'

She had hardly moved since the conversation began, hands lying tidily on top of each other. Her body was completely under control and, unlike most people, she wasn't afraid of silence. Most of us cram every gap in a conversation with excess words, but she was on her best behaviour like a well-raised child, speaking only when she was spoken to.

'But you're still campaigning to get out, aren't you? Still defending your innocence.'

She gave another loud, scoffing laugh. Laughter seemed to be the only impulse she couldn't suppress.

'I can't stop my supporters gathering their petitions, if they want to. But that's not why you're here, is it?'

For a moment I almost felt sorry for her. Blindness had made her vulnerable. She must have known we were staring at her, subjecting her to our scrutiny, but she had no way of guarding herself. Maybe that was why she had developed that mask-like expression.

'I'd like to talk to you about the hostel, if that's okay.'

'How did I guess?' Benson's mouth twitched. 'You want to know about Ray, don't you?'

'I want as much detail as you can give me.'

'I know why you're here.' Her blank eyes skated past my face. 'I heard what happened at Crossbones on the news.'

'You've been to Crossbones, have you, Marie?'

'Course I have, I lived just round the corner. It's the prostitutes' graveyard, isn't it?'

'Not exactly. It's just a piece of unhallowed ground where the bodies of sex workers were dumped, because the Church didn't approve. No headstones, and the graves weren't even numbered.'

Benson's expression remained as blank as ever, but her body language gave her away. She was leaning forward in her chair, as if she was expecting a morsel of prime gossip.

'Tell me what the hostel was like, Marie. I hear it was full, every day. All those rough sleepers must have thought they'd landed in heaven.'

She gave a narrow smile then crossed her arms. 'Do you know how many people have visited me over the years, Dr Quentin, digging for information?'

'Dozens, I expect.'

'Hundreds, more like. Police, shrinks, journalists. And it's been worse since Ray went. Now there's just me to chuck your questions at.'

'Who knew, Marie?'

'Knew what?'

'About your special rules. Keep them in the dark, gagged and blindfolded, no food, no water, all those little scars. You told someone, didn't you? It was too much to carry on your own.'

'I didn't know a thing, Dr Quentin,' Benson whispered. 'Ray ran the place, and he told me those girls had packed their bags and moved on. I had my head down, cooking, scrubbing floors, making beds. The cellar was Ray's empire. He made furniture down there, when we first got married. He never let on where he kept the key.'

Benson's words came out like a mantra. Maybe she had repeated them so often she believed them herself.

'Five girls are still unaccounted for, aren't they, Marie?'

'So they tell me.' Her hand flew up to her crucifix. 'But how can I say where they are, if I don't know?'

'That cross comforts you, doesn't it?'

'I'll be wearing it when they put me in the ground.' She covered the cross protectively with the flat of her hand. 'It reminds me I'm not alone.'

'And what about your husband, Marie, did you see him before he died?'

'The judge wanted us kept apart. We couldn't see each other or use the phone. He said we were a toxic combination.' The idea seemed to amuse her. 'Bloody ridiculous. I worked my guts out in that place. No thanks from anyone.' Benson looked aggrieved, like she was still waiting for someone to give her a promotion.

'We'd better leave you in peace.'

'Leave me with Sergeant Alvarez, if you like.' She twisted her body in his direction, giving her best open-mouthed smile, blank eyes trying to pinpoint him.

Alvarez's expression was even more hostile than usual.

'You're out of luck, Marie,' I said. 'He's married.'

'Pity.'

'Here's my card. Call me if you feel like talking.' I placed the card in her outstretched hand, taking care not to touch her.

'I might just do that. It helps pass the time.'

Benson looked disappointed when we got up to leave. In her position any kind of human contact must have been better than none.

'It's not me you should talk to,' she called as I opened the door. 'Sergeant Alvarez knows exactly what Ray got up to in his spare time.'

Her eyes made direct contact with mine, and for a second I wondered if her blindness was just another lie.

'What did she mean about you knowing Ray Benson?' I asked Alvarez when we got back to the car.

He seemed reluctant to answer, as if he was admitting to something shameful. 'It was me that heard Ray Benson's confession. Fourteen hours, over two days. We picked him up at eleven o'clock from a pub in Borough. He was paying for last orders.'

'And you grilled him all night?'

'Off and on.' Alvarez looked straight ahead, hands balanced on the dashboard.

'That's one hell of a conversation.'

'He took twelve hours to break. Then the last two hours I couldn't shut him up if I tried. He told me what he did to eight of the girls, every detail.'

'But not the other five.'

'He stopped talking and that was that,' Alvarez frowned. 'He hanged himself at Broadmoor five years later.'

'Jesus.'

'And that bitch could tell us exactly where those girls are buried right now, if she wanted to.' A muscle twitched, just above his jaw.

'What do you mean?'

'I thought you knew.' Alvarez stared at me. 'Ray was only following her instructions. She wrote down the time she wanted it to take, the knives she wanted him to use.'

I closed my eyes and Marie Benson appeared out of nowhere, with her empty face and nondescript clothes. It was hard to imagine her possessing the energy to damage anyone. Maybe that was why she made someone else carry out her plans.

'Did you get any counselling after listening to all of that?' I asked.

He shook his head. 'No need.'

'Of course not. That would be *una pérdida de honor*, wouldn't it?'

He gave a low laugh. 'Go on then, diagnose me, Dr Alice, I can see you're dying to.'

'Post-traumatic stress disorder. But you knew that already, didn't you? You've checked your symptoms on the net.'

Alvarez shook his head and leaned back in the driver's seat. 'Very smart. Except you're a mile wide of the mark. And now I expect you want a ride home, don't you?'

We didn't speak on the way back. My head was busy cleansing itself, putting things back in their place. When we got to

Providence Square I thanked Alvarez for the lift and tried to open the door. The handle rattled but wouldn't budge.

'Your lock's broken.'

He leaned across me, his shoulder pressing against mine. 'It just takes a bit of force, that's all.'

His face was so close I could have kissed his cheek without moving a muscle. It was a struggle to remember my rule about not sleeping with married men. When the door finally swung open I leapt out of the car and said goodbye, before there was time to change my mind.

IO

Lola's belongings were scattered across every room when I hauled myself out of bed the next morning. Her purple scarf was draped over a chair in the hall, a pair of leopard-skin boots by the settee, cartons of Chinese takeaway littering the kitchen counter. Already she was more at home in the flat than I was. Comfortable enough to leave a trail of glamorous jewellery in the bathroom, and finish my most expensive face cream. But somehow when she emerged from the spare room it was impossible to stay annoyed. She was so delighted to see me.

'Al! Where've you been?' She looked gorgeous and dishevelled, a sea of dark red curls flowing across her shoulders.

'You don't want to know.'

'I do, actually.' Lola curled herself into a kitchen chair, clutching her knees.

'Wasting my time talking to vicious psychopaths.'

'You're kidding.'

'Unfortunately not. I had to interview Marie Benson last night.'

'God, how creepy.'

'Creepy's an understatement.' I put a cup of coffee in front of her. 'She's like an alien species. What have you been up to anyway?'

'Not much.' She rested her head on her hand, as if it was a burden to carry. 'I had an audition, for a dance job in Covent Garden.'

'Any luck?'

'The director liked me, I think. But I haven't heard a dicky-bird.'

I sipped my coffee. 'You will, today, I bet you.'

'This came for you, by the way.' Lola rooted through a pile of junk mail that had accumulated on the kitchen table, then dropped a white envelope beside my cup. 'I meant to put it under your bedroom door.'

'Shit. It's from him.'

'Who?'

'The weirdo who sent me the death threats.'

'God, Al, why didn't you tell me?' Lola grabbed the envelope from my hand and peered at it. 'Funny handwriting for a bloke. My aunt writes like that. She's so uptight, every word has to be perfect, or she rips it up and starts again.'

Lola used a long, scarlet fingernail to slice open the letter. Her expression changed from curiosity to horror as she scanned the page.

'Jesus, Al. The sick bastard.'

'Go on, read it out for me, please. I had to deal with the first one on my own.'

'If I must.' She took a deep breath and began to read.

Dear Alice,

Do you really think you can mend the great cracks running through your patients' minds? How can you, when you're a fraud? You're weaker than they are, just a little girl, tottering on high heels you can't even walk in. You want to hurt me, Alice, and you'll pay for that. You don't know what real pain feels like yet. Soon you'll understand.

Lola's hand shook as she put the sheet of paper back on the counter.

'Who would send you something like that, for fuck's sake?'

'God alone knows.'

'He's stalking you, Al.' Lola's green eyes were round with panic. 'He's got your address, and he says he wants to hurt you. Promise me you'll tell the police.'

I held my hands up. 'All right, all right.'

'Today. Promise me.'

After a dramatic pause Lola refilled her coffee cup and headed to her room before I had time to tell her about my flirtation with Alvarez.

Someone knocked on the front door just as I was dialling the police station. The face that appeared in the spy-hole made me do a double-take. I stepped away then looked again, to reassure myself before letting him in. My brother looked like a different person. He was wearing clean black trousers and a smart jacket I hadn't seen before. Even his face looked different. His dark blond hair had been cut short and he was clean-shaven. His eyes still looked spooked and bloodshot, but if someone met him for the first time, they would never guess he lived in a van.

'My God, you look great, Will! Ten years younger.'

'Thanks,' he said quietly. His mouth twitched into an anxious smile.

'Where did you get the clothes?'

'Oxfam. Lola took me yesterday.' He ran his hand across his forehead self-consciously. 'And her friend cut my hair.'

'She's transformed you.' I touched his shoulder for a second, felt his collarbone under my thumb, only a thin layer of skin covering it.

Will fished in his pocket and brought out matches and a pouch of tobacco. I had given up the fight about smoking indoors, it was always a losing battle. His hands trembled as he dropped a trail of brown leaves on to the cigarette paper.

'I'm going to start again, Al.' He said the words tentatively, trying them on for size. 'It's not too late. I'm only thirty-five.'

'That's brilliant, Will. Where are you off to?'

'I'm seeing this therapist Lola's friend told me about.' His foot tapped out a rhythm on the wooden floor, as if he was listening to dance music no one else could hear.

'So that's why you look so smart.'

'Partly,' he agreed, then took a long drag on his roll-up. 'I want to show her I mean business.'

'She'll know that as soon as she talks to you. What time's your appointment?'

'Ten o'clock, in Clapham.'

'What kind of therapy is it?'

Will shrugged. 'She uses crystals and stuff. She's amazing, apparently.'

My optimism evaporated. There were so many charlatans in the phone book, promising expensive cures to the desperate, with nothing to offer except hot oils, vitamin pills and incantations. God knows what kind of therapist thought she could cure bipolar disorder by balancing rocks on someone's skin. I bit my lip.

'I hope it helps, Will. Maybe it'll relax you.'

He stubbed out his cigarette. 'The thing is, I need to borrow some cash.'

'How much do you need?'

I was breaking all my own rules. Normally I bought him things; filled his van with diesel every few weeks and encouraged him to eat my food, but I never gave him money. The idea of him using it to buy drugs that might kill him was more than I could bear.

'Eighty quid. Forty for the assessment, then forty for the first session.'

'I'll make out a cheque if you tell me her name.'

'Can't remember.' He scrabbled in the pocket of his jacket and pulled out a scrap of paper. 'I've only got her address.'

'Okay, let's go to the cashpoint then. Give me a minute to get ready.'

I went into my room and pulled on my running things, packing my work clothes into my rucksack.

'Ready?'

Will was sitting exactly where I'd left him, perched on an uncomfortable stool. When he followed me to the door I noticed that even his walk had changed. In the old days he strode along so fast that I couldn't keep up. Now even his pace was unreliable. He seemed to have forgotten how to measure his steps.

'Maybe they'll give me my old job back,' he mumbled as we crossed Providence Square.

I smiled at him. 'Or you could try something completely new.'

He shook his head vehemently. 'There's no time, Al. *Carpe diem*, Lola says.'

Carpe diem had been Lola's motto ever since we saw *Dead Poets Society* at an impressionable age. Maybe she hadn't worked out that it didn't apply to Will – he would have to bring himself back under control before anything stayed in his hands. We walked along Tower Bridge Road together, until we came to the cashpoint. Will tucked the twenty-pound notes carefully into the pocket of his new jacket. His eyes were brimming.

'Thanks, Al,' he muttered. 'I won't let you down.'

'I know.' I touched his cheek for a moment. 'Where are you going now? It's a long time till your appointment.'

'Back to yours. I'm making breakfast for Lola.'

'Sounds like you've got a new best friend.'

'She's brilliant, Al.' His face lit up. 'I never realised.'

I gave him a brief hug, then watched him hurry away with his odd, unsteady gait. He looked as if the first strong breeze could bring him down.

Tower Bridge Road was already solid with traffic, Mercedes and Audis spitting out fumes as they piled into the City, in search of even bigger bonuses. I jogged left, into the heart of the old leather industry. The street names in Southwark had taught me more local history than visiting a museum could ever have done. Mason Close, Tanner Street, Leathermarket Street. I pictured the leather workers as I ran, in their long aprons, up to their elbows in grease, skin stained with a hundred different dyes. The city's idea of industry had changed completely in a hundred years. Factories had become designer flats, people flooding out of them every morning, heading for the Square Mile and another day behind their computers, then the tube home, without once raising a sweat. No wonder everyone was depressed. Cutting through the back streets behind London Bridge Station, I saw a man sleeping in a doorway, a border collie standing guard at his feet. At Borough High Street I slowed down. There was no choice. The pavements teemed with people, waiting for buses and collecting takeaway coffee from the Greek and Turkish cafés the area specialised in.

The receptionist at the police station was prim but officious, her grey hair permed into hundreds of rigid curls that a force nine gale wouldn't have disturbed. She spent a long time explaining that members of the public couldn't just walk in and demand to see the station's most senior officer.

Her manner softened when Alvarez appeared; suddenly she became everyone's favourite granny.

'It's okay, Sheila,' he explained. 'Alice works with us. She's a psychologist.'

The woman looked at my shabby running gear in horror, proof positive that the medical profession was in terminal decline.

Alvarez led me down the corridor, walking even faster than normal, as if he would have been more comfortable sprinting. When we reached his office, I dropped the two letters on his desk before he could say anything.

'Some light reading for you.'

Alvarez stood beside me, and his shoulder brushed mine as he scanned them.

'Charming,' he muttered. 'And you got the second one today, did you?'

'Yesterday. My friend forgot to give it to me.'

Alvarez raised his eyebrows. 'You've received two death threats, but you didn't bother to bring them in?'

'I told Burns, but I didn't want to give the bastard the reaction he was after.' I crossed my arms. 'He wanted me to be afraid. In fact, he wanted me to shit myself. Why give him the pleasure?'

Alvarez observed me, as if I was one of life's great mysteries, before stepping out into the corridor. It gave me the chance to snoop around his office. A poster of a lush green landscape filled the space behind his desk, the sun hovering over mountains, a haze of blue water in the distance. It was positioned to greet him each morning, like he was stepping into Shangri-la. His desk was covered with files, stacked in separate heaps, keeping chaos at bay. There were two photographs of the same woman on top of his filing cabinet, in plain silver frames. For some reason my breath caught in my throat.

She was standing on a beach in a red dress, dark hair flowing in the breeze, beaming at the person behind the lens. The second was a wedding photo, on the steps of a church. She was almost as tall as Alvarez, her long-fingered hand resting on his chest, a flutter of confetti falling around them. Before I could get a closer look the door swung open.

'It's sorted,' Alvarez said. 'Someone's checking them out right now.'

'And there's one more thing,' I said. 'The evidence from the Benson investigation.'

'What about it?'

'I need to see it,' I snapped. 'Burns asked me to help, remember?'

'We're not talking about a couple of files, Alice. There's enough paper to fill a room.'

Alvarez stood in front of the seaside landscape, like he was advertising the virtues of Spain as a holiday destination.

'Those pictures of your wife are gorgeous, by the way.' I kept my voice expressionless. His gaze shifted away from my face. It was clear that he had no intention of defending himself. 'Just arrange access to the Benson archive for me, please. I'll come back when I have time.'

I closed the door harder than was strictly necessary on my way out. Not hard enough to shatter the glass, but with enough force to demonstrate that I didn't appreciate men who cheated on their wives.

11

It was after eleven by the time I got back to the clinic. Hari's door was open and he beckoned me in, his beatific smile spreading across his face. There was a heaped plate of pastries beside his phone.

'Alice, just in time for a snack.'

I chose an apple turnover, sticky with sugar and cinnamon. 'Do you actually do any exercise, Hari?'

'Not if I can help it.'

'So you're completely cerebral. A mind without a body. Total disconnection.'

'Pretty much.' Hari's smile widened. 'Tejo makes me walk the dog occasionally, but that's as far as it goes.'

'How is Tejo?'

'Furious with me, as a matter of fact.'

'I don't believe you.' In the five years I worked with Tejo, she never once lost her cool, even when the registrars were doing their best to put us in our place.

'She wants you to come to dinner. Apparently I've been remiss.'

'Ready and willing,' I smiled, and stood up to go. 'I'd cross deserts for one of your meals.'

Hari rubbed his hands together. 'Good, we'll fix a date.'

'See you later.'

He called me back just as I was stepping into the corridor. 'Your policeman friend rang. I wrote down the message somewhere.' He hunted through a heap of coloured paper beside his phone.

'Burns?'

'That's the one. He wants to book some of your time.'

I gave a cautious nod. 'That's okay.'

'You're sure you want to?'

'I haven't got a choice on this one.'

'Of course you do.' Hari waved his hand nonchalantly. 'Just like I choose not to play tennis. You're allowed to turn things down, Alice.'

I returned his smile. 'Not this time. I've already committed myself.'

The afternoon contained three out-patient appointments: an elderly woman struggling with depression; a middle-aged man recovering from a stress-induced breakdown; and a teenaged boy suffering from acute social phobia. He spent the whole session humming to himself and hiding behind his fringe. After he left I ran down to Ruskin Ward to check on Laura Wallis, but she had visitors. Two girls were sitting on the edge of her bed, making her laugh. It was a shock to see how tiny she appeared by comparison. Her friends looked like amazons, easily twice her size. But at least Laura seemed relieved that she hadn't been forgotten, and she already looked stronger than when she was admitted, with a glimmer of pink in her cheeks.

It was beginning to sleet by the time I was ready to leave. My Outlook account was still full to capacity: two hundred and thirty-nine questions waiting to be answered. I closed my eyes and tried to imagine two hundred and thirty-nine people queuing along the corridor, waiting for me to fix their lives. The thought made me queasy. It was too cold to walk home so I slipped back into my running gear. My T-shirt felt unpleasantly clammy, so I raced down the stairs even faster than

normal to warm myself up. As usual the stairwell was empty.
God knows what would happen if I ever encountered someone during my descent. It would be like colliding at full speed
off-piste. I skirted through crowds of people going home late,
faces grimed by the cold city air. Sleet landed on my face,
wetting my lips and blurring my vision. My running top was
drenched in seconds, but already I was warm enough not to
care, the river slipping past to my left, disappearing between
buildings, as if it was imaginary.

Will's van was nowhere to be seen. I ripped off my running
gear and draped my bathrobe across the towel rail to get it
warm. My plan was to step straight into the shower, rinse
the day away, then lounge around, doing absolutely nothing.
A note from Lola was waiting for me on the kitchen table.
'Celebration!!! Meet me at Vinopolis at nine. Do not be late.'
One of her auditions must have come up trumps. I screwed
up the pale green envelope she had scribbled on and curled
up on the sofa, determined not to let anything get in the way
of my quiet night at home.

I must have dozed for a while, because the next time I looked
at my watch it was half past eight, and a pang of guilt hit me.
Lola had been so good with Will. Somehow she had made him
see life differently, just by taking an interest. It was an effort,
but I finally forced myself up off the sofa. The mirror in my
bedroom reflected a woman who needed to take better care of
herself, washed out, with damp hair in need of styling. It was
too much effort to replace the make-up I had washed off, so
I pulled on a pair of jeans, biker boots and black V-neck and
headed for the door.

The square was completely deserted. Fortunately no one
was mad enough to venture out into the cold except me. No
crazed psychopaths were waiting to explain the meaning of
pain, before hacking me to bits. I jumped on my bike and

pedalled at full speed along Tooley Street, cursing Lola without moving my lips.

Vinopolis was heaving. Couples were huddled over tables just large enough for a bottle of wine, a candle and a dish of tapas. A waiter shepherded me through the packed cellar, while my eyes got used to the dark. He sat me in a corner to wait for Lola, but by ten past nine there was still no sign of her. Another waiter deposited a bottle of Sauvignon Blanc on my table, with a plate of tapas. I surveyed the dishes of haricot beans in tomato sauce, cubes of Spanish omelette, and white anchovies swimming in oil.

'I didn't order this.'

He smiled at me. 'You didn't have to, someone ordered for you.'

Lola must have arrived before me and gone to the bar, but I couldn't see her anywhere. Apart from the candles guttering on each table the place was completely unlit. It felt like a dungeon, rather than a wine cellar. No windows, crammed with people, and it was a long way to the exit. My chest started to tighten, so I tried the tapas to distract myself. The anchovies delivered a heavy shot of salt and brine, followed by the garlicky sweetness of the beans.

Suddenly a spotlight flicked on in front of me. A tall woman in a long black dress stepped on to a small platform, a microphone hovering by her mouth. I rubbed my eyes. Lola was wearing a slash of crimson lipstick. I reeled backwards in my seat. To my knowledge she had never sung anywhere, except in the bath. A piano picked out a few lazy notes and she spoke seductively to her audience, as if she had been a chanteuse all her life.

'Why don't we forget it's winter out there, if we can?'

She launched into a slow, smoky version of 'Summertime', and a ripple of applause went round the room. As usual Lola had pulled it off. That's what I admired about her: if life as an actress didn't work out, she became a dancer, and if that failed, she taught herself to sing. Clusters of men gazed at her adoringly, while she smouldered through another torch song.

And that's when I spotted Sean. He was sitting at a table on the far side of the room, his back to the bare brick wall, deep in conversation with a pretty, dark-haired girl. Her head was tipped back, laughing as if he was the funniest man alive. Her hand was resting on his forearm. Maybe she needed to remind herself that such a dreamboat was flesh and blood. I looked for the nearest exit while Lola sang one of my favourite Nina Simone ballads. There's no explaining why I was so upset. Maybe I'd been keeping him in reserve without realising. I glanced in his direction again. By now they were holding hands. No doubt he wouldn't waste any time getting her back to his flat, demonstrating his bedside manner. Or maybe he already had. He was still ridiculously handsome, like all those actors in *ER*, who look like they spend every waking moment in the gym.

He glanced up and saw me watching him. He jerked upright in his seat and dropped the girl's hand like a hot coal. I forced myself to give Lola my undivided attention for the next ten minutes. As soon as there was a break between songs I escaped. The winter air cleared my head immediately, freezing my self-pity in its tracks.

'Alice, wait.' Sean appeared just as I was unchaining my bike from the railings.

'Go back,' I smiled. 'Don't let me spoil your evening.'

'It's not how it looks. She asked me to come along, to cheer me up, that's all. It doesn't mean anything.'

'Bollocks.'

'It's true.' He frowned at me, his hand resting on the saddle of my bike. 'It's you who keeps me awake every fucking night. You don't know what you've done to me. Most of the time I can't think about anything else.'

'Look, Sean. It's great that you've found someone. Now, can I have my bike back please?'

'The least you can do is let me have my say.'

I dug my freezing hands deeper into my pockets. 'Go on then.'

'Sooner or later, it'll catch up with you.'

'Sorry?'

'The way you use people.' His face contorted with anger. 'Before long someone won't accept being thrown away like a piece of trash, without an explanation.' He was standing over me, shaking either from cold or rage. Then he stepped backwards suddenly. Maybe he was frightened of what he might do. By now he looked confused, as if he couldn't decide whether to kiss me, or punch me in the mouth.

Neither option attracted me, so it was a relief to race away into the cold when he finally let me go. I felt guilty all the way home, because he had a point. Why let myself get dragged into relationships if I couldn't deliver? I kept trying, but the outcome stayed the same.

Back at the flat I sent Will a text, congratulating him on going to his therapist, but there was no answer. I checked again before crawling into bed, but his van was still nowhere to be seen. God knows where he had gone. He was capable of pulling up the drawbridge for months, if he chose to.

The Monica Ali novel that had been sitting on my bedside table for weeks didn't tempt me. I switched off the light, but the image of Sean's face distorted with anger kept appearing in my mind. Eventually I fell asleep, but something woke me just after three o'clock. The sound was unmistakable, coming through the thin wall. Giggling, and then a few minutes later a man's low moan, bedsprings squeaking. Lola had brought someone back, to celebrate her triumphant career change. There was no choice but to stare at the ceiling and listen to them enjoying themselves, gritting my teeth.

Tomorrow I would have to stop at Boots on my way to work and invest in a packet of super-strength earplugs.

12

Fortunately Lola and her new man were taking a break from their sexual marathon when the alarm went off the next morning. The constant battering of the headboard against the wall had finally stopped. I stood by the fridge and drank a glass of icy, full-fat milk. There's something about milk that always improves my mood. Maybe it's the clean white innocence of it. Or memories of primary school, when the future never extended past break-time and no decisions had to be made. I fried two eggs in a pool of melted butter then sandwiched them between slices of rye bread, crisp with caraway seeds.

The local free newspaper told me about a community I had never noticed before: jumble sales in church halls, a campaign for speed bumps on Tooley Street, a new art gallery opening on China Wharf. The flats all around mine must be a hive of activity. People were getting together, opening businesses, improving things.

A naked man stepped into the hallway as I finished my breakfast. He turned towards me just as I was admiring his rangy, tennis player's physique.

'Looking for the bathroom?' I asked.

'Please.' His smile was completely relaxed. Maybe he didn't bother with clothes, nudity was his normal state.

'Last door on the left.'

He gave a polite wave then sauntered along the hall like he had all the time in the world. Lola emerged a second later, wearing a man's shirt and a brilliant smile.

'Pleasant evening?' I asked.

She fell into the chair opposite and let her blissed-out body language tell the story.

'As good as that?'

'Better.' Her eyes were even more sleepy and cat-like than normal. Any second now she would begin to purr.

'Go on then. What's his name and where did you find him?'

'Lars. He runs the bar at Vinopolis.'

'And let me guess. He's Danish, right?'

'Swedish.'

I nodded. 'That explains why he's so comfortable in the buff.'

'All that rolling around in the snow, beating yourself with twigs,' Lola giggled.

'Coffee?'

'Go on then, and do one for Lars please, darling.'

I filled the kettle. 'Your singing was amazing last night, by the way.'

'How do you know?' she pouted. 'You buggered off halfway through my set.'

'Sorry. There was an old flame I needed to escape from. You were great though, I had no idea you could sing.'

Lola grinned. 'I was just doing my Bette Midler impersonation.'

Out of the corner of my eye Lars was strolling back into the spare room. Ash-blond, tall and perfectly formed.

'Did you see much of Will yesterday?' I asked.

'Not really.' Lola gazed out of the window, looking for his van. 'He went for his reiki session.'

'What exactly is reiki?'

'They rest their hands on your pressure points, gets rid of your stress.'

'I bet. Rub someone's forehead for half an hour and hey presto, you're forty quid richer. That would lower my stress levels too.'

'Don't knock it, Al,' Lola tutted. 'You should go with him, or you'll explode one day, like that fat bloke in *La Grande Bouffe*.'

She smiled cheerily, picked up the mugs of coffee, then dashed back into the spare room.

It was still dark when I set off for my run, frost sparkling on the road, as if someone had dusted it with glitter. My good intentions about distance and speed were soon abandoned, because my breakfast was doing cartwheels in my stomach. Halfway across Tower Bridge I stopped to take in the view. The river widened downstream as it flowed past Wapping, slate grey, sequinned with reflections from car headlights, half a dozen tugs cutting its surface to ribbons. I slowed down again a few minutes later to admire the harbour master's house in St Katharine's Dock. It's my favourite building in the whole of London, bay windows on both floors with uninterrupted river views. I wanted to break in and curl up on a window seat, watch the sun rise over the city's wharves and spires. By Wapping Wall my pace was improving, and I could taste the salty pungency of the river at high tide. Lights were beginning to come on in the windows of flats at Limehouse Basin. Thank God I didn't live there. The lock was awash with litter, empty fag packets and dozens of lager cans drifting by the gates.

It was a relief to get back on to the river path, Canary Wharf floating ahead of me, tower blocks glowing like a financier's version of Las Vegas. Every building was branded with the name of a different bank, picked out in coloured lights. Will never convinced me of his reasons for becoming a trader. It seemed to involve juggling huge numbers for clients he never met. Maybe he wanted to build a wall of money so impenetrable, he would never feel a draught again.

A pair of joggers ran towards me. Each man gave me the same smile, slightly embarrassed, as if we had been caught doing something that no one else would understand. Maybe they were right. Running before daybreak is a kind of masochism; part of your brain constantly asking why you're not in bed, enjoying a lie-in, like a normal person. An old man tottered towards me, leaning heavily on his stick. Maybe it was the only thing left in his world that he could still rely on.

The mirrored buildings of Canary Wharf began to turn pink. I wanted to run until they were within touching distance, but there was no time, so I stopped by the railings and counted the churches on the opposite bank. They were hiding behind the wharves, only their needle-sharp spires giving them away.

I jogged back more leisurely, enjoying the clean-slate sensation a long run always gives, tension evaporating through my pores. It made me wonder how I'd let things get so out of proportion. By Tanner Street, everything was solved. Who cared if Sean was in love with someone else? Lola was welcome to spend the next six months shagging her boyfriend at high volume, and sooner or later all my brother's problems would be fixed.

Will's van was back in my parking space in Providence Square, which seemed like a good omen. My brain was still in hazy post-exercise mode. I tapped on the passenger door and tried to peer inside, but the faded blue curtains were firmly closed. There was no sound at all when I pressed my ear to the glass. Yesterday must have exhausted him. After so long without anyone touching him, it would have felt strange to be comforted.

Crossing the square towards the flats, I glanced back, expecting to see him, bleary-eyed at the window, cursing whoever had interrupted his dreams. A heap of black rubbish bags was lying on the pavement a few metres from the van. They would be the first thing Will saw when he drew back his curtains. I went back to clear them away, but the black shape turned out to be a roll of polythene. When I tugged one end it unwound itself. I covered my mouth with the back of my hand, but it was too late to shield myself from the stench of urine and excrement. The pavement reeled up to greet me. The blood soon rushed back to my brain, my vision gradually clearing. Then I made myself look again.

The naked body was skeletal, older than the girl at Crossbones Yard. I recognised the scar on her abdomen as an appendectomy, faded to a thin silver line. But all the other scars were fresh, a network of livid crosses covering her body. Only her face had been spared. She must have been beautiful once – a delicate snub nose, heart-shaped face, fine black eyebrows. Her mouth gaped, as if she had been in the middle of laughing. But her last seconds must have been terrifying, gasping for air like a fish out of water, lungs collapsing in her chest. Soon she would be lying beside the Crossbones girl, in the freezer at Guy's, comparing wounds.

A wave of nausea hit me and I took a step backwards. It dawned on me that the killer had dumped the body just a few feet behind Will's van. I ran to the driver's window and pounded on the glass with both fists. When I tugged at the handle, the door swung open, and my heart turned over in my chest. Maybe he was still safe and he had just forgotten to lock it. I knelt on the driver's seat and forced myself to look into the dark interior of the van. His bed was empty and there was no sign that he had been disturbed. In fact there was evidence that he was trying to turn over a new leaf. He had thrown away the heaps of newspapers, folded his clothes into piles, pairs of shoes lined up under his bunk. He must be safe somewhere, keeping warm.

I pulled the black plastic sheet back across the woman's body. My wrist touched her ice-cold face. She must have been dumped there in the middle of the night, left on the pavement to freeze. Calling the police on my mobile only took a few minutes, but by now people were flooding out of the flats. Mothers in cashmere jackets and kitten heels were piling their children into the Audis and BMWs that lined the square. They stared at me as I stood guard. Ruffians like me blocking the pavement in our cheap running gear were responsible for lowering the tone.

Burns was the first to arrive, in his grubby blue Mondeo. He squeezed out from behind the steering wheel then struggled across the square. By the time he reached me he was panting for breath. His face was colourless, apart from the dark red veins floating against the whites of his eyes.

'Here we go again, Alice.'

'Sorry, Don. I seem to be making a habit of this.'

'Are you okay?' He shunted his thick glasses back on to the bridge of his nose to take a better look at me.

'I'm not sure. I think so.'

I checked my hands. Even though it was freezing they weren't shaking. My mind had emptied itself, and the outline of the woman's body in her plastic shroud didn't scare me at all. There was no reaction, just a gap where my thoughts should have been.

'Let's take a look at her.' Burns leaned down and peered at the woman's face.

She stared straight past him, trying to catch my eye. A siren grew louder until it screamed to a halt a few metres away. He carried on studying the woman's face intently. 'Poor wee thing,' he muttered, crossing himself as he stood up. His Scots roots obviously came to the fore under pressure.

Suddenly the square was humming with activity. An ambulance had arrived, two police vans and a squad car.

Someone had blocked the road with a line of cones. A hand touched the small of my back. When I turned round it was Alvarez, overstepping the boundaries as usual, managing to look handsome, unkempt and angry, all at the same time. His mouth was set in an immovable line, as if every human experience demanded the same neutrality.

'You don't look too good,' he said quietly. 'Want to sit down?'

My shoulders were beginning to shake, so there was no point in protesting. He guided me to a bench beside the entrance to my block.

'It doesn't make sense,' I told him. 'I got up early, went for a run, and there she was. Wrapped up like a birthday present for me to find.'

'You don't know that,' he said. 'Maybe you've just been unlucky.'

'Nobody's that unlucky twice.'

My fingers were doing an uncontrollable St Vitus's dance in my lap. Alvarez rested his hand over mine and I didn't have the strength to pull away. It gave me the chance to study his wedding ring – a thick, square-edged chunk of white gold, with no markings, apart from the nicks and scratches that come with time. He must have worn it for years, but for some reason his wife didn't even cross my mind. Anyone looking at us at that moment would have thought we were a couple, trying to hold our marriage together. A big, solidly built man, and his little blonde wife, doing her best not to cry.

13

Lola and her new man were sitting at the kitchen table when I got back inside, feeding each other pieces of croissant.

'Al! I thought you'd gone to work.' Lola was still wrapped in Lars's cornflower-blue shirt.

'I've been out there.' I nodded at the window.

The square was thronging with people. A white tent had been erected beside Will's van, over the place where the girl's body was lying. Police cars were coming and going, one of them blocking the road, hazard lights flashing.

'Is something going on?' Lars's immaculate smile flicked on effortlessly. Maybe Alvarez could pay him for lessons in charm.

'Didn't you hear the sirens?'

Lola shook her head dreamily. She looked as if she had been drugged and was only just surfacing.

'Turn on the radio.' I gritted my teeth. 'It'll be on the news.'

In the bathroom I was desperate to throw myself under the jet of water. Tipping my head back, my sight blurred then cleared again. By the time I had dried myself my heart rate was beginning to slow down.

The passenger door of Alvarez's car was slightly ajar when I got back downstairs. He had to manoeuvre carefully out of the square, edging between half a dozen squad cars. My mind still wasn't working properly. It was a struggle to remember exactly what I'd seen. I stared out of the window blankly, until the car swung left into Leathermarket Street, interrupting a stream of Japanese tourists busy photographing everything they saw. A man leaned down and took our picture with an old-fashioned camera, as if we were celebrities. I wondered what he would see when the film was developed: my shocked white face, and Alvarez with his indelible frown.

I phoned Hari, just as we pulled into the car park of the police station. There was a moment's silence while his brain did calculations. I hardly ever called him, because sick days weren't my speciality.

'I found a woman's body this morning,' I told him.

'A body?' he echoed, taking care not to sound shocked.

I stifled a laugh. 'It's okay, Hari. No need to use your sympathetic repetition technique on me. I'll survive.'

'Of course you will. But is anyone helping you?'

'The police. I'm going to the station now.'

'Would you like me to come with you?'

'I'll be fine. Just cancel my appointments please. I don't know when I'll be in.'

'Of course.' Hari's voice was as gentle as always, as if words were things to be given out cautiously, like knives.

Maybe it was my imagination, but Alvarez's swagger seemed less pronounced that day. His walk was slower, like a boxing manager waiting for a fight he had staked his whole future on. When we got inside he led me in the opposite direction from his office, into a meeting room buzzing with people and computers. The air reeked of coffee and adrenalin. Maybe they had spent the night on lockdown, no one allowed to go home. A dozen people were milling around, some of them gazing at their screens, others standing by a large pinboard, which was covered with photos and documents. A tall man quizzed Alvarez earnestly as soon as we walked through the door.

I wandered over to the wall display. My photo had been placed right in the centre. Someone had downloaded it from Facebook. It was taken at Oludeniz in Turkey four summers ago. I looked young and tanned and giggly. Lola had caught me at an unguarded moment, just as we were about to fling off our T-shirts and run into the sea. A picture of the dead girl at Crossbones Yard was pasted beside me, our photos almost touching. Her face was chalk white, still wrapped in her make-shift shroud, like the woman I had just found.

Alvarez appeared again, with two cups of coffee.

'Can I have a biscuit with that? I feel a bit woozy.'

He dumped a polystyrene cup in my hand and hurried across the busy room, stealing a packet of Jaffa Cakes from someone's desk on the way.

We ended up in a cubicle just large enough for a white Formica table and two of the hard plastic chairs the police always use, as if discomfort is their official policy. The space was hardly bigger than a lift, but at least it had a glass wall, which gave the illusion that escape was still an option. The incident room bustled with activity while Alvarez flicked through a sheaf of papers. There was no sign of Burns. Maybe he was still in Providence Square, keeping his eye on the forensics team. Alvarez dropped a blank sheet of paper in front of me.

'If you feel up to it, we need some information, Alice.'

I bit into another Jaffa Cake and waited for him to explain. The rise in blood sugar was helping things to make sense again.

'I need a list of your boyfriends.' Alvarez shuffled his papers awkwardly.

'Sorry?'

'All your partners. With dates, if possible.'

'No problem.' I stared at him. 'Provided you sit here and do the same for me.'

'It's standard procedure, Alice.' Alvarez got to his feet. 'You've discovered too many dead bodies recently.'

'You honestly think I went out with a serial killer, do you?'

'We don't know at this stage. But we have to rule it out, so I'll leave you to it.' He hovered by the door. 'Give me a shout if you need more paper.'

'Ha bloody ha.' I stared at the empty sheet.

The task took nearly an hour. Not because I've had hundreds of lovers, but because my brain was on slowdown. The people in the incident room distracted me, spinning between the phone desk and the wall chart, as if they were taking part in an elaborate dance. Watching them was far more interesting than my sexual history. The first name on my list was Jamie Mitchell. The relationship lasted thirty minutes and involved a lot of frantic fumbling with zips and condoms, when I was sixteen years old, under a monkey puzzle tree in Greenwich Park. Afterwards I examined my face in the bathroom mirror to see if my expression was suddenly grown-up, feeling nothing, except relief not to be a virgin any more. My longest relationship finished after nearly a year, when I was training at the Maudsley. It was great at first, but his mother began dropping hints about July being the best month for honeymoons, so I had to leave. When the list was complete there were nine names on the sheet, in chronological order. Not very impressive for a thirty-two-year-old. I decided not to include the rugby player I had sex with in a broom cupboard on the night I graduated, largely because I couldn't remember his name.

Alvarez appeared in the doorway while I was checking the dates of my conquests.

'Finished?' he asked.

He pulled up a chair, so close our thighs were almost touching.

'Didn't anyone ever teach you about personal space?' I asked. 'You're meant to give people room to breathe.'

He moved his chair a centimetre away then turned to face me. His eyes were so dark it was hard to see where his pupils began and ended.

'Now I need another list of your friends, family and colleagues.'

'This is ridiculous. It's got to be a stranger. I've never seen that handwriting in my life.'

'Nine times out of ten letters like this come from someone you're connected with.' He turned his attention back to my list. 'Do you still see these men?'

'Only the last three.' I pointed to each name in turn. 'I went to his wedding last summer, I meet him for dinner now and then, and Sean's a colleague at Guy's.'

'And who ended the relationships?'

'Shouldn't Burns be doing this?' I peered across the incident room. 'He's the one in charge, isn't he?'

'Technically that's true, I suppose. But he had a heart attack six months ago. He's only just come back.'

'So you do the legwork to reduce his stress.'

'It's not that simple. He's helped me a lot in the past.' Alvarez leaned across the table. 'Look, Alice, if you tell me who ended these relationships, I'll leave you in peace.'

'I did.'

'Which ones?'

'All of them. Every one.'

Alvarez looked up from the list. I watched his expression change. He was busy redrawing his picture of me as a ditsy female who couldn't look after herself, to a witch who destroyed every man on her radar.

★   ★   ★

It didn't take long to name my family members: my mother and Will, a frail aunt who I saw every other Christmas, and two cousins who had moved to the Dordogne, to run a holiday company. I was beginning to wish they'd taken me with them. The list of friends and colleagues proved more difficult. Trying to remember names, dates and contexts was giving me a headache.

It was almost lunchtime when Burns finally arrived. Maybe he had spent the morning dozing in his office while Alvarez conducted the action in the incident room, like a ringmaster. The plastic chair creaked ominously as he sat down. Burns let himself recover for a few seconds before mopping his forehead with one of his favourite white cotton hankies.

'We know who this one is,' he panted. 'Suzanne Wilkes. Her husband reported her missing six weeks ago. She worked for a charity called Street Safe.'

'I've heard of them. They've got a bus, haven't they?'

'A load of *Guardian*-reading do-gooders' – Burns wrinkled his nose – 'giving out sandwiches to druggies, and finding them jobs they'll never hold down.'

'That's your world view, is it?'

He didn't answer. His face was the definition of tired. His skin glistened with a sweat that came from the sheer effort of staying on his feet.

'Any news on the girl at Crossbones?' I asked.

'Not a whisper. Chances are she came over without a visa, slept rough, never found a job. She didn't appear on anyone's radar.'

'And her family back home never find out she's dead.'

'We're not giving up.' Burns's microscopic eyes pinpointed me, as if I might try to fly away.

Over his shoulder developments were happening in the incident room. My scrawled list of conquests had been typed up and magnified to A3 size. It was tacked to the pinboard, for everyone to scrutinise.

'I've got something to show you,' Burns said. He pulled a bundle of papers from the file he was carrying. 'It's the graphologist's report on the letters you gave us.'

Burns heaved himself to his feet again and left me to peruse the report. I've never had much time for graphology, a mixture of nonsense and pseudo-science. But the report was better than I expected. It started with a list of facts. The writer had used a steel-tipped fountain pen, and applied an unusual degree of pressure to incise each word into the paper. The line spacing and gaps between words were unexpectedly regular. Then the report gave a checklist of personality attributes. The writer was organised and obsessive, and the backward-sloping letters meant that he was passive aggressive, waiting to vent the rage he held inside. Photocopies of both letters were stapled to the report. I glanced at the handwriting again, veering to the left, immaculately controlled. Then my eyes flicked back to the first page.

I'd missed the most interesting part. The report explained that the writing was similar to Ray Benson's. A snippet from a letter I had never seen before had been pasted into the report. Although it was addressed to Marie, the writing was just like my unhinged pen-pal's. The killer must have hunted through newspapers and the Internet for snippets of Benson's handwriting that were published by the press. I closed my eyes and tried to take it all in. The report suggested that there was less than ten per cent probability that the killer was writing naturally. He was mimicking Ray Benson's style. I tried to visualise a man hunched over a desk, patiently transcribing death threats for hours at a time, but the picture refused to take shape.

14

By lunchtime I was on information overload. My head felt dangerously full, and there was an odd throbbing pain behind my eyes. A policeman who looked about fifteen years old offered me a cup of tea, then disappeared abruptly. Clearly he hadn't yet mastered the art of small talk. Alvarez was still at the eye of the storm. People circled him in the incident room, asking questions, and offering him pieces of paper. His response was the same each time. He listened carefully then gave a brief reply, never raising a smile. His colleagues probably had dozens of nicknames for him: Mr Happy, Smiler, Sweetness and Light. When the fifteen-year-old boy returned with my tea, it was so thick with sugar that it was undrinkable.

I fished in my bag to check my phone. Three texts and a phone message were waiting for me. Two of the texts were from Lola, but the third was a cryptic one from Sean, inviting me out for dinner, which was baffling. In his shoes I'd have been relieved to move on to someone less complicated. My answering service had registered Will's number, but only a couple of garbled words had been recorded. His voice was strained and a pitch too high, as if his vocal cords were permanently tense. When I called back there was no reply. By now he must have returned to his van and been sent away by Burns's forensics team, in case he contaminated their crime scene.

'You can go home, if you want.' Alvarez arrived while I was looking at my phone. 'Are you okay?'

'Never better.' I rubbed the back of my neck. 'Except my brother worries me.'

'I meant to ask about him.' Alvarez flicked through his sheaf of papers. 'You didn't give us his address.'

'That's right,' I nodded.

'So where does he live?'

'Nowhere.'

Alvarez closed his eyes, as if my sarcasm had finally broken him.

'It's not a joke,' I said. 'Normally he uses my address, but he doesn't own a property.'

'But he must rent somewhere, right?'

'No. That's the thing. Most nights he sleeps in his van.'

'Your brother's homeless?' Alvarez's mouth hung open, as though he had swallowed something unpleasant. He tried to return his expression to neutral, but it was a struggle. Not only was I a danger to my boyfriends, but I was cold-hearted enough to let my brother sleep outside in the middle of winter.

'I see him all the time,' I blustered. 'He's got a key to my flat, he comes by most days.'

'So why are you worried?'

'He hasn't been around since yesterday. His van's in my space, but I don't know if he slept there.'

'Let's get this straight.' Alvarez tried to massage the frown from his forehead. 'Your brother could have spent the night on the same street as the murder victim?'

'Maybe, but at least I know he's safe. He called me this morning.'

'What's wrong with you?' Alvarez slammed down his papers on the desk. 'Why didn't you tell us?'

'There's nothing to tell. He's unpredictable, that's all.'

'It's not him I'm worried about.' He marched back into the incident room, leaving the glass door swinging on its hinges.

Another hour passed without anyone telling me anything. Maybe it was paranoia, but people were looking in my direction more often, peering at me through the glass wall, like I was a specimen in an aquarium. By now every one of them was an expert on my sexual history, and now they had heard that my brother was half-crazy too. It was hard to tell whether their glances were curious, outraged or pitying. The headache that had started behind my eyes had spread to the base of my skull.

I began to scribble on a piece of paper to distract myself. I used the same approach when I saw a patient for the first time, listing every trait or verbal tic that could help my diagnosis. The thing that interested me most was the killer's use of the Benson murders as a prototype, or a form of hero worship. Depending on his illness, he might even believe he could become Ray Benson. Mimicry would allow him to borrow a stronger man's identity.

By the time Burns returned I had filled several sheets of A4 paper with diagrams, scribbles and bullet point lists. He looked exhausted, even though he had managed to avoid the incident room for most of the day.

'It's got to stop, Alice.' He studied me closely, as if I might be dangerous.

'What has?'

'You've upset my deputy again. He's been in my office, moaning his head off. He says you're concealing things.'

'Rubbish.'

'I can see where he's coming from.'

'Look, I've already explained. My brother's mentally ill, he disappears all the time. Last year he cleared off for months without telling me where he'd gone.'

'It doesn't look good, Alice.' Burns blew a long jet of air out of his pursed lips, as if he was playing an invisible trumpet. 'We need to interview him, and now he's done a bunk.'

'Nonsense. Will's probably at my flat right now.'

'He's not.' Burns peered at a computer printout he had spread across the table. 'And you didn't tell us about his criminal record. It's quite impressive, isn't it?'

'Don't exaggerate.'

'Affray, shoplifting, abusing a police officer,' Burns read from the printout, 'not to mention criminal damage and resisting arrest.'

I leaned back in my chair, arms folded. 'Until eight years ago Will was a model citizen, then he got ill. Simple as that.'

'I know.' Burns jabbed at his glasses. 'And that's why he's got off lightly until now.'

'Look, Don. He was turning a corner, there's no way he's got anything to do with this. He wouldn't harm a fly.'

He appraised me thoughtfully. 'All right, Alice, let's get you out of here.'

The crowds made way for Burns in the incident room, like the parting of the Red Sea. A wall of blank faces turned to watch me leave. We headed down a corridor that looked different from the pristine ones at the front of the building. Here the walls were a dirty sepia, the colour of pub ceilings in the days before smoking was outlawed. Burns produced an old-fashioned key from his pocket and opened a large wooden door. The room was almost dark; a narrow stream of light fell from a high window, teeming with dust motes.

'Sorry about the mess,' he muttered. 'No one's been here for a while.'

He tried the light switch several times. It flickered for a few seconds then made a fizzing noise and died. The room was so crowded with junk it was impossible to move: dented cardboard boxes were stacked beside files and heaps of manila envelopes; four or five antiquated computers were piled in a corner; a table groaned under the weight of ring-binders and notepads.

'What is all this?' I asked.

'The Benson archive. You wanted to see it, didn't you?'

I drew in a long breath. 'Jesus, I had no idea there was so much.'

'Witness reports, forensic records, transcripts of interviews. The whole nine yards. Thirty of us doing overtime all year.'

'Can I take a look?'

'You've been here long enough, you should go home.'

'But the answer's here, isn't it? Our man's the secretary of the Bensons' fan club.'

He looked exasperated. 'We're not even sure there's a link between the murders and the letters you've been getting. There's no hard evidence.'

'Half an hour, Don, please.'

Burns rolled his eyes at me, like I was a demanding ten-year-old. 'All right. At least you can't get up to any mischief in here.'

After a few minutes of fussing he left me to my own devices. I dusted down a chair and positioned it under the room's only window, then collected a box-file from the table. It was crammed with photographs. Names and numbers had been printed on the back of each picture of the Bensons' eight victims, and the five who were suspected dead, but never found. The parade of girls looked back at me. Some of them had produced a broad smile for the camera, but others refused to meet my eye. Ray Benson didn't seem to have a type, apart from the fact that they were all young. One of them looked about sixteen. I remembered her face from the news bulletins, a teenage runaway from the west coast of Ireland who came to London for the glamour, but ended up preserved in a layer of concrete under the Bensons' patio. She had a mane of black curls and a neon smile. It was hard to imagine what Alvarez must have felt, listening to Benson describe what he did to each girl down in that cellar. No wonder he'd forgotten how to smile.

Burns came back just as I was replacing the file. He looked wistfully at the chair next to mine, calculating the energy needed to stand up against the comfort of sitting down.

'All right, Alice. Here's how it's going to work. Someone's going to drive you home, and from now on you're not going anywhere without an escort. And when that brother of yours gets in contact, call me immediately. Understand?'

'Of course,' I nodded, too tired to argue.

'And stay away from Ben Alvarez, in case there's an explosion of some kind.'

The ride home was peaceful. My driver was the monosyllabic fifteen-year-old, so there was no need to make conversation, and I didn't miss Alvarez's mixture of disapproval and machismo. The white tent was still standing over the place where the girl's body had been dumped, but the square was empty, except for Will's van.

I flopped into a chair in the kitchen. There were hardly any lights on in the flats opposite. Maybe people were staying with friends, unsettled by the news. There was no sign of Lola anywhere. Either she had gone out, or she and Lars were locked in the spare room, indulging in quiet sex, to see if silence increased their pleasure. The red light on my answer-machine winked urgently.

'Alice, what on earth's going on? The police have been here, looking for your brother.' For once the smooth surface of my mother's voice sounded ruffled. 'I hope you're not in trouble.'

'That makes two of us.'

I stabbed the delete button with my finger before taking off my coat.

15

My mind had wiped itself clean the morning after I stumbled across Suzanne Wilkes's body. For the first minute or two it was a normal day, with time to lie in bed before jumping in the shower. Then the memories reassembled, and closing my eyes didn't make them go away. I saw the deep wounds on her skin, Alvarez's frown, and Burns's face, grey with defeat. It was a relief to hear Lola and Lars chatting in the room next door; proof that other people's lives were carrying on as normal.

By seven thirty I was ready to leave, but my police escort hadn't arrived. Outside the window a squad car was parked beside Will's van, two coppers sleeping like babies in the front seats. I decided to give them ten more minutes of dream time before running downstairs and demanding my lift.

Someone knocked on the door just as I was making my packed lunch. It wasn't my brother's familiar rapping, loud enough to wake the whole neighbourhood, just a couple of quiet taps, like the caller didn't really want to be heard. I checked the spy-hole then wrenched open the door. Will was talking to an invisible friend in a serious voice. He seemed to be trying to persuade him to do something against his better judgement.

'Come in.' I held out my arms. 'Let's get you warm.'

He looked straight through me, still dressed in the second-hand clothes Lola had bought him, black trousers covered in splatters of mud. God alone knew where he had spent the last couple of nights. I rested my hand on his arm. The material of his jacket was soaked, no wonder he was shivering. He whispered a jumble of unconnected words, impossible to decipher.

'Lola's here. Don't you want to see her?' I asked.

His shoulders twitched. For a second he was with me, still staring straight ahead, but I knew he could hear.

'She's got a new job, singing in a bar.'

Will hummed a few tuneless notes.

'That's right. She's not bad either, somewhere between Piaf and Billie Holiday.'

He gave a high squealing laugh, as if the idea delighted him. I tried again to lead him indoors, but he edged away.

'Stay there, Will,' I said quietly. 'Please don't leave.'

Back in the flat I hovered outside the spare room.

'Lola? I need your help.'

Seconds later she emerged. Without her make-up she was pink-cheeked and freckled, about seventeen years old. She padded along the hallway barefoot, and I stepped into the kitchen to let her do her magic.

'Sweetheart,' she exclaimed. 'How lovely, you've come to see me.'

Will's reply was too quiet to hear.

'Of course I'll sing for you, darling, but only if you have breakfast with me. Look, the door's open when you're ready.'

Lola looked shaken when she came back inside.

'Jesus, Al. He's in a hell of a state,' she whispered. 'I don't even know if he'll come in.'

After a few minutes Will ventured through the door. Lola took his hand and led him to the kitchen table, while I made a pile of toast. At least it excused me from having to watch him, twitching from head to toe, muttering to himself. If he had been a patient it would have been easy. I could have observed him calmly, written down a list of anti-psychotic drugs to try, then signed him up for the full battery of support, to keep him going until the medication kicked in.

'You want a song before I've even had breakfast?' Lola teased. 'My God, you're a hard taskmaster.'

She began to croon 'God Bless the Child'. When I turned round, Will's shaking had stopped, his gaze fixed on Lola, chin propped on his hand, as though he could listen for ever. I put a plate of toast in front of him, and he ate without shifting his attention for a beat. When the song finished he didn't say thank you, he just carried on staring. I sat down at the table and tried to catch his attention.

'Listen, Will. After breakfast we have to get a taxi. The police need to talk to us.'

His body language changed immediately. The conversation he had been having with himself started up again, lips moving in an urgent whisper.

'I'll come too, if you like.' Lola squeezed his hand.

'It's not a big deal,' I added. 'They just want to know where you've been, that's all.'

'With my friend,' Will said quietly. Suddenly his eyes narrowed with anger. 'You were wrong about him, Al. He cooked for me and gave me stuff. But you never let me have friends, do you?'

'Of course I do. I just don't like the ones who give you drugs, that's all. What's your friend's name anyway?'

Lola put her hand on Will's collar. 'This is all wet, darling. Why don't I put it on the radiator?' She slipped out into the hall, holding his jacket.

Will ignored me, slathering jam on to his toast.

'So what's your friend like, Will?' I pictured a middle-aged do-gooder with a Samaritan complex, working overtime to keep his conscience clean.

'He's interested in me, and sometimes he asks questions about you too, Al.' He gave me a sly look, out of the corner of his eye.

A prickling sensation travelled across my skin. 'What does he want to know about me, Will?'

He began to hum quietly to himself, eyes fixed on the window, as if I had ceased to exist.

My legs were trembling as I left the kitchen. Lola had slung Will's jacket across the radiator. There was a bulge in one of the pockets. Maybe his friend wasn't a Samaritan after all. He'd given him a cocktail of new drugs to try. Slipping my hand under the flap, I expected to find a packet, or a syringe, but my fingers closed around a shaft of metal. I pulled out the flick-knife I had seen in his rucksack. It was tempting to throw it away, but he would be incensed if I stole something that belonged to him.

Lola appeared as I was trying to decide what to do.

'What's that?' She stared down at the knife's ornate silver handle. If it hadn't been so lethal, it would have been a thing of beauty.

'It was in his pocket,' I whispered.

She took it from my hand before I could stop her.

Back in the kitchen Will was still lost in his own world, taking long, noisy gulps of juice. Lola settled herself in a chair and put the knife on the table beside him.

'This fell out of your pocket, darling. Where on earth did you get it?'

Will carried on drinking until his glass was empty. 'A friend gave it to me,' he muttered. 'It was a present.'

'Knives give me the spooks.' She gave a mock shudder. 'Why don't you leave it here? You could hurt yourself with the nasty great thing.'

Will nodded obediently, and I marvelled again at Lola's power to make men do exactly what she wanted. If I'd tried to confiscate it there would have been an all-out war.

'Now, I'll put some clothes on and we'll get going. Okay?' Lola stooped to kiss Will's forehead and he closed his eyes in rapture.

The peace didn't last for long. While Lola was in the bathroom, Lars wandered in as I made coffee. He was in his usual state of undress, bare-chested, with a towel wrapped round his waist. Will's whole body tensed, like a child when a stranger gets too close.

'Who are you?' he asked.

Lars smiled and held out his hand. 'Lola's boyfriend.'

Will jumped up so quickly that his chair fell backwards, clattering on the floor. Yelling after him was no use. The knife had disappeared from the table, and his feet were already pounding down the stairs.

'Fuck,' I muttered.

'That didn't go so well, did it?' Lars treated me to another effortless smile.

Burns was not impressed when I rang him from my mobile. I tried to explain that I had planned to bring Will to the station myself, in case he panicked, but his voice was thick with sleep and outrage. Tooley Street went by in a blur. The policemen had finally agreed to run me to work. I could hear Burns grinding his teeth at the other end of the line.

'Just so you know, Alice, forensics are starting work on your brother's van today.'

I took a deep breath. 'You're not seriously telling me Will's a suspect, are you?'

There was a long pause. 'Better safe than sorry, that's all.'

'I don't fucking believe this.'

'It'll be better for him in the long run.'

'Why, Don? Why will it be better? He hasn't done anything.'

'Calm down, Alice. The sooner we check him out, the sooner he gets on with his life.'

On this occasion Burns's accent, with its blend of Scotland and Thames estuary, had lost its power to calm me down.

The policemen dropped me at work just after nine, which meant that I had to jog up the stairs, rather than pace myself. Hari was standing by the reception desk when I arrived, chatting to one of the mental health nurses like he had all the time in the world. He gave me a grave smile, and asked me to join him in his office. It was easy to forecast what he was going to say. Go home, rest, look after yourself.

'Sit down, please.' He nodded at the chair his patients always sat in.

'I don't need a therapy session, Hari, honestly.'

'Maybe you do.' He studied me carefully, as if all my secrets were visible. 'You've witnessed something terrible, Alice.'

'Not really. What about the soldiers we treat? They've watched hundreds of people die.'

'But you're not a soldier. You're a psychologist.'

'I know. Believe it or not, I hadn't forgotten.'

Hari appeared to be searching for the best way to share bad news. 'You haven't been yourself for the last few months, Alice. You've seemed distracted, maybe even depressed.'

'You would say that. It's your specialism.'

He studied me for at least a minute, without moving a muscle. 'The thing is, you have a high pain threshold, don't you?'

'Meaning?'

'You know exactly what I mean. You internalise it. You don't offload enough on to your friends or colleagues, even during supervision.'

I looked out of the window. 'And what would you put that down to?'

'Witnessing too much suffering as a child, maybe.' His chocolate-brown eyes settled on my face.

'But I'm a grown-up now. It's behind me.'

Hari looked amazed. 'Nothing's ever behind us, Alice. You know that as well as I do.'

'Patients to see, but thanks for the warning about my latent depression.' I got to my feet.

'One more thing.'

I paused by the door, expecting another warning about my fragile mental health.

'Dinner, tomorrow night, eight o'clock.'

'Try and keep me away,' I smiled.

I gave myself a break from email that day, making a policy decision to avoid frustration. If someone wanted me badly enough they could phone, or send a letter.

The morning was crammed with appointments. My chat with Hari made me fifteen minutes late for my first consultation, so it was a game of catch-up, trying not to keep people waiting. The most interesting person I saw was a man suffering from hysterical blindness. Under stress, he lost the ability to see, or imagined he did. Either way it made his life impossible. He couldn't trust himself to drive, in case the lights went out suddenly on a busy road, with his kids in the back seat. We agreed he would keep a diary, pinpoint the triggers for each attack, increase the amount of exercise he took, begin twelve weeks of therapy.

After lunch I went to see Laura Wallis. She was curled up on her bed, leafing through a novel with a bright pink cover. I perched on a visitor's chair.

'Good book?'

She wrinkled her nose. 'Not really, it's a bit too soppy.'

I glanced at the cover. 'Mills and Boon.'

'Mum loves them. She's got hundreds at home.'

I remembered Mrs Wallis's anxious expression. The poor woman must be desperate for a world where things ended happily.

Laura's chart showed that she had gained another pound. 'You're doing great. Soon you'll be on target.'

She beamed, as though she'd been given a gold star. 'I have to be home for my birthday.'

'When's that?'

'A week on Monday.'

'Better start asking for double portions of pudding then.'

She screwed up her face in horror, as if she had been told to eat a domestic animal.

When I got back to my office the city had disappeared, nothing there except a layer of fog, smothering my window like a sheet of grubby cotton wool. I was about to get on with a list of GP referrals when the phone rang.

'Alice, can you get down here, pronto? There's a car waiting outside.' Burns's voice sounded urgent, even more out of breath than usual.

They must have found Will, and by now he'd be bouncing off the walls of his holding cell. I let the phone drop back on to its cradle before Burns could finish his statement, sprinting down fourteen flights of stairs before I remembered that my coat was still hanging behind my door. But by then the momentum was driving me. There was no option but to carry on.

16

Burns was drinking tea in his office at the station. He looked smug, as if he had been given the promotion of his dreams.

'We've caught him,' he announced proudly.

'Who?'

'Morris Cley.'

My heart rate slowed to normal. All the way to the station I had been picturing Will, screaming at the walls of an empty room.

'Where's he been?'

'Ramsgate, staying with his auntie. So he says.'

'What's he been arrested for?'

'Assault. He knocked you out cold, remember?' Burns appraised me through his pebble-thick glasses. 'And he travelled back the same night Suzanne Wilkes's body was dumped. The CCTV at London Bridge Station picked him up.'

'I didn't press charges.'

'But you will.' Burns's eyes had the fixed, obsessive look football fans get a minute before victory. 'He killed a prostitute right here in Southwark, Alice. We can't exactly rule him out.'

'He can't even drive. How could he dump a body? And Suzanne was taken six weeks before he got out of Wandsworth.'

'He's not acting alone, obviously.' Burns's smile had evaporated, as if I had missed the punchline. 'All you have to do is watch the interview, see what you can gather.'

The room Burns led me to was no bigger than a broom cupboard.

'Can we keep the door open?' I asked. 'I'm not great with confined spaces.'

For a second he looked at me like I was mad, then his expression softened. 'My wife's got a thing about tall buildings. Anything over six floors is beyond her, and one sign of a spider's web and she's frothing at the mouth.'

I thought Burns might give me the full list of his wife's phobias, but he was distracted by a light flicking on in front of us. Through the smoked glass panel there was an empty room that looked like a film set, waiting for the cameras to roll. Alvarez entered first. It was a relief that there was a one-way window between us, so I could observe him without being seen. He looked like the lead man in a Spanish melodrama, thickset with untidy hair and a permanently serious expression. Maybe he was nursing a secret so grave, no one could prise it out of him.

After a few seconds a middle-aged blonde escorted Cley into the room. I hoped she was ex-directory, otherwise Cley would be paying her one of his midnight visits. He looked exactly as I remembered him: thin and wiry, with protruding teeth and a storm cloud of frizzy grey hair. The colour had drained from his face, and he spoke to his solicitor in an anxious whisper. She gave him a reassuring smile before Alvarez leaned over and flicked on the tape recorder.

'We talked to your aunt, Morris. She says you left Ramsgate around six o'clock. Where did you go when you got back to London Bridge?'

Cley stared down at his knees. 'The park on Druid Street.'

'I know the one, right by Tower Bridge.' Alvarez leaned back in his chair. His body language was relaxed, as if he was chatting to a friend. 'Poor old you, that place is always full of druggies and winos. Why did you come back, Morris? You could have stayed by the sea with your aunt, couldn't you?'

Cley was silent for so long that his solicitor leaned across and whispered something to him. 'She's too old to look after me, she says.' His eyes were fixed on his clenched hands.

Alvarez shifted uncomfortably in his chair. Clearly he would have preferred an equal to spar with. There was no pleasure in attacking a weakling, like a playground bully. He gave Cley a few minutes to collect himself, and when the questions began again, his tone had softened.

'What did you get up to in Ramsgate, Morris?'

Cley looked puzzled. 'Watched TV most days.'

'Indoors with the old lady, the whole time.' Alvarez raised his eyebrows. 'But you called your friends. You used a phone box, didn't you? Where did you go to ring your mates, Morris?'

Cley shook his head solemnly, like a child denying truancy to the headmaster. 'I never went out.'

Alvarez spent another half-hour trying to coax information from him, but it was an uphill struggle. Eventually he looked up at us, as though he could see through the mirrored glass. He looked exhausted, like a boxer whose championship days are over.

'He's got to be concealing something,' Burns said under his breath.

'I doubt it.' I held his gaze. 'Cley hasn't got the intellect to lure a woman into a trap, let alone torture her to death.'

'But his mates have. Don't be fooled by the village idiot act. He knew the Bensons, remember? This guy's hung out with the scum of the earth.'

'So why aren't you chasing up all the people who stayed at the Bensons' hostel?'

'We are.' Burns jabbed his glasses back on to the bridge of his nose. 'Except most of them gave false names. Keeping records wasn't Ray's number one priority.'

'I still think you're barking up the wrong tree. You can tell from his body language. He's got nothing to conceal.'

'We'll have to agree to differ.' Burns folded his arms tightly. 'I reckon he's in it up to his neck.'

'How long can you hold him?'

'Thirty-six hours,' he replied. 'We'll be pushing our luck if we can keep him for another night.'

I thought about telling Burns that he was exhibiting classic signs of obsessionality, imagining things that couldn't be real, but his expression was tense with conviction. There's no way he would have heard me.

'What are you doing for the next few hours, Alice?' he asked.

I glanced at my watch. 'Getting a takeaway, then going home to a big glass of Muscadet.'

Somehow Burns persuaded me to put my relaxation plan on hold. As usual his car smelled of cigarettes and fast food; an empty McDonald's bag and half a dozen cans of Coke were littered across the back seat.

'You don't actually drink that stuff, do you?' I asked.

'Not guilty. I just haven't got round to binning the kids' rubbish.'

'So you're a healthy eating freak, are you?'

'No way.' He kept his eyes fixed on the road. 'But you can't beat a triple bypass to get you on a diet. I've lost two stone in the last three months.'

'That's amazing.' I glanced at him. He probably had five or six more to lose before he stopped being morbidly obese. His long-suffering wife must have spent weeks weaning him on to salads and couscous. I wondered how she would react if she knew he was sneaking the odd smoke when her back was turned. 'So who are you taking me to see anyway?'

'Cheryl Martin. The only surviving victim of the Bensons.'

'How did she escape?'

Burns concentrated on crossing Bishopsgate. Crowds of rain-soaked commuters were shivering on the kerb outside Liverpool Street, waiting for the lights to change.

'Pure luck. She was in the cellar when we picked Ray Benson up. We kept hearing this tapping, but it took hours to figure it out. The entrance was through a trapdoor in his shed, five combination locks on the door. It was like those stupid horror films you don't let the kids watch. He'd built a cell, six feet long, three feet high. Not big enough to stand up in, freezing cold.'

'How long was she down there?' I asked.

'Fifteen days.' Burns sucked air through his teeth. 'She spent six months in hospital after what those bastards did to her.'

He parked in Wilmer Gardens, a narrow cul-de-sac lined with low blocks of 1970s council flats. They looked out on well-kept communal gardens, cherry trees, balconies for every flat.

'Not bad,' I commented. 'And she's got herself a trendy postcode.'

'We asked the housing association to give her something decent. The playschool she works at isn't far from here.'

I followed Burns up two pristine flights of stairs. It made perfect sense why someone like Cheryl Martin would want to look after children. No one had looked after her, so she had turned the tables, decided to nurture everyone else.

Burns paused on the landing, drawing in huge breaths as though he'd just swum the Channel. The door sprang open before he had time to knock. A young woman with a cloud of dark curls framing her face threw her arms around Burns. She was dressed in paint-spattered jeans and a sweatshirt.

'Been paintballing, Cheryl?' he smiled.

'I'm doing my bedroom. The colour's a bit sickly though.'

So far she hadn't acknowledged me, too busy welcoming Burns like a long-lost father.

'This is Alice.' Burns nodded at me. 'She's working for me.'

The girl held out her hand. She must have been in her mid-twenties but the dimples in her cheeks made her look about eighteen.

'Are you any good at colour schemes?' she asked hopefully.

'Not great, I'm afraid. I always go for white, so things don't clash.'

'Come and take a look anyway. I think I could be making a big mistake.'

Cheryl led the way along a pale pink corridor. Stylised pictures of flowers and kittens hung on both walls. It looked like a ten-year-old girl had been given free rein to decorate the place exactly as she pleased. She showed us into a small bedroom, where a patch of vivid lilac paint was beginning to spread across a grubby beige wall.

'What do you reckon?' Cheryl waited anxiously, as though she expected to be given a low mark.

'Good choice,' I replied. 'Really clean and fresh.'

Burns inspected her handiwork carefully. 'You're doing a grand job, Cheryl, not a smear in sight.'

She gave him another impulsive hug.

'Give over.' Burns patted her back gingerly, his expression a mixture of pleasure and embarrassment.

We sat in Cheryl's lounge while she made us a cup of tea. It was obvious she had no money, but she was still trying hard to improve things. A large coffee table took pride of place in the centre of the room. She must have decorated it herself, with stencilled silver leaves curling across the white surface.

'Is this a social call then?' Cheryl placed a tea tray in front of us.

'Not quite,' Burns admitted.

She let out a long sigh. 'It was six years ago, Don. I've stopped thinking about it.' Her expression had changed from eager to please to anxious in the space of a second.

'The thing is, Cheryl, two girls have been killed, and we reckon there's a connection with the hostel. The people involved must have lived there, or been mates of the Bensons.'

'You're kidding.' She twisted a brown curl between her fingers, staring at him in disbelief. 'They were psychos, Don. They didn't have friends.'

'You must have been very young when you stayed there,' I said quietly.

She turned to face me. 'I was seventeen. Mum had just chucked me out. She had a new boyfriend, and I'd been smoking too much dope. I was a pain in the arse, probably.'

'But you've done well in the last few years, haven't you?'

'I got myself to college, thanks to Don. He phoned every week, helped with the application forms, nagged me to get my coursework done.'

Burns looked mortified, as if compassion was a sacking offence.

'What was it like at the hostel?' I asked.

Cheryl studied the contents of her cup. 'Okay to begin with. I'd been sleeping in squats, so it was a relief to be somewhere warm. Ray and Marie seemed pretty normal at first. I just thought they were trying to do their bit.' Her eyes went out of focus, as if she was looking at something a long distance away. 'I must have been so fucking naive.'

'You don't have to talk about this now, love,' Burns interrupted. 'We can come back.'

'No, Don,' she snapped. 'I'd rather get it over with.'

'Did Ray and Marie employ anyone to help them?' I asked.

'God no, they were cheapskates.' Cheryl screwed up her face in disgust. 'Marie made us do all the work round the place. Cooking or washing up, cleaning the loos. Anyone who didn't got chucked out.'

'The thing is, someone's got insider information. Someone very disturbed,' Burns frowned.

'Everyone was fucked up in that place, Don.' Cheryl sounded exhausted. 'I mean, it was a doss house. You only go to places like that if you're desperate. One girl just sat in the corner of the day room, rocking. They picked the most vulnerable people they could find.'

'You don't seem vulnerable,' I commented.

'I was back then. The youngest kid in the hostel, no one looking out for me.' She passed her hand across her eyes like she was trying to clear her vision. 'There was one bloke they had a soft spot for. I can't remember his name. He used to hang about in the garden. I just thought he went out there for a fag, but he was their doorman, I'm sure of it. They must have paid him to stop people poking about.'

'Or escaping?' I asked.

'Fat chance.' Cheryl shivered. 'I used to hear Ray coming for me, undoing all the locks.'

Her face contorted again. It was hard to tell whether she was going to cry or scream.

'It's all right, love,' Burns muttered.

'It's not, Don.' Her soft voice was shrill with distress. 'And do you know what keeps me awake? It's not what he did to me, it's what I didn't do to him.'

'No one could have stopped it,' I replied.

'I should have fought though.' She covered her face with her hands. 'I should have killed him when I had the chance.'

The sleeve of her sweatshirt fell back as she wiped her face, revealing half a dozen crosses, scattered across her wrist and forearm. They had faded to narrow silver scars, each one a few centimetres in diameter. I shifted my eyes to the window while Burns comforted her. God knows how many times Ray Benson had carved his hallmark into her skin. It was impossible to imagine how she must have felt when they pulled her from the trap, naked and covered in wounds.

17

Lola was nowhere to be seen in the morning, but the spare room door was firmly shut, bedsprings groaning as I walked along the hall. Maybe Lars had moved in without my noticing. I poured myself a glass of apple juice and looked at Will's van through the window. It was still shrouded by a huge white awning. Burns's men must have spent yesterday inspecting his dirty clothes and worn-out shoes, hunting for drugs under the driving seat. Hopefully he was safe somewhere, lying low, with his mystery friend.

Back in my room I got into my tracksuit and tried to decide which circuit to choose. It was a toss-up between laps of Southwark Park or a long straight sprint to Blackfriars Bridge, before the city woke up. As usual the river won and I was setting off across the square when someone called after me.

'Where do you think you're going?' Alvarez emerged from his car.

'What does it look like?'

'Solitary jogging is off limits, I'm afraid.'

'I don't jog, I run.'

'Same difference.'

'All that power must go to your head, mustn't it?'

Alvarez didn't answer. As usual his expression was neutral, coal-black eyes studying my mouth. For a moment it crossed my mind to invite him upstairs for a different kind of exercise.

'You're under police protection,' he said. 'We couldn't guar-
antee your safety.'

'Come with me then.'

'Not in this suit.' His mouth twitched, as though he was
trying to smile. 'Another time maybe.'

I turned on my heel without saying goodbye. Alvarez had
found the perfect job. It allowed him to be arrogant, rude and
controlling all at the same time.

After fuming quietly over a cup of coffee I dragged my
bike downstairs. Alvarez's car pulled out behind me, in hot
pursuit along Tooley Street. It reminded me of the cat and
mouse game Will taught me in the garden when we were
kids. He was always the cat, hiding behind a tree, waiting to
pounce, just when I had forgotten he was there. At the hospital
Alvarez appeared again in the corner of my eye, while I chatted to a nurse from the fifth floor. He stood by the entrance,
broad-shouldered and thuggish, refusing to leave me alone.
I decided to sprint upstairs, which killed two birds with one
stone. It gave me the workout I needed, and left him stranded,
hundreds of feet below.

It was eight o'clock when I sat down at my desk, leaving
me an hour to catch up with the two hundred and nine emails
in my inbox. Deleting the reminders to renew subscriptions
to professional journals was the easy part. If they wanted my
money badly enough they could always post me a bill. The next
task was to wipe every message copied to me for information
only, normally because someone was covering their back in
case a diagnosis turned out to be spectacularly wrong. After
forty minutes my incoming mail had been whittled down to
sixteen messages to be answered today, and another twenty that
could wait. I was still basking in relief when the phone rang.

'Is that Dr Quentin?' The female voice was oddly familiar, a
deep monotone, roughened by a lifetime's cigarettes.

'Who is this, please?'

'Marie Benson. You said I could call you for a chat.'

'That's right,' I floundered. For some reason it wasn't Benson's face I saw when I closed my eyes, it was Myra Hindley's, with her deep-set eyes and sullen pout. Marie had never looked like anyone's idea of a murderer. 'This is a surprise, Marie. How can I help you?'

There was a quiet, rasping sound, like she was struggling to breathe. Or maybe she was laughing.

'You asked *me* for help, remember?'

'I did. But I wasn't expecting to get it, to be honest.'

'Underestimated me then, didn't you?'

Her game plan was becoming obvious. All she wanted to do was dangle clues in front of me, then pull them away as soon as I reached out.

'Marie, I haven't got much time, I'm afraid. Is there something you want to tell me?'

'In a rush, are we?' She sounded affronted.

'I've got an appointment soon, but if you want a longer talk I'll call back.'

'It's just an invitation, Dr Quentin.' The teasing tone had made a comeback. 'You could visit me, if you like. Maybe we could help each other out.'

'I'm not following you.'

'We could share some information, tit for tat.' She laughed again, a grating sound, like fingernails being dragged across the receiver.

'Women are getting killed, Marie. That's all I know. The police don't share their findings with me. I wouldn't have anything to trade.'

A long pause was punctuated by Marie's measured breathing. 'If you were a bit more open, Dr Quentin, we could find so much common ground.'

'Meaning?'

'You give me a clue, then I give you something in return.'

'I can't do that, I'm afraid.'

'Pity,' she sighed. 'You know where I am if you change your mind.'

'Thank you.'

'Think about it, Dr Quentin,' she murmured. 'We've got so many friends in common, you know.'

The static on the line buzzed for a few seconds, but the white noise failed to clear my thoughts.

Hari put his head round the door as I hung up. He was wearing his immaculate saffron turban, and his ever-present smile. He told me that he and Tejo had spent hours preparing a feast for that evening, and that I should arrive by eight.

'She's invited someone for you, by the way,' he said.

'Oh God, no.' I covered my eyes with my hands. 'I'm not coming.'

'He lives near us. The perfect match, she says.'

'That's not fair, Hari. I haven't been on a blind date since I was twelve.'

'So it's definitely time you went on another.' For a second his smile pulsed even more brightly, then the door clicked shut behind him.

There was no sign of Lars when I got home from work. Lola was curled up on the sofa, like a cat after a large meal.

'Where's lover boy?' I asked.

'Sainsbury's. We ran out of cornflakes.' She giggled. 'He's beyond gorgeous, isn't he?'

'He is. And he's reduced you to a state of adolescent frenzy, hasn't he?'

'I know. But what about you?' She examined me more closely. 'The last few days must have been absolute crap.'

I slumped on the sofa beside her. 'You could say that. The fucking police won't let me out of their sight. I can't even go for a run.'

'But that's good, Al. Thank God they're taking it seriously.'

'One way to look at it, I suppose.'

'Why don't you eat with us tonight? Lars is making some Swedish thing with mackerel and potatoes.'

'Jesus, it must be love. No thanks, I'm going out.'

'You don't look thrilled about it.'

'It's a set-up, that's why. They've dug up some weirdo for me.'

'A sixty-two-year-old lawyer who likes kinky sex?'

'Or a stamp-collecting librarian with bad skin.'

Lola rolled her eyes. 'Ever the optimist, Al.'

After my shower I decided to make an effort, slipping on a grey silk dress which exposed a little too much cleavage, and my favourite chunky silver jewellery. Whoever Tejo had chosen would at least get a run for his money. I even bothered to blow dry my hair, rather than running a comb through and letting it frizz. My make-up was subdued, smoky eyes and dark pink lips.

'You look amazing.' Lola came into the hall and helped me on with my coat. 'Go on, girl. Get sozzled and have a good flirt.'

'They're Sikhs, Lo. There won't be any booze.'

Lola's face froze in horror as she tried to imagine enduring a stone-cold-sober blind date.

The taxi was revving its engine when I got downstairs, but there was no sign of Alvarez, or the squad car that had been trailing me for days. Maybe they had forgotten about me, decided to enjoy their Friday night, go to the pictures instead. The car headed south, along Southwark Bridge Road, past three boarded-up pubs for every one still in business. The smokers of south London must have gone home in a sulk, to get pissed in the comfort of their own homes. It was a relief to watch the streets spin past. Life was getting back to normal, with no chaperones watching my every move. Maybe my pen-pal had grown bored of his project and moved on to someone else. The taxi driver talked non-stop as he wove through Camberwell, delivering a gruff rant about the state of the nation. He held strong convictions about everything, from house prices and gangs taking over the neighbourhood, to his passion for Leonard Cohen.

The tsunami of conversation finally came to a halt when we reached Deepdene Road. Hari and Tejo had been renovating their redbrick Victorian semi for years. It looked glossy and prosperous, two perfectly clipped box bushes guarding the porch like sentinels. I lifted the brass door knocker and waited to be admitted.

'Hello, stranger,' Tejo beamed. She looked effortlessly beautiful as always, in a pale blue shalwar kameez covered in delicate silver stitching.

'My God, you're pregnant!' I exclaimed.

'You beast.' She wagged her finger at Hari. 'I thought you told her.'

'And I thought you did.' He looked apologetic then kissed me on both cheeks.

'IVF,' Tejo whispered as they led me along the hall.

'That's brilliant! Congratulations.'

'Four months to go,' she grimaced, 'and I'm already as big as a bus.'

The kitchen door swung open, and I took a deep breath. After I sat down there was just one vacant chair next to mine at the large wooden table, nine people smiling and chatting to each other. A few of them I already knew: Hari's sister and her husband, some familiar faces from Guy's. Tejo passed round a platter of samosas and pakoras.

'Don't let Alice near them,' Hari laughed. 'She'll scoff the lot.'

'It's true I'm afraid,' I nodded.

'Who are we waiting for?' someone asked.

Tejo smirked. 'Alice's date.'

'I can't believe you've set me up.' I covered my face with my hands.

The woman next to me gave me a sympathetic look. She was Japanese, with fine grey hair swept back from her face, a network of laughter lines circling her eyes. 'Are you divorced?' she asked.

'Single.'

'That's okay then.' She gave a gentle smile. 'Not too much baggage to carry around.'

I laughed. 'You'd be surprised.'

Before she could tell me her name Tejo struck her glass with a fork, as if she was making a toast.

'An announcement, everyone, about our missing guest. Be gentle with him, won't you? He's had a bad time.'

'Of course we will,' a balding man opposite me replied solemnly. 'If you tell us what's happened to him.'

Tejo gave an enigmatic smile. 'He'll tell you himself, if he wants to.'

Hari helped himself to another bhaji. 'You'll like him. Shy, but interesting.'

God knows why Tejo was so keen to introduce me to a man who was caught up in some terrible personal trauma. Luckily the Japanese woman was interesting enough to keep my thoughts occupied. She told me that her name was Kyoko and she worked at the British Museum as a conservator.

'What does that involve?' I asked.

'I mend broken porcelain and china. Today I was working on a twelve-hundred-year-old vase. It'll take weeks to mend, maybe months.'

'It must be satisfying when it's finished.'

She looked surprised, then smiled at me as if I had misunderstood. 'It's the carrying on I enjoy, not the finishing.' Her small hands mimed the slow piecing together of fragments. Something about the gesture reminded me of my own job. Except we're meant to fix people in double-quick time, glue them back together, then send them out of the door, before they're too expensive to mend.

Out of the corner of my eye I saw the mystery man arrive, standing with his back to me by the kitchen door.

'He's handsome,' Kyoko whispered. 'You'll love him.'

When I turned round again, Alvarez was sitting beside me. My initial reaction was outrage. He must have showed Tejo his ID card, bluffed his way inside. I was about to deliver a piece of my mind when Hari gave me his usual innocent grin.

'Alice, I want you to meet our good friend Ben.'

The shock took a moment to register. Then my pakora dropped out of my hand, showering the table with crumbs.

18

Alvarez had undergone a personality change. He was wearing a crumpled blue linen shirt and worn-out jeans, as if he had made a conscious decision not to be a policeman for the evening.

'Tell me this isn't happening,' I muttered.

'I'm afraid it is.' Alvarez looked like he could smile at any minute. 'It's all your nightmares rolled into one, isn't it?'

'Pretty much. The only thing that could be worse is getting stuck in a lift with you.'

'I don't know.' He lounged in his chair, his gaze travelling across my body. 'I can think of worse ways to spend an afternoon.'

On the other side of the table Tejo looked smug, as though she had won a medal for successful matchmaking. Alvarez carried on watching me, like a cat appraising a bowl of cream. My only option was to be polite until I could think of an excuse and leave.

'So, how do you know Hari?' I asked.

'It's Tejo I know best actually. She's been unbelievable. Definitely not your common-or-garden shrink.' Alvarez glanced at his plate.

He was interrupted before he could elaborate. The woman sitting to his right finally managed to grab his attention.

'Did I hear you say something about gardens?' she purred. 'I'm passionate about them, always have been.'

Alvarez twisted round to talk to her. She was a well-built brunette, with a pink, animated face. She must have prepared herself for the evening's lack of alcohol by visiting the pub first. Her words slurred as she tried to connect with Alvarez. Soon she was simpering about the virtues of perennials over annuals, fluttering her eyelashes as she explained that she needed help with digging out a buddleia that had taken hold beside her patio.

Kyoko gave me a sympathetic look, then leaned over to whisper something.

'Don't worry. It's you he likes, not her.'

I shrugged. 'It doesn't matter. He's married anyway.'

Kyoko raised her eyebrows. 'You're not seeing the whole picture, Alice.' She held up her finger and thumb like she was holding a fragment of glass. 'Only a little piece of it.'

'Sorry?'

She gave a gentle smile. 'Men wear wedding rings for all sorts of different reasons, don't they?' Then she turned away to chat to someone else.

Alvarez was still locked in conversation with the brunette, who had balanced her cleavage on the table for him to admire. I concentrated on eating. Tejo had remembered my favourites from our flat-sharing days: lentil curry, ochra, naan bread oozing with coconut. I was still trying to work out why Alvarez would advertise himself as married if he was divorced, when he turned to face me again.

'Great meal,' he commented, dipping a piece of bread into a dish of raita. 'But I'm surprised you like it.'

'Why?'

'It's not very English. But you are to the core, aren't you?'

'I know where this is going.' I rolled my eyes. 'You're going to give me the whole spiel about Brits loving the Queen and not expressing their emotions, right?'

'I wouldn't dream of it.' He held up his hands innocently. 'I'd say the English aren't that different to the Spanish – loyal, defiant, a bit arrogant sometimes. The only difference is that you can't cook or dance.'

'Rubbish. I'm a great dancer.'

He helped himself to a spoonful of lime pickle. It gave me an opportunity to study him. His messy hair was swept back from his forehead, the usual fine growth of stubble visible against his skin. The thin vertical line between his eyebrows was still there. For some reason I wanted to reach out and touch it. It was a fight to keep my hands still.

'Go on then, tell me how you ended up in London,' I said. 'There's no chance of escape, so you might as well.'

'I'd hate to bore you, Alice. I know you have a short attention span when it comes to male company.'

'If it gets tedious I'll let you know.'

He balanced his fork on his plate. 'My father grew up in a little seaside town, north of Valencia. People grow oranges there and take a lot of siestas.'

'Sounds perfect.'

'Not for him. He was looking for adventure, so he hitch-hiked to Madrid, became a journalist for *El País*, and met my mother.'

'What was she doing?'

'She's from London. She was studying languages at the university.'

'So this anti-English thing is just a con. In reality, you're a Brit.'

'I never denied it.' He caught my eye. 'You jumped to conclusions, Alice. I spent a long time in Spain, but I've lived here since my teens.'

He leaned against the arm of my chair, close enough for me to study the way his eyelashes swept against his cheek.

Thank God we weren't on our own. Alvarez drew back and my breathing returned to normal. It annoyed me that he could affect me so much, even when I was as sober as a judge.

'Your turn,' he said. 'Give me your life story. I don't know the first thing about you.'

'Rubbish. You've got the name and address of every man I've ever said hello to.' I frowned. 'And don't kid yourself I've forgiven you for that, by the way.'

'I don't.' He held my eye for a beat longer than necessary.

'What do you want to know, anyway?'

'Everything, starting at the beginning.' He was so attentive I thought he might pull a notebook from his pocket and start writing things down.

I took a deep breath. 'Well, I grew up in Blackheath.'

'Very classy.'

'Not really.' I stared at my upturned hand, lying on the table like a fish out of water. For some reason my voice had dried up on me.

'That's all you've got to say about your childhood. Five words?'

'It's a dinner party for God's sake.'

He raised his eyebrows. 'That's what people do at parties, Alice. They chat about themselves, get to know each other.'

I folded my arms. 'There's nothing to tell. My parents weren't happy and things got complicated. End of story.'

'And your brother got caught in the middle?'

'Something like that, yeah.'

'It's strange you don't like to talk.' Alvarez studied me thoughtfully. 'You collect people's stories, but you won't tell your own.'

'Because I don't want to,' I shrugged. 'I hear conversations all day. When I'm off duty I want to run, and dance, and eat, and—'

'And what?' He held my gaze.

'I want to live in my body, not my head.'

His eyes narrowed. Under the table I felt his hand brush my skin, travelling up the length of my thigh, pulling back the silk of my dress. I drew in a quick gasp of breath.

His hand closed round mine. 'Come on, we're leaving.'

'We can't just go before the dessert.'

'Yes, we can,' he insisted.

The next few minutes went into overdrive. Alvarez skirted round the crowded kitchen and leaned down to talk to Tejo. She glanced at me, smiling, then patted him on the shoulder. The faces of the other guests held a range of expressions as we said goodbye. Kyoko beamed approvingly, but the brunette looked outraged, as if I had stolen her fiancé. We made it to the front door before touching each other again. Then the kiss went on for ever. It was completely different from Sean, more urgent, like he couldn't have stopped himself, even if he tried. His hands tugged at the belt of my dress.

'You could get arrested for this, you know,' I whispered.

'Worth it, definitely.' He buried his face in the nape of my neck, hands closing around my waist. 'Where are we going?'

'Yours?'

'It's a mess.' His expression was unreadable under the streetlight. 'Let's go to yours.'

'No way. The square's crawling with your mates.'

'Not tonight.' Alvarez shook his head. 'I said I'd take care of you until morning.'

'You presumptuous bastard.'

'We could stop, but you don't want to, do you?' He kissed me again.

I didn't have enough breath to reply.

'My place is only ten minutes away,' he whispered. 'I'll grab my stuff then I'll drive you.'

We didn't talk as we walked past Ruskin Park, but his hand held mine so tightly that my knuckles hurt. A couple of times he pulled me into the shadows and kissed me until my head spun. After a few minutes we arrived at Kemerton Road.

'This is it. Home sweet home,' he said.

'Nice,' I nodded. The house was a tall Victorian end of terrace with a bay window, elegant but slightly shabby.

'Want to come in while I grab some stuff?' He leaned down to kiss me again.

I shook my head. 'I'll wait here.'

Alvarez jogged up the steps to his house and my phone began to vibrate in my coat pocket. I thought about turning it off, but it was bound to be Will. By now he would have come to his senses and need me to pick him up. I didn't recognise the number, but it had to be him. Who else would ring me so late at night? He was sobbing into the receiver.

'It's okay, Will. Where are you? I'll come and get you.'

He was trying to keep it together, clearing his throat to explain. But when the voice finally started to speak, it didn't belong to my brother.

'Something terrible's happened.' For once my mother's ice maiden act had melted. Her voice shook like a child's after a bad dream.

Alvarez emerged from his house with a bag slung over his shoulder just as I was stuffing the phone back into my pocket.

'I've got to go to the hospital,' I muttered. 'It's urgent.'

'I'll take you.' He was already heading across the street to his car, but a taxi was driving towards us.

'I'd better go on my own, I'm sorry.'

As the taxi pulled away I pressed my hand against the window but he didn't bother to wave. He just stood beside his car. It looked like he was trying to decide whether to follow me, or let me disappear.

19

The taxi ride took for ever, crawling down the Old Kent Road, past a procession of cafés and the tiny shops Tejo and I visited when we were students, with bolts of gaudy Indian silks stacked to the ceiling. They were locked behind metal grilles, as though they wouldn't survive the night without body armour. The driver dropped me on the wrong side of the square, and I kept my mind empty as I ran across the quadrangle to Bermondsey Wing. There was no point in guessing what had happened until my mother gave me the full story.

She was waiting in the corridor on the third floor. There was no sign that she had allowed herself to shed a tear. She was dressed in a velvet jacket, patent leather shoes, not a hair out of place. Maybe she had been at the theatre, or having dinner with friends when the phone call came. She flinched as I leaned down to kiss her cheek. I perched next to her on the bench.

'What happened, Mum?'

She pursed her lips. 'They won't say how he got his injuries.'

'I thought he collapsed. You didn't tell me he'd been hurt.'

'How could I? You hung up before I could finish.' Her grey eyes had frosted over. 'They think he may have fallen.'

'Fallen from what?'

'Stop it, Alice. How can I think straight with you repeating everything I say?'

'Sorry, go ahead.'

'Thank you.' She fixed me with her best librarian's glare. 'He was found in a car park. Someone heard him screaming and called an ambulance.' She pressed her fingers to her mouth, trying to hold back the words.

I forced myself to take deep breaths. 'Just tell me what you know.'

'Like I said, they took him away for X-rays. I haven't seen him.' Her face was expressionless, but the strip lights were punishing. The wrinkles and age spots she normally concealed so skilfully stood out like a sore thumb. 'The police keep asking if he's come round, so they can interview him. What on earth's been going on, Alice?'

For a moment I considered giving her the full story: I had stumbled across two dead women in as many weeks, and someone was sending me psychotic love letters.

'Nothing.' I shook my head. 'Nothing at all.'

She was about to argue when a familiar voice greeted me. Things were shifting from bad to worse. Sean was standing there in his favourite Savile Row suit, looking puzzled. 'I didn't know you'd been called.'

'I haven't. I'm here to see my brother Will.'

Sean did a double-take. It took a moment for his impeccable professional manner to re-establish itself.

'Could we talk privately, please?' He bent down and spoke to my mother in a respectful murmur. 'Nothing to worry about, Mrs Quentin, your son's being well looked after.'

My mother looked relieved to be spared the medical details. She had always been squeamish. We ate meat every day when I was a child, but she always refused to touch it. It sat in the fridge under a thick layer of cellophane, sliced into neat pink cubes by the butcher.

Sean led me to his consulting room beside operating

theatre one. Ancient rock music throbbed through the wall:
Aerosmith or Bon Jovi. One of the surgeons always played the
worst music he could find, to annoy his interns. Sean looked
awkward. Maybe he didn't know whether to treat me like a
patient, or someone he used to have sex with every day.

'Look, Sean, just tell me what happened please.'

He dug his hands into the pockets of his jacket. 'The first
thing is that he's serious but stable.'

I let out a long breath. At least that meant he was likely to
survive.

'But he'll need several operations. His back's okay. I was
worried he had a lumbar fracture at first. But the thing is,
Alice, there's no way we can operate tonight.'

'How come?'

'We need the bloods back from toxicology.' His gaze drifted
back to my face. 'He was hallucinating when he came in. Do
you know what he's been taking?'

I took a deep breath. 'Heroin, methadone, ketamine,
crystal meth. You name it. He's a walking pharmaceutical
laboratory.'

'Jesus, Alice.' Sean's expression was a mix of rage and frustration. 'Why the fuck didn't you tell me?'

The answer stuck in my throat. I was sick of talking about
it, to an army of GPs and social workers and drug counsel-
lors and probation officers. Watching it happen had been hard
enough, like seeing the same train derailing every day, carriage
by carriage, in slow motion.

'Do you want to see the X-rays? It's not a pretty sight I'm
afraid.' Sean flicked on the light box and the images made me
wince. He studied me coldly as I stared at them. 'Your brother
couldn't tell us what happened, but he must have fallen quite
a distance to do that much damage.'

I forced myself to look at the X-rays again. One leg had

two clean breaks, but the other was a complete mess, shin and thigh bones in fragments. Even with expert surgery, he wouldn't be able to stand for months.

I was shaking when I let myself out of the consulting room, and halfway along the corridor before I remembered that I hadn't said goodbye. My mother was sitting in exactly the same position as before, clutching her expensive handbag, as if someone might try to wrestle it from her hands. She seemed reluctant to move, but eventually she followed me along the corridor.

Will was in a room just big enough for his bed, an oxygen tank and the supply of diamorphine he was hooked up to. He was fast asleep, white face burrowed into the pillow, his ruined legs hidden under a metal frame, protecting them from the weight of the bedding.

'Is he conscious?' my mother whispered.

'Sedated,' I replied, 'until the morning.'

My mother inspected her son's face in silence before turning to me. 'I trusted you,' she said quietly.

'Sorry?'

'He parked his van outside your flat,' she hissed. 'He wanted your help, but you did absolutely nothing.'

'So this is all down to me, is it?'

My mother's eyes glittered like wet pebbles. 'It's you he reached out to, Alice, not me.'

'Displacement,' I replied.

'Pardon?' My mother reacted like I had sworn at her. She had been enjoying her rampage down the warpath, but the word had thrown her off track.

'You didn't protect us when we were kids, and now it's easier to blame someone else. Anyone, but never yourself.'

'Don't bring up the past.' She was trying not to shout. 'Now is not the time.'

'Exactly,' I agreed. Will shifted uncomfortably in his

drug-induced sleep, as if the tension was infecting his dreams. 'Go home, Mum. There's nothing you can do.'

Her protests were short-lived. She was desperate to jump in her car, breathe in the lemon air freshener she always used.

After she had gone I sat with Will, even though he wouldn't come round for hours. His cheekbones were even sharper than before, eye sockets blacker. When I squeezed his hand his eyelids fluttered, but he was too far under to respond.

Don Burns was chatting to a nurse at the far end of the corridor when I stepped outside. His silhouette was impossible to miss, grey and circular, blocking out the light. I escaped into the stairwell before he could see me.

Outside in the quadrangle, I pulled in long gulps of fresh air. It was just after 3 a.m., and my mind wasn't working properly. The sensible thing would have been to find a cab on Great Maze Pond, but my feet took me in the opposite direction. I stopped at a cashpoint on Borough High Street, then headed in the direction of Sean's flat. By now the Angel pub was deserted. Even the landlord must have hit the sack, lights out in every window. I sat down on the brick wall and waited. Several cars crawled by; one man even rolled down his window and asked me for a price.

'Fuck off,' I yelled, and his grubby SUV disappeared with an angry screech of brakes.

Twenty minutes later the person I had been waiting for arrived. Michelle spilled out of a brand-new yellow sports car. Maybe some businessman had decided to treat himself to a bit of rough while the wife was out of town. She was wearing six-inch heels and a black leather mini skirt. She must have consulted the Internet to see what kind of get-up attracted the highest price.

'You don't remember me, do you?' I asked.

She peered at my face. 'Not another fucking social worker, are you?'

'I talked to you last week, when I was out running.'

'Oh yeah, I remember. I thought you'd croak on me.' She lit a cigarette and inhaled for ever, like smoke was a better life source than oxygen. 'Enjoy our little chat, did you?' Her pupils were as big as saucers in her pinched white face. She looked like a child that's been left by itself for days. Out of the corner of my eye I could see cars trailing past, rolling down their windows to check what was on offer, slowly moving off again.

'The thing is, Michelle, my brother got hurt tonight.'

'Yeah?' Tears welled in her eyes immediately. She must have forgotten how to protect herself from other people's concerns.

'He'll be in hospital for weeks.'

'There are some sick bastards about.' She glanced around, as though she were afraid someone might be eavesdropping. 'This bloke picked up my friend yesterday. He kept saying stuff to her.'

'What kind of stuff?'

'How he was going to hurt her, she didn't deserve to be alive. She had to fight her way out.'

'But you're still here.'

'No choice.' She stared straight ahead, a curtain of dyed black hair obscuring her face.

'Go home.' I pulled a hundred pounds out of my pocket. 'Take a taxi. It's not safe out here, for any of you.'

She hesitated for a moment, then reached out for the money. Her expression was uncertain. Maybe it was too hard to believe that she was getting something without having to pay anything in return.

'Tell me your name again.'

'Alice.'

'You're an angel, Alice.' She flung her arms round me, then teetered towards the night bus stop like a kid learning to use stilts, turning back several times to wave goodbye.

I sat on the wall, gathering my energy for the walk home in the opposite direction. God knows what Alvarez would say if he could see me chatting to prostitutes in the middle of the night. My head spun. It was hard not to smile when I remembered the way he kissed me, as if he had forgotten how to breathe.

20

It was impossible to sleep. Lars and Lola were trying out a new sexual style. They had graduated from fast and furious to experimental, and seemed to be aiming for the longest orgasm of all time. I finally drifted off to the sound of Lola repeating Lars's name, like she was afraid he might disappear before the act was complete. A nightmare woke me a few hours later. I was locked out of the flat wearing only a T-shirt, my feet bare on the frozen road, staring through the windows of Will's empty van. The black tarpaulin was there again, rolled up like a huge cigar. Even though I knew what was inside, the temptation to look was irresistible. But when the fabric pulled apart, the white face that gazed up at me didn't belong to Suzanne Wilkes. It belonged to Will. His eyes were fixed on the sky, the wound in his throat gaping. My heart rate slowed as soon as I opened my eyes. At least Will was alive and, given the downward spiral he'd been following, hospital was the safest place for him.

Lola listened to a potted version of events while she made coffee. Her spoon clattered into the sink when she heard about Will.

'Will he be able to walk?' She glanced down at her mile-long legs in horror. For someone who made a living on the stage, his injuries must have seemed like the end of the world.

'Probably. But it'll be a long time.'

'The poor soul. It makes me feel guilty. You're both going through all this, while I'm mooning around, singing stupid songs in a bar.'

'Don't knock it. It sounds great to me.'

'It is.' She buried her hands in her red curls. 'It's more than I deserve.'

I smiled at her. 'Lucky beast.'

'Lars is taking me to Malmö, to meet his family.'

'Oh my God,' I groaned. 'You'll be eating reindeer and living in a log cabin before you can say Ikea.'

Lola giggled, then her face grew serious again, as if it was a crime to seem happy. 'What ward is Will on?'

'Bermondsey.'

She scribbled the word down on the back of an envelope, then wrapped her arms round me. She smelled of the Scandinavian aftershave Lars wafted around the bathroom: pine cones, lavender and sea air.

I set off down the stairs at ten o'clock, mentally preparing myself to see Will. By now he would be coming to, trying to find ways to cope with the pain.

Burns was waiting by the gate when I opened the security door, blowing clouds of hot air into the cold, smoking a fantasy cigarette.

'Morning, Alice. I'm sorry about your brother.' His pinhole eyes peered at me through his thick lenses.

'What are you after, Don?'

'You know me too well.' Burns's small mouth broke into a smile. 'I want you to meet someone.'

'It's Saturday. Don't you believe in weekends?'

'They're cancelled for the time being,' he said. He was already beginning the difficult job of squeezing himself into his car.

I wondered if Alvarez had told him about our flirtation the night before; another piece of my complicated sexual history to add to the official jigsaw.

Burns focused on his driving as we turned right on to Tower Bridge Road.

'Your brother had a lucky escape,' he commented.

'You're kidding. He'll be in pain for months, and the physio will be agony.' I could have gone on arguing, but there was no point. The car was stuck in traffic on Tower Bridge, giving me the chance to take in my favourite view. The Thames swung left towards the Houses of Parliament, but there was no glitter today, just acres of mud-brown water, currents twisting under its surface, like sinews under skin.

'I mean he's lucky they left it at that.' Burns hunched uncomfortably over the wheel.

'I'm not following you.'

'There's a witness.' He glanced across at me. 'She saw a car pull up round the back of her flats in Stockwell late yesterday afternoon. A bloke dragged him off the back seat, dumped him by the rubbish bins and drove away.'

'Fucking bastard,' I muttered.

'The dozy cow didn't get the licence number. Too shocked, apparently.'

Burns headed right towards the East End. When I was growing up people told you never to go there alone, even in daylight, unless you wanted to get mugged or shot in the back. These days Wapping High Street was failing to live up to its shady reputation. Gangster hideouts and dark alleyways had given way to delicatessens, estate agents and Pizza Express. I closed my eyes and tried to make sense of what Burns had said. Someone had pushed Will from the roof of a building, scooped him into the back of their car and left him in a car park, on a day when it was cold enough to snow. It was hard to fathom why anyone would want to inflict that much pain.

'At least this means Will's in the clear, doesn't it?' I said.

'Not if there's a gang of them.' Burns avoided my gaze. 'We'll see what he's got to say when he comes round.'

There was no point in contradicting him. Disagreement just made Burns even more determined to fly in the face of logic. We drove through narrow, gentrified streets, lined with Smart cars and Prius estates – well-heeled young couples doing their bit to save the planet. He parked outside a converted Victorian factory. It looked different from the neighbouring buildings. Decades of East End grime had been scrubbed away, restoring the bricks to their original pink. It stuck out, like a baby surrounded by adults. As we walked towards the entrance Burns warned me who we were about to visit.

'Brace yourself,' he said. 'He's not great company at the minute.'

Mark Wilkes took forever to answer the doorbell. A pair of dull brown eyes inspected us through the gap before he finally let us in. A tornado had passed through his flat. Clothes were lying in abandoned heaps in the hall, and an assortment of books, cups and takeaway food cartons were scattered across every surface. The sitting room smelled of coffee and stale air, and a pile of bedding was heaped in the corner. Wilkes looked even worse than his flat. His T-shirt had seen better days and his greasy brown hair clearly hadn't been washed for some time. The rings under his eyes were so dark that he looked like he'd been punched. When he traipsed away to make us a drink I opened the window a few centimetres to air the room. A Siamese cat appeared out of nowhere and rubbed against my legs, mewing a high-pitched greeting. She curled up beside me on the sofa, purring loudly. When Wilkes came back there was no clear space on his coffee table, so he dumped the mugs on the floor.

'The cat's Suzanne's,' he said. 'Fuck knows what I'll do with her now.'

Wilkes's voice was flat-lining. The tone was instantly recognisable. Depressives always sound the same. At its worst the illness reduces their speech to a monotone, as if nothing could ever surprise or please them again. Burns was minding his own business, balancing himself precariously on a tiny stool. Wilkes sat cross-legged on the floor, like a primary school child, waiting to be told what to do. He started talking before I had the chance to ask a question.

'I told her to give up that fucking job, wasting her time with street people. Scum, the lot of them.'

His hands were balled into fists, clenching and unclenching, like he was preparing for a fight. Maybe he would carry on yelling at the walls long after we'd gone. Burns looked shaken, as though the torrent of words had knocked him sideways, but for me it was business as usual. No one chooses to visit a psychologist unless they're prepared to shout their problems down.

'I don't know what I'm meant to do,' he said, on the verge of tears. 'They won't even give her back to me.'

I tried not to think about the two women I'd found, side by side in the freezer at Guy's. A picture of Suzanne Wilkes was balanced on a table beside me, next to a tumbler of whisky, covered in smeared fingerprints. The smell of alcohol so early in the day made me feel queasy. The photo looked nothing like the woman I had found beside Will's van. She was standing beside her husband, arms slung round each other's shoulders, beaming, as if they'd been out on the tiles. She must have been my height, the top of her head barely reaching his shoulder, a cap of sleek black hair framing her delicate face.

'How long were you married?' I asked.

Wilkes began to speak more calmly. Maybe my question was a welcome distraction. 'Since June. The wedding was in

Cyprus. She sorted the whole thing, sent out the invitations, booked the hotel.'

Sooner or later someone would have to make phone calls, tell the relatives. Burns sat next to me and tried to catch Wilkes's eye. Eventually he got a word in edgeways, and began to scribble down Wilkes's garbled answers. I observed his reactions, and tried to work out why Burns was so keen for me to spend my Saturday in his company. There was little to learn about Wilkes's state of mind except that he was in denial, stuck in the first stage of grief, which could last for months.

I got up and went to the bathroom. It was just as Suzanne had left it. The cabinet was crammed with pots of nail varnish, eye make-up, moisturiser: dozens of Superdrug reminders for Mark Wilkes that his wife wasn't coming home.

There were more photos in the hall. I spotted one of Suzanne at the centre of a sea of faces and did a double-take. I recognised one of them instantly. Morris Cley was standing beside her, waving, as if he'd never been happier. It must have been taken before he went to prison. He looked like a different person, less grey and careworn. Eight or nine people were clustered around Suzanne in an overgrown garden, and there must have been more, because the photo had been cropped to fit the frame. For some reason my heart was pumping too quickly, but there were a dozen innocent reasons why Cley would know her. Her job would have brought her into contact not just with rough sleepers, but with many of Southwark's most vulnerable people.

Burns slumped on the wall when we got outside. He was panting so hard, it sounded like he'd run a marathon.

'Poor bastard.' He took off his glasses and massaged the bridge of his nose. 'I'm glad we saw him though. Take a guess where Suzanne used to work, Alice.'

'Surprise me.'

'The Bensons' place. Street Safe sent her in to help the punters get job interviews.'

'Yet another connection,' I murmured.

The East End disappeared in the wing mirror and I let the sights of London wash over me, like a tourist who's just touched down. A queue had gathered outside the Tower of London, all waiting to pay an extortionate sum to be dazzled by the world's biggest collection of bling. Burns was talking non-stop in his soothing hybrid accent. As usual he was asking me to do something unpleasant.

'You can go tomorrow, can't you? It won't take all day.'

'Why would I want to waste my Sunday on Marie Benson?'

Burns frowned. 'She knows what's going on, Alice. You were right about our man being chairman of the Benson fan club. She's got to know who he is.'

'She won't tell me a thing, Don. Withholding information's the only power she's got left.'

I felt like pointing out that the murderer was just as likely to be a complete unknown, who got off on all the gory stories the press told about the Bensons' deeds when he was a kid. And who knew how much information had been leaked at the time? But there was no point in trying to reason with Burns when he had the bit between his teeth. When I finally agreed to visit her he looked smug. Yet again he'd managed to persuade me to do something against my better judgement. His technique never failed, he just carried on begging until I crumbled.

It was lunchtime when Burns dropped me at the hospital. I was steeling myself to face visiting Will when Laura Wallis came into my mind. I decided to call on her as a delaying tactic. I knew it would cheer me up to read how much more weight she'd gained.

When I got to Ruskin Ward another patient was asleep in Laura's bed, and there was no sign of her ever-present mother. I spoke to the first nurse I saw.

'Do you know which ward Laura Wallis has gone to, please?'

She looked confused. 'Sorry, I've just come on duty, I'll have to check.'

She scurried away to ask the ward sister, but I already knew what must have happened. Laura had nagged some well-meaning intern into sending her home, even though she was still below her target weight. She was probably lounging on the sofa right now, calling her mates, arranging her birthday party. The ward sister bustled towards me.

'I left a message on your voicemail, Dr Quentin. Would you like to come in here for a minute?'

I followed her into the airless cubbyhole she used for an office. She had a brisk, pleasant manner, and a broad Belfast accent. It was clear she didn't believe in beating around the bush.

'We lost her last night, I'm afraid.'

'Lost her?' My brain was lagging at least two steps behind.

'Laura had an arrhythmia. They took her to ITC but it was too late.'

'Her kidney function was improving,' I stuttered. 'She was gaining weight.'

The sister gave a sympathetic nod. 'I know, but the heart muscle was damaged. That's anorexia for you.'

Something snapped inside me. I felt it go, like the sound runners hear when their Achilles tendon breaks. Maybe we're all held together by invisible elastic bands that we don't notice until it's too late.

The sister put her hand on my shoulder. 'Stay here till you feel better.' She closed the door and trotted away to deal with her empire.

It didn't take long for the walls to fold in on me. Two minutes later I was galloping down the stairs, throwing up on a patch of grass. I don't know why it upset me so much. Maybe it was because she had been trying so hard to get home to her friends, or because I hadn't done enough. I tried not to think about her shell-shocked mother. Leaning against the wall of the building, I rummaged for a hankie to wipe my face. Breath flowed more steadily into my lungs and gradually my thoughts stopped racing.

There was no point in breaking down. That wouldn't bring any of them back. It was too late to help the girl at Crossbones Yard, and Laura, and Suzanne Wilkes, but it wasn't too late to stop the killer. I gritted my teeth. From now on I'd have to work harder, do everything in my power to help Burns and Alvarez track him down, before another girl was lost.

I let the cold air bring me round, then walked across the quadrangle. The climb to Bermondsey Ward took a long time, because my legs had lost their strength. When I peered through the window into Will's room, Lola was sitting in the chair beside his bed, with her back to the door. He still hadn't regained consciousness, but Sean had been busy. A huge wound ran down the length of his right leg, deftly sewn together, surgical cages pinning his shattered bones into place. There was no point in barging in, but I stood there watching them. Lola was holding Will's hand, humming quietly, and my eyes filled again. She was singing him a lullaby, even though he was already asleep.

Hari didn't answer when I called his mobile, so I left a message, explaining that I needed a week off, asking him to call me on Monday. For once, the walk home unfolded slowly, instead of racing by in a blur. The river was thick with winter fog, a pale sheet suspended above the water, shrouding the opposite bank. I did something I never normally let myself do, and stopped at the most expensive café on Butler's Wharf. A waiter brought me hot chocolate, and I watched swathes of fog travelling in from the sea. Lighters were sounding their horns as they lurched upstream. The combination of sugar and calm finally gave me enough strength for the last part of my walk.

When I got home, I lay on the sofa without bothering to take off my shoes.

It was dark when I woke up, and my phone was buzzing. But the tapping on my door was harder to ignore, quiet but insistent. The caller obviously had no intention of going away. The face that appeared in the spy-hole was distorted. A jumble of dark hair and shadows, a familiar scowl.

'I think we should do this properly.' Alvarez stood on the doormat. 'Let's go out for a drink, like normal people.'

He carried on standing there, not moving a muscle, while I made up my mind. He looked solid and calm, as if he could have waited until the end of time.

21

Alvarez's five o'clock shadow had disappeared, and for once he looked as though he might be prepared to take no for an answer.

'What if I said I was too tired?' I asked.

'Then I'd have made a wasted journey. But it wouldn't put me off, I'd just keep turning up, like a bad penny.' His expression was impossible to read, either grave or mocking. I let the door swing open reluctantly.

'I'm warning you, I'm not at my best.'

'That's why I came.' His stare had the same effect as always. I didn't know whether to be embarrassed, or grab his hand and kick open the bedroom door.

The mirror wasn't doing me any favours when I got changed. Grey shadows had pooled under my eyes, and it was hard to tell whether the butterflies in my stomach were the result of hunger or anxiety about spending an evening with Alvarez. Either way, I made sure not to look like I'd gone to any trouble, pulling on a dark blue shirt, my oldest Levi's, flat-heeled boots. He had disappeared when I came out. Hunkered down behind the sofa, he was examining the contents of my shelves.

'What do you think you're doing?' I asked.

'Worrying about your musical taste.' He held a CD by the corner as if it might explode. 'Boy George is the biggest concern.'

'For God's sake. That was a birthday present when I was twelve.'

He gave a contemptuous sniff. 'Miles Davis redeems you, but only just.'

Eventually he prised himself away from my music collection. On the way out I spotted one of Lola's notes on the kitchen table.

'Party at Lars's tonight. 9 p.m. Wear your silver dress!'

A row of kisses was scrawled under her huge, looping words. A graphologist would have had a field day, defining her personality as dangerously unstable.

'Do you have to go?' Alvarez peered at the note over my shoulder.

'No way. I've never felt less like dancing.'

He didn't say where he was taking me, but it was a relief to be a passenger for once, not making decisions for anyone. He kept his hand in the small of my back as we walked down to the river, passing New Concordia Wharf. Light was spilling from every window. The whole of London had decided to avoid the cold, watching their state-of-the-art TVs. Fog was still hovering over the river, wrapping the boats in tissue, muffling every sound.

There was a sign for the Blueprint Café by the Design Museum, and Alvarez led me up a narrow flight of stairs. We emerged into a dimly lit room. Waiters were dashing between tables, juggling trays of drinks on their fingertips. He chose a sofa beside the huge panoramic window. On a clear night you could have counted the factories and spires as far as Whitechapel, but tonight there was just a solid mass of cloud, pressing against the glass.

'Nothing to look at,' I commented.

'I wouldn't say that.' Alvarez observed me as one of the acrobatic waiters placed the beers he had ordered on the table in front of us.

I returned his stare. 'What do you think Burns would say, if he knew you were here?'

'Lucky sod, probably.' He shrugged. 'I wouldn't get the sack, if that's what you mean. He needs me too much.'

Fog swirled past the window, and I tried to decide what to do. We could go on flirting all night. Or I could pitch him a direct question and change the evening completely. I took a deep breath and fired.

'So, tell me, how long ago did you lose your wife?'

His face tensed then relaxed again, like a boxer reacting to a blow. 'I didn't lose her,' he said quietly. 'She was at home when she died. Losing her makes it sound like she fell out of my pocket somewhere, without me noticing.'

I didn't respond. Hari told me once that the best skill a psychologist can acquire is passivity. Don't say a word when someone is in full flow, just let your body language show you're listening.

'She got depressed, that was the first symptom of the brain tumour. That's how we met Tejo. The neurologist told us it was inoperable, but she counselled Luisa for months, helped her come to terms with it.' He was watching the fog, as if he could see straight through it. 'God knows how we'd have coped without her help.'

'I'm sorry,' I said quietly.

'Everyone is. When people said that at the start it used to make my blood boil. I must have pissed off a lot of friends, telling them to shove their pointless sympathy.'

'I doubt it. You can say what you like when you're grieving. The normal rules don't apply.'

He rubbed his temple. 'I'm not great at following rules at the best of times.'

'I noticed. How long did you know Luisa?'

'For ever.' He said it without missing a beat.

'Since the dawn of time?'

'Pretty much. I met her when I was fifteen, two Spanish kids surrounded by Londoners. The only time we were apart after that was at college. I stayed in London to do law, and she went back to Spain to study interior design. Poor girl probably thought she'd seen the back of me. But when I finished my degree I wanted to do something practical instead of sitting in an office all day. We got married a few days after I joined the force. It took a lot of persuading to get her to live in England again.'

I looked out of the window. The lights on the opposite bank kept appearing then vanishing again. It was hard to imagine anyone having the guts to get married that young. Sometimes it felt like I'd never committed myself to anything in my whole life. Alvarez was lounging in his seat, observing me again.

'You shouldn't do that,' I said. 'Staring's considered rude in this country, you know.'

'A man can look, can't he? And anyway, I'm not just watching, I'm waiting. There's an outside chance you'll tell me something about yourself.'

'Only if I get pissed.'

Alvarez beckoned the waiter who scurried over with two more glasses of beer.

'Go on then, drink that, and see if you can say something personal.' He kept his arms crossed as he threw down the challenge. 'Anything you like.'

'I have to be in the mood.'

Alvarez rolled his eyes. 'Have you always been locked up like this, with a big sign over your head saying do not disturb?'

'Is that how you see me?'

He kept his arms crossed. 'It's not how I see you, Alice. It's how you are.'

'What do you want to know?' The band around my chest started to constrict, like I was stepping into a lift.

'Tell me about your brother.'

I took a long gulp of beer. 'Will was a phenomenon, IQ off the scale, first-class degree in economics from Cambridge, hundreds of friends, great job in the City. You name it, he had the lot. But he overdid it, I suppose, flew a bit too near the sun.'

'Must have been tough on your parents.'

'My father died when he was nineteen, but they were never close.'

'You're kidding.' Alvarez looked shocked. 'If I forgot my father's birthday my brothers would fly over and beat me to a pulp.'

I laughed. 'Anyway, that's enough personal stuff. One piece of information is all you get.'

He shook his head in amazement, but he listened attentively while I talked about everything else, and he almost smiled when he heard about Lola's ecstatic new romance. And then the bar emptied and he leaned across and kissed me. Something flipped over in my chest, as if my heart was attempting a quick exit. His shoulder felt bulky and solid under my hand. God knows where his muscles came from, he claimed to be allergic to the gym.

'You keep grabbing me, every time I see you,' I said.

'Someone's got to.'

Four strong beers had gone to my head. The room shifted when I stood up, like an earthquake was in progress, but no one else had noticed. At least the fog was clearing. The barges had reappeared, moored in their usual cluster around Capital Wharf.

The fresh air and the chill hit me as soon as we got outside. It felt like I'd been sitting in a pub all day, knocking back shots.

'Are you okay?' Alvarez's voice was being fed through an echo machine.

'Dizzy. I haven't eaten anything.'

'You'll have to hang on to me then, won't you?'

He put his arm round my waist, and I got the chance to admire him without him noticing. In profile he was a bona fide Spanish aristocrat, black hair spilling across his eyes, Roman nose, full mouth. I reached for him without thinking, my hand on his lapel. He seemed surprised at first, maybe he thought he would always have to make the first move. It didn't take long for him to kiss me back. His hand strayed inside my coat, tracing the curve of my waist, cold fingers on the nape of my neck.

'Come home with me,' I said.

'You're drunk, Alice. You should eat something then go to sleep.'

He didn't touch me again until we got back to the square. When he bent down to kiss me goodbye his eyes were too dark to read.

'You could change your mind,' I whispered.

'I'd love to, believe me.' He kissed me again. 'But I want you to remember me in the morning.'

He smoothed a strand of hair behind my ear. He looked like he was questioning his willpower, so I said goodnight. He walked away without glancing back.

The security door refused to close behind me, even though I wrestled with it. The mechanism was broken, so I left it ajar and reeled up the stairs. If Lola had been at home I could have spilled the beans, but she would spend the night dancing with Lars, before passing out at dawn on his bed.

I sat on one of the hard chairs in the kitchen and tried to sober up. Maybe a stern talking-to was all that was required. My bathroom routine was more vigorous than normal.

I washed my face with soap and water, scrubbed my teeth relentlessly, hoping that cleanliness could banish confusion. But I still couldn't shake Alvarez off. He was there when I closed my eyes, impossibly macho, eyebrows raised in permanent disbelief. I knew I should call him tomorrow and tell him it had been a mistake, yet all I wanted to do was to dash out and buy new underwear, discover ways to make him smile.

Something woke me while it was still dark. Maybe it was just the remains of a nightmare, but I thought I heard a sound. And then it came again, more definite this time. An odd, scuffling noise. It was the opposite of the racket Lola normally made. She always switched on the lights and clattered about, forgetting I might be asleep. Someone was standing there, planning their next move. For some reason, there was no panic at all. Maybe that's what happens when the danger is real. I fumbled in the dark for my phone, but it must have been in the pocket of my coat, hanging in the hall. Then the sound came again. The tiptoe of someone moving silently from room to room.

I climbed out of bed as quietly as possible, then pulled on my jeans and took a chance. It took all my strength to shunt the chest of drawers in front of the door. I ran out on to the balcony. My mouth was so dry that when I yelled there was hardly any sound. No one came running, and no lights flicked on in the neighbouring flats. My breath formed clouds in front of my face, bare feet freezing on the concrete platform.

The door handle was twisting, the chest of drawers slowly edging across the floor. I had a minute, maybe less. My voice had formed a solid mass in my throat. I didn't let myself look down, because the vertigo would paralyse me, and leave me cowering on the balcony. The image of the Crossbones girl covered in hundreds of scars made me scramble over the metal railing. Then I took a deep breath and hurled myself into space.

22

It felt like flight. I travelled across seven or eight feet of winter air, nothing below me except the pavement and a thirty-foot drop. My hands grabbed the railing of the balcony of the flat next to mine and I hung there, legs swinging, like it was a playground adventure. My fingers were losing their grip on the metal bar, but I couldn't look down, too busy trying not to fall. Then a hand closed around my wrist and a man's voice cursed. He hauled me over the railing and I lay on the decking, gasping for breath, too exhausted to say thank you.

'What the fuck do you think you're doing?' The man who saved my life must have been in his early twenties, wearing nothing except a pair of boxer shorts and an outraged expression.

'Call the police,' I whispered. Then the fog closed in out of nowhere, and I forgot to breathe.

The young man was dressed by the time I came round, and his girlfriend was hovering over me. After they recovered from the shock of finding me dangling from their balcony, screaming my head off, they dealt with the situation brilliantly, providing biscuits and sympathy until the police arrived. The girl looked like a china doll, with perfect skin and corkscrew ringlets.

'You mean someone's been stalking you?' Her eyes were round with amazement.

I nodded. 'Except I've never seen him. God knows what he looks like.'

'Must be someone you know,' she said confidently.

'Why?'

She looked at me kindly, as if I was a slow learner. 'He had a key, didn't he?'

It took a few seconds for the idea to register. She was right, of course. Whoever it was had let himself in. But no one had a key to the flat except me, Will and Lola. Sean had suggested once that we should swap keys, but I had conveniently forgotten to get one cut.

Two uniformed policemen arrived while I was finishing another chocolate digestive, trying to restore my blood sugar. They looked like extras from *The Bill*, tired and middle-aged, desperate to retire on their fiftieth birthdays. They sat on my neighbour's black leather sofa, looking sceptical. Maybe they thought I was making it all up just to inconvenience them. After a few minutes the older one excused himself and stepped out into the corridor, muttering into his walkie-talkie, asking for an identity check. He was shamefaced when he came back, the radio on his lapel spluttering like a badly trained parrot. But I didn't blame him; in his shoes I'd have done the same. My life was beginning to sound like something you couldn't make up, yet for some reason I felt elated. Maybe it was simply relief at being alive, rather than scattered in bits across the road.

Police officers were buzzing around my flat like bluebottles when I was finally allowed to return. One was working on my front door, applying dust to the lock with a large brush. Two others were crawling all over the hall. Burns arrived while I was resisting the urge to shoo them out, counting to ten under my breath. His eyes were as tiny as currants in the pale dough of his face.

'You again, Alice.' He looked disappointed, like his favourite pupil had let herself down, but he still listened patiently while I explained what had happened.

'So you thought you'd do your own stunts, did you? Get yourself ready for the next James Bond.'

'There wasn't much choice,' I protested.

He gave a concerned frown. 'You didn't hurt yourself, did you?'

I shook my head, but my palms were beginning to tingle. They had been grazed raw during my adventure. Shock must have stopped the pain from registering.

'Your friend Lola's got a key to this place, has she?'

'Yes. I should call her and Lars, let them know what's happened.'

'Lars?' Burns's small eyes snapped open, like a camera's aperture.

'Lola's boyfriend.'

'What's his last name?'

'Jansen.'

He scribbled the word in his bulging notebook.

'But it's not him, for God's sake. Lola only met him a few days ago.'

The sofa groaned loudly under Burns's shifting weight. 'Someone got into your flat, Alice.' He spoke so slowly, he might have been explaining something complex to a child. 'So they either borrowed a key, or they stole one.'

'Well, you can forget about Lars. He's as laid back as they come.'

'And so are you.' He frowned. 'You're too bloody calm for my liking, Alice.'

'Disassociation.'

'Sorry?'

'People do it when they're in denial. It keeps anxiety at bay, you intellectualise things, instead of panicking.'

Burns took off his glasses and his face briefly came into focus. He must have been handsome once, back in the days when his cheekbones were still visible. 'But you should be panicking. Without your flying circus trick, you'd be in the boot of his car by now, and the next thing you know, you're at Crossbones, wrapped in black plastic.'

It was easy to imagine what kind of father he was: protective to the point of smothering. Something had sent his guardian instincts into overdrive.

'But there's no point in being scared, is there? All I can do is keep my wits about me.'

'Jesus.' Burns gave a low whistle. 'You should jack in psychology. They'd love you in the commandos.'

'Thanks for the careers advice. So, what should I do about the key? I need a locksmith, don't I?'

Burns blinked at me. 'You're not serious.'

'Of course I am. I can't stay here until the locks are changed. He can get in any time he likes.'

'You can't stay here full stop,' he said firmly. 'From now on, you're under full police protection.'

After a while I gave up protesting. Burns had made up his mind, and the more I argued, the more dogged he became. He waited while I packed a bag, a serious expression on his face, like he was taking a dangerous criminal into custody.

'By the way, we talked to your ex today.'

'Sean?'

'For a couple of hours down at the station, then we let him go again. He's a proper gent, isn't he?' Burns's mouth puckered in disgust.

'Is it his charm that offends you?'

'Smarmy. We'll be keeping an eye on him.' The maniacal look was back on Burns's face, his eyes round and focused, like a child in a sweetshop, trying to taste everything at once.

For some reason I didn't try to plead Sean's case. While I was with him he had seemed so well adjusted it was frightening, but nothing made sense any more. I kept picturing him outside Vinopolis, hands shaking, so enraged I hardly recognised him. All I'd wanted to do was jump on my bike and put a safe distance between us.

Burns watched me climb into the back of a squad car. Maybe he was afraid I'd wrench open the door while we were in transit and make my escape. The policeman didn't say a word, probably conserving his energy in case I misbehaved. It was dawn by the time he escorted me up the steps of a large, corporate hotel called the Regency, in Bankside.

The officer checked me in under an assumed name, and I had to bite my lip to stop myself laughing. Maybe it was the combination of shock, hunger and disbelief, but none of the day's events seemed real. My nightcap with Alvarez could have happened years ago. I was too tired to protest about using the lift to the fifth floor. The usual surge of panic washed over me when we stepped inside, but fortunately the lift shot upwards quickly, and I kept my eyes firmly closed. As soon as we got to the suite the officer installed himself on the sofa and began to explore the satellite channels on the flat-screen TV. He seemed perfectly content. Anything must have been preferable to another cold night patrolling the freezing streets, looking for miscreants to arrest.

I bolted the bedroom door behind me. It was just a reflex reaction, but after what had happened there was no way I could sleep in a bedroom without a solid lock. London was already waking up, as if nothing unusual had happened. To the east the sky was turning pink over Canary Wharf. From that distance the skyscrapers looked like an illusion, as thin as gravestones. The cupola of St Paul's was visible through chinks between the buildings. I wondered what advice Christopher Wren would have given me. None, was the likely answer. He wouldn't even have looked up from his desk – too busy finishing a drawing, flogging himself through another twenty-hour day. I sent Lola a text, then closed the curtains, ignoring the tremor in my hands, and climbed into bed for the second time that day.

23

Burns's idea of full police protection meant a complete denial of privacy, and keeping me indoors at all times. In the morning my bodyguards changed hands. The world-weary copper from the night before was replaced by a perky young woman who resembled a pixie. She was even smaller than me, with a delicate face and cropped strawberry-blonde hair. It was a surprise every time she spoke, because she had a gruff east London accent. Her name was Angie, and she traipsed down the stairs behind me with surprising goodwill. On an ordinary day I would have warmed to her, but two hours' sleep and an overload of worry had cancelled my sense of humour.

'Don't you do lifts then?' she asked cheerily.

'Not if I can help it.'

'Bet you're not mad on the London Eye, are you?'

Angie carried on gushing, like a tap with a faulty washer. By the time we reached the ground floor I knew all about her dad's sciatica, her mum's desire to live in Cyprus, and her belief that the force was no place to work if you wanted kids. She was keen to join me for breakfast, but I told her politely that someone was meeting me. She looked horrified. Maybe she hunted down a companion for every meal, so conversation could flow seamlessly from dawn till dusk.

The hotel dining room was cavernous. It looked like an aircraft hangar, which someone had tried to humanise by hanging dubious artworks on the wall. The breakfast buffet was languishing on hotplates, getting more desiccated by the minute, but I was too hungry to refuse. I loaded my plate and headed for a table by the wall. Angie loitered a few metres away, yammering happily into her mobile phone. Fifteen minutes later, Lola made a dramatic entrance, Pre-Raphaelite curls flying.

'Sorry I'm late, Al.' She threw her arms round me. 'They've got Lars at the police station. That fucking detective pitched up at seven this morning.'

'Which one do you mean?'

'You know, the big thug with the wedding ring.'

'Alvarez.' I took a bite of fried bread and tried not to meet her eye.

Lola leaned across the table, as though she was about to share a state secret. 'Anyway, he may be God's gift to women, but he's also a complete shit. He's been grilling Lars for hours. DNA sample, phone calls to Sweden, you name it.' Her lower lip quivered. 'It's a disaster. I've got a huge audition, and they won't even let me collect my clothes from yours.'

It was an effort not to smile. Lola had been exactly the same at school: an even mix of kindness and self-interest, with no grey area in between. In her eyes missing a showbiz opportunity was worse than a psychopath arriving in your bedroom in the middle of the night, or your boyfriend getting slammed in jail.

'Have you seen Will?' I asked.

Lola's expression changed immediately, as if she'd clicked back into reality. 'He's not good, Al. The poor thing's spouting all this weird stuff about heaven and hell. He's even more paranoid than before.'

'It'll be a rough few months,' I said quietly.

'And the fucking police have been hassling him too.'

I was beginning to lose patience. 'What are they meant to do, Lola? It's their job to ask questions. They don't do it for fun,' I snapped.

Her lip was trembling again, which was always a sign that the full waterworks could start at any minute.

'Look, you stay there, Lo. I'll get us some coffee.'

She had collected herself by the time I got back, and the double espresso improved her mood immediately. She dashed away as quickly as she'd arrived, in search of someone to lend her dance gear for the audition. For the time being everything else was put on hold, while she pursued her theatrical dream.

At least the walk back to the suite was quieter than the descent. Angie tried to keep the conversation going, but by the third floor she was struggling for breath. When we finally got to my suite she needed a cup of tea to help her recover. Even with floor to ceiling windows, the room felt airless. The ventilation system wasn't doing much, except shifting stale air from room to room. I went into the bedroom to escape Angie's wedding plans. Apparently the bridesmaids had chosen midnight-blue satin, and they were looking into the cost of hiring a Rolls-Royce. Outside the window a family of pigeons were admiring the view past St Paul's to Bishopsgate, as fat and satisfied as old women at a bus stop. They looked happy to sit on the ledge all day, but I was going quietly mad, aching to break the rules and go for a run. Overnight I had gone from complete independence to having to justify everything I did. I couldn't even leave the hotel to buy a newspaper without someone tagging behind. My mobile rang just as I was plotting my getaway.

'PC Meads here, Dr Quentin. I'm your driver for the afternoon.'

The promise Burns had squeezed out of me had completely slipped my mind, but the idea seemed more appealing now.

Anything was better than spending the whole afternoon indoors, kicking my heels. PC Meads turned out to be the baby-faced plod who drove me home from the station after I found Suzanne Wilkes's body. He was as monosyllabic as ever, his uniform two sizes too big, as though he was trying on a fancy dress outfit for a party at school. But at least it would mean a break from the hotel. A view of the streets racing by was preferable to four walls closing in on me.

Alvarez called just as we were crossing London Bridge.

'Sorry, I can't speak to you,' I said sharply. 'Lola says you're giving her boyfriend a hard time.'

'A hard time?' Alvarez sounded incredulous. 'I could have unscrewed the light bulb and refused him food.'

'I thought as much.'

'Why didn't you call me last night?' His voice was different on the phone, deeper and more guttural, like he might break into Spanish at any minute.

'Believe it or not, I was quite busy, trying to stay alive.'

He exhaled loudly. 'I knew I should have taken you back to mine.'

'Missed your chance, didn't you?'

'There'll be another.' His tone was completely confident, as if no logical argument could be made. 'Listen, Alice, I need to know where your brother keeps his key to your flat.'

I thought for a moment. We were driving through Stoke Newington, past parents corralling their kids towards Clissold Park, chivvying them to keep up.

'In his pocket normally. He hasn't got many other places to hide it. Why?'

'Someone handed in a bag last night. It was in some bushes, near where he was found.'

My heart turned over in my chest. 'Grey canvas, with his name inside the flap.'

'That's the one. And the thing is, Alice, we found a weapon in it.'

I took a deep breath. 'A flick-knife, with a silver handle.'

'You knew.' Alvarez cursed quietly under his breath. 'Who in their right mind would let someone as sick as your brother walk around with a weapon?'

'What was I meant to do? I tried to take it off him, but he grabbed it back.'

'Bullshit,' Alvarez muttered. 'You were too scared to follow through.'

There was no easy reply, so I switched off my phone. The car was chasing north through the suburbs now, past chains of down-at-heel terraces. Alvarez had hit the nail on the head. Fear had stopped me from helping Will. There had been so many days when I booked hospital appointments and tried to make him go. Coaxing, cajoling and bribery had all failed. Maybe I should have stood my ground, but he could flip without any provocation. Suddenly he would be uncontainable, beating the wall with his fists, calling me every name under the sun. The echoes of my father's behaviour terrified me. His illness made him react in exactly the same way. Our childhood must have been a training ground. Countless times Will had cowered in the living room, watching my father lose control. When he was drunk the violence began for no reason, in the blink of an eye. He needed Will to understand the enjoyment he got from hurting my mother and me. I rubbed my temples, trying to remove the disloyal thoughts from my mind. After all, none of it had been Will's fault. A twelve-year-old boy couldn't have fought a grown man, but it was still hard to understand why he didn't even try.

The hinterlands disappeared as we joined the A1. My brain seized the chance to make up its sleep deficit, and I woke up to hear Meads telling me we were nearly there. I peered out of the window. Rampton hadn't changed since my visit three years before, when I interviewed a team of psychiatrists on their methods for treating aggression in psychotic patients. From the approach road it looked more like a holiday camp than a secure mental hospital, low-rise buildings scattered across acres of open land. But the entrance gates were like Checkpoint Charlie. Eventually we were waved through and entered what looked like a village.

When the place was first built, all the staff lived on site, walking across the green from their pleasant villas to work at the bedlam every day. The governor spoiled them. He built a swimming pool, dance hall, tennis courts. He even paid for a bowling green. The inmates were kept in padded cells, in isolation much of the time. Hardly any treatments were available apart from dopamine, lithium and ECT. In the seventies the place nearly closed, because inspectors said the regime was barbaric. They made sure that all the staff perks were removed. Even the swimming pool had been filled in, replaced by a garden for the inmates to tend.

Meads looked even more like an anxious choirboy when he got out of the car. Maybe he was afraid someone would run out and straitjacket him.

'What's this place for, anyway?' he asked.

'It's a cross between a prison and a hospital. There's a mix of men and women. Some of them are criminally insane, and others are kept under the Mental Health Act.'

'Lovely.' His eyes widened. 'They've got that bloke here, haven't they? The one who killed the two little girls.'

'Ian Huntley. Not any more, he's at Wakefield Prison, overweight and smoking himself to death.'

'Couldn't happen to a nicer bloke,' Meads muttered. 'Who else is in there?'

'They had the most dangerous man in the UK for a while, Charles Bronson. And Beverley Allitt. The tabloids called her the angel of death.'

'How come?' He was hanging on my every word. Maybe he dashed home from work every night to pore over true crime magazines.

'She was a pretty blonde nurse, but she killed four of her patients. She tried to finish off a lot more, but they caught her on video.'

Meads was wide-eyed with amazement. 'Isn't it asking for trouble, keeping a load of nutters in one place?'

'Not really. There are four members of staff to every inmate, and they get assessed all the time. There hasn't been any bother here for years.'

Despite the reassurance Meads was reluctant to come inside. His skin looked waxy as he struggled to breathe. People often react like that. They're afraid to come into contact with madness, in case it's infectious, or the sight of it is damaging in some way. Meads traipsed along the corridor, trying not to look right or left in case a lunatic appeared in his line of vision. On the surface the place was like any other hospital, with blank magnolia walls, tasteless patterned curtains. The only difference was that the windows were sealed, reinforced-glass doors clicking shut behind us. A kick of adrenalin stirred under my ribcage. If the place went into lockdown, no one would ever escape.

Eventually we arrived at a door with a small glass window. Marie Benson was deep in conversation with someone. She looked different from the last time I'd seen her, rejuvenated, lips parted in her trademark gap-toothed smile. Her grin stayed put for several minutes. The man was doing a good job of keeping her amused. Whenever she spoke he listened attentively, then scribbled on a clipboard. Eventually he stood up to leave, and Marie looked crestfallen. I couldn't guess who the man was, but his jeans and corduroy jacket were too relaxed for a psychiatrist. He paused in the corridor, smiling and holding out a hand for me to shake.

'Marie's expecting you,' he said. 'I'm Gareth, her writing tutor.'

He lounged against the wall, as if he could have chatted all day. Thank God Lola wasn't there, she would have fancied him immediately. He was tall and rangy, with one of those mobile faces that change all the time, switching from joy to despair in a micro-second. His eyes were the type of blue I longed for as a child, so vivid they were almost turquoise.

'Must be a challenging job,' I commented.

He laughed. 'That's one way to describe it. It's pretty intense. Most of my work's one to one.'

'What kind of writing does Marie do?'

He hugged his clipboard closer to his chest. 'This year it's poems, but last year she was working on short stories.'

'And you help her improve them?'

'Most of the time she's pretty sure about what she wants to say. I'll scribe for her then read it back, until she's satisfied. I'm sure she'd be happy for you to see some of her stuff.' He nodded earnestly.

It was hard to imagine the tales Marie would dream up. Probably not ideal bedtime reading for your kids.

The man smiled again. 'I'd better get moving. Another student to see.'

I wondered how he could spend his days with the most violent, unpredictable people in Britain, yet look so calm. He fished in his pocket then handed me a card. His name and details were laid out in simple green letters: Gareth Wright-Phillips, Creativity Trainer.

'Drop me an email if you'd like to see Marie's poems.'

I watched him walk away, his stride loose and confident. Meads smirked to himself, admiring my pulling technique.

'Are you coming?' I asked.

'No ta.' He shook his head firmly. 'I'll wait here.'

Marie Benson was in an upbeat mood. 'Nice to see you, Dr Quentin. I enjoyed our chat last time, and I get so few visitors these days. But where's Sergeant Alvarez?'

'Busy, I'm afraid.'

'Pity, but I'm sure he'll come another time.'

I wondered what made her so certain that Alvarez was keen to see her. She must have been looking forward to his arrival more than mine. It's hard to identify what made her company so unsettling. Maybe it was her stillness. She was the opposite of a fidget, every drop of energy was being kept in reserve, and she was completely motionless for minutes at a time. Only her eyes flickered constantly from object to object, hoping to land on something she could see.

'I think you could unlock everything, if you wanted to, Marie,' I commented.

Her odd smile pulsed on unexpectedly, like the filament in a light bulb. When she was younger it must have been dazzling. 'There's not much I can unlock from in here.'

'What were you writing about today?' I asked.

The smile switched off again. 'Just a bit of verse. Not much good probably.'

I tried to imagine her reading her poems to an audience. Her crackling, chain-smoker's voice would be compelling enough to draw a crowd. 'But you like working with Gareth, do you?'

'He's wonderful.' For a second her face relaxed. 'A real soul mate. I could talk to him all day.'

I had the feeling she could have waxed lyrical about her

writing tutor for hours. 'Listen, Marie, you said you wanted me to visit. What did you want to talk about?'

'You know.' She smiled coyly.

Maybe I should have invented some new stories about grisly murders, just to see her reaction. The mask would have slipped, and she would have been unable to hide her delight.

'I don't know how the investigation's going. But I went to see Suzanne Wilkes's husband this week. You knew Suzanne, didn't you? She came to your hostel every week in the last year or two.'

'Terrible, isn't it?' Marie simpered. 'I heard about it on the news. He must be in bits.'

I suppressed a smile. Psychopaths are so skilled. They train themselves to react correctly, until they can simulate any emotion you can name: grief, sympathy, shame. Most of them have an incredible repertoire.

'And Suzanne's the link between us, isn't she? You and Ray knew her, and her body was dumped outside my flat.'

'She's not the only link.' Her eyes settled on mine, as if she'd suddenly regained the power to see. 'There's one much closer to home.'

'Is there?'

'You'll work it out soon enough,' she grinned.

'Why not tell me now?'

'Then you wouldn't come back and see me again, would you?' Marie fluttered her eyelashes then turned her head away. 'Poor little Suzanne,' she cooed.

If my eyes had been closed, she would almost have had me convinced. Her tone was full of sympathy. Only her expression let her down. It made me wonder if she was capable of experiencing any human feelings at all.

24

When I woke up the next morning I couldn't get Marie Benson's peculiar smile out of my head. Outside the hotel window London looked ridiculously inviting. It was just after six, but the working day had begun already, dozens of people scuttling along the street towards Waterloo. Cleaners, postmen and tube drivers, preparing for another nine hours of drudgery, but at that moment I would happily have traded places with any of them. I rested my hand on the window frame. It was vacuum-sealed, no sign of a draught. The en-suite bathroom was badly lit and windowless. I took a deep breath and forced myself into the tiny shower. By the time I had finished, every breath of air had been replaced by steam. I grabbed the door handle, but nothing happened. The door rattled against its frame, refusing to budge. My heart thumped unevenly against my ribs, and I wondered how long it took to die of oxygen starvation. Eventually my frantic struggling released the lock, and I spilled out, gasping for air. My system flooded with the familiar feeling of shame, for failing so spectacularly to control myself. If I had been wearing shoes I could have kicked the wall, vented my frustration on the immaculate paintwork.

Angie was waiting for me when I opened the door, curled up on the sofa with a mug of coffee. I tried to look pleased to see her, but my enthusiasm wore out immediately. Her stream-of-consciousness monologue rattled over my head as we ate our breakfast, and I wondered if I should change my ways. Maybe if we both talked nineteen to the dozen we would cancel each other out and end up with silence.

'I must make a quick call,' I said.

The nurse who answered the phone was cool, bordering on officious. When I asked about Will I heard the crisp rustle of pages while she consulted his case notes. He was no worse and no better than the day before, she explained. The sedatives were having little impact. Other patients had been complaining about the noise he made, but he didn't seem able to control himself.

'Sounds like he needs more pain relief,' I suggested.

There was an outraged silence. Eventually she gave me a curt warning not to visit for at least an hour, because they had only just managed to get him off to sleep.

Angie was ploughing through another mound of toast when I got back. God knows how she stayed so thin, without exercising. She obviously had the same compulsive relationship with food as with conversation. Orally fixated, Freud would say. Only happy if her mouth was full of words, or coffee or bread.

'Everything okay?' she asked.

'It's been better.'

'Yeah?' Her attention was already fixed on her next slice, thickly loaded with butter and marmalade.

'I have to go to the hospital when you're ready, to see my brother.'

'No can do, I'm afraid. We're staying here till eleven.' She popped another crust into her mouth and chewed briskly. 'The station just called.'

I forced myself to take a deep breath. 'But I have to see him. He's sick.'

'We can visit later.' She gave an apologetic shrug.

I got up to leave. 'Then I'll go for a quick run while I'm waiting.'

'No you will not,' she snarled. Angie's expression had changed from pleasant schoolgirl to cornered Rottweiler. 'Let's get something straight, Alice. It's my job to keep you safe. Where you go, I go. Are you reading me?' Her expression was ferocious.

'I am,' I nodded. 'But I'm telling you, if I don't get some exercise soon, I'm going to lose it, in a big way.'

'We'll see about that,' she muttered. 'Now, if you're so keen to run about, why not get me some more bacon? Two rashers'll do nicely.'

After breakfast Angie tutted under her breath as she tagged me back down to the ground floor. A row of treadmills was pressed against the window in the hotel gym, but the glass must have been mirrored. Passers-by kept slowing down to admire themselves or adjust their hair. It was a relief to hear the whirr of the treadmill, my feet pounding on the narrow track. I had the place to myself, apart from Angie and a gym assistant who was keeping her company, while I tried to sweat the last few days out of my system. On the other side of the window a varied cast of characters were going about their business. A *Big Issue* seller was having no luck by the crossroads, failing to catch anyone's eye. An old woman tottered past, her back so stooped she seemed determined to watch her feet taking each step. Slivers of the Thames were trapped between the buildings. The river had faded to a dull pewter, in need of polish.

Sweat was coursing down my back by the time Burns's car pulled up outside the hotel. He parked on the double yellow lines and winced as he heaved himself upright. No doubt he had joint problems by now, cartilages fraying under the daily pressure. I hit the emergency stop and the treadmill juddered to a halt. Angie watched me walk past as she chatted to her new friend. In the changing room I stuck my head under the tap, letting cold water gush across the back of my neck.

Burns was waiting for us in reception, comfortably filling one of the mock Chippendale sofas. Angie made her way over to the magazine rack, keeping me in viewing distance, even though Burns had told her to take a break.

'That girl's like superglue,' I moaned.

'One of our best,' Burns nodded. 'You're safe with Angie, that's for sure. Top of her year at training school.'

'I bet.' I tried to look impressed. 'So what's been happening?'

'We've had a few developments from forensics.' He fiddled with a loose button on his outsized white shirt.

'Spit it out, Don.'

'You're not going to like it.' Burns heaved in a deep breath, as though he was about to go under water for a long time. 'The results came back from your brother's van, and there's evidence he was involved.'

I blinked. 'Don't be ridiculous.'

He glanced down at his scuffed black shoes. 'The van's full of it, Alice. A blanket with hair and skin cells from both girls. A piece of the rope Suzanne Wilkes was tied up with.'

'So you've already made up your mind.'

'Of course not.' Burns repositioned his glasses on the bridge of his nose with a pudgy forefinger, eyes like pinpricks behind the thick lenses. 'But I've got to look at the proof, haven't I? And at the moment there's a hell of a lot of it.'

'Such as?'

'We've been talking to people, like your friend Lola. She says she couldn't believe the change in him.' He flicked through his notebook and read out a sentence in a calm, sing-song voice that made me want to slap him. 'One minute he's fine, then he loses it. You never know which way he's going to turn.'

'That's out of context. Lola knows better than anyone that Will wouldn't hurt a soul.'

Burns's eyes fixed on me. 'If he's such a sweetheart, why's he carrying a blade that could slice you into barbecue steak?'

'Look, Don. It doesn't make sense. You're not telling me Will sent the letters, are you, for God's sake? He's bombed out of his head on whatever he's taken that day. He's not calm enough to do something like that, even if he wanted to.'

'I've told you, there's a gang of them. We're sure of it. Maybe he fell out with them, and that's why he got hurt.' Burns pressed his lips together firmly, like there was nothing more to say.

'And what's Will's take on all this crap?'

'We haven't interviewed him yet.' Burns looked sheepish. 'The hospital says we've got to wait till he's himself again.'

'You'll have a bloody long wait then. He hasn't been himself for eight years. Some bastard pushed him off a roof, but you're not bothered about that, are you?'

'I know it's hard to take in.' He shot me a sympathetic glance. 'But we're keeping you here till the threat's over. You don't have to worry.'

Before I could think of a reply, Burns gathered his jacket and notebook and hoisted himself into a breathless standing position. He made a getaway before I could give him another piece of my mind.

Angie was unusually quiet when she escorted me back to my room. We were passing the magazine stand when something caught my eye. A face I recognised stared at me from the front page of the *Southwark Gazette*. The picture must have been taken a few years ago, before the drugs and booze took hold, but it was definitely her. She was wearing her slightly too trusting smile, and the same dark fringe, which almost hid her eyes. There was no escaping the fact that the photo was a black and white version of Michelle, the prostitute I had paid to stay at home.

25

The headline wasn't exactly original. SOUTHWARK RIPPER STRIKES AGAIN? The *Gazette* was milking the story for every ounce of pathos: 'Michelle Yeats, 27, was last seen getting into a saloon car outside the Angel pub in Southwark late on Friday evening. None of her friends have heard from her since. Her mother Lesley says that Michelle has recently turned her life around, and is on an NHS drug rehabilitation programme, in an attempt to win back custody of her six-year-old daughter Liane.'

I dropped the paper on to a coffee table without finishing the article. Angie peered at the photo over my shoulder.

'So young, isn't she?' she cooed. 'Poor girl.'

The impulse to tell her to fuck off was overwhelming. I rubbed my eyes, but the image of Michelle by herself in the dark, clawing at a brick wall, refused to disappear. The bastard must have got hold of her on Friday night, just after I gave her the money to stay at home. Maybe he even saw us sitting on the wall together. The thought gave me a queasy feeling in the pit of my stomach.

I glanced at my watch. It was ten thirty on Monday morning. If the killer was holding her, she'd be growing weaker by now. He'd had more than forty-eight hours to carve his favourite symbols into her skin. But there was no use phoning Burns to point out that his theory had fallen apart. Even though Will was languishing in hospital while women carried on being abducted, there would still be a way to prove he was implicated.

Angie was reluctant to do what I asked, until I told her that the order came from Burns. Then she snapped her heels together and sprang into action, terrified of jeopardising her chances of promotion. The drive took less than ten minutes, the sky threatening to snow at any minute. Half a dozen cyclists queued beside us at the lights, in an assortment of Day-Glo Lycra outfits. The tenacity of London's long-distance bike riders has never failed to impress me. Dozens of them get killed and injured every year, yet you still see them, out in all weathers, battling with the juggernauts.

Bermondsey Ward was quiet when we arrived. Two policemen were sitting outside Will's room, as though they expected him to barge out of the door and race to freedom. Lola must have visited recently. She had left a bag of peaches on the table beside his bed and a card ordering him to get well immediately, rows of kisses underneath her name. I touched Will's forehead. His skin was clammy and feverish. So far he hadn't noticed me. His eyes were fixed on the closed window, trying to count the clouds. I sat on the edge of his bed and attempted to catch one of his hands, but they were in constant motion, fluttering from his chest to his face. Maybe the room was full of flies that only he could see. The veins in his neck stood out like cords, bulging under his skin. He spoke quietly to himself, like an actor reading a part for the first time.

'Can you hear me, Will?'

His chatter continued without a let-up. He had travelled a long distance since the last time I saw him. Even if I yelled at the top of my voice, he still wouldn't have heard me. But at least the metal frame over his legs was anchoring him safely to the bed. I covered my mouth with my hands. In that state it must have been impossible for him to sleep. The drug chart on his bed recorded regular doses of the sedative Nembutal and Xodol for the pain, which explained his twitching. All the painkillers and sedatives in the world wouldn't do the trick. Without methadone he was going cold turkey. When he came to his senses, he had two weeks of hell to look forward to.

Sean appeared out of nowhere. He must have passed under Angie's safety radar in his white coat. She was out in the corridor, gossiping with a junior doctor as if her life depended on it.

'He's making progress,' Sean said quietly.

I kept my eyes on Will's face. His expression kept changing, grinning then convulsing in pain, like someone was forcing him to watch a horror film again and again.

'That's not exactly what I'd call it.'

'This must be hellish for you.' Sean stood next to me, his arm almost touching my shoulder. 'Did you hear that your police friends interviewed me? They wanted all the gory details about us.'

He was still ridiculously good-looking, like a fairytale hero, on the hunt for damsels to rescue. When he leaned down and kissed me I was too shocked to push him away at first, but something about his touch scared me. Too deliberate, as if he'd been planning it for days, his fingers cold around my wrist.

'Stop it, Sean.' I jerked my hand away. His expression was confused. Maybe rejection was a completely new experience for him.

'It's your fault, Alice. I can't think straight any more.' His dark blue eyes bored into me. 'My head's completely fucked.'

It was a struggle to think of a reply. 'I'm sorry the police have been bothering you.' I shifted my attention back to Will. 'But this is what I have to focus on now.'

'Why not let me help you, Alice?' He carried on talking, but by now I had turned away. A minute later the door clicked shut.

The sound startled Will, his gaze sharpening for a second, like a telescope focusing.

'Can you see them, Al?' he whispered.

'What, sweetheart?'

'Outside.' He was smiling now, pointing at the window. 'Dozens of them.'

I peered through the window. There was nothing except a view of the mortuary and a strip of wintry sky.

I touched the back of his hand. 'It's okay. There's nothing to worry about out there.'

His eyes widened. 'The angels have come back, Al. Open the window.'

'I don't want you to catch cold.'

'Let them in.' His voice was rising to a shout, so I slid the glass back by a few centimetres, the freezing draught chilling my face. 'Wider!'

Will's whole body strained towards the clean air, arms outstretched. The expression on his face had changed too. The best word to describe it is rapture: poised and expectant, preparing himself to fly. Tears blurred my vision. Fortunately there was a box of tissues next to his bed so I could wipe my face. I got myself out of the door without looking back. Over the years I must have treated hundreds of delusional patients: a man who thought he was John Lennon; a young girl who believed she was so ugly that people ran from her in the street; and a pensioner who woke up one day, convinced his wife had been replaced by a total stranger. But it's different when it's someone you love. It's like bereavement, except you're not allowed to grieve.

Burns was waiting for me in the corridor. He didn't attempt to get to his feet, obviously rationing his energy for something more important. Behind the door Will began to wail. A high fluting sound, then a fully fledged howl. Maybe the fact that he couldn't soar out of the window, or skim across the roofs and treetops had finally hit him. A nurse scuttled along the corridor to silence him.

'He didn't want you to leave,' Burns commented.

'I don't think he even clocked I'd arrived.'

'Did you get any sense out of him?' He peered at me as if I might be withholding something vital.

'Not a word.' I shook my head. 'He's having a psychotic episode. It could be the pain that's caused it, or trauma, or a reaction to the drugs he's taken.'

'And how long will it last?'

'God knows. Days or months. People don't always come back from a drug-induced psychosis, their personalities change. Remember Syd Barrett from Pink Floyd?'

'Jesus wept.' Burns removed his glasses in despair.

'And there's another thing, Don, about that girl who's gone missing.'

Burns's gimlet eyes snapped open again. 'Michelle Yeats.'

'I saw her on Friday night.'

'How come?' Burns looked stunned, as if a new side to my personality had been revealed. He seemed so exhausted I decided to keep my explanation as short as possible.

'I bumped into her once before, when I was out running. I saw her again on Friday night after Will was admitted.'

'Did you speak to her?'

I nodded. 'I gave her some cash, to get home safely.'

'God almighty,' he groaned. 'Give a druggie money and they don't go home for an early night and a cup of cocoa, Alice. They buy a bag of crack.'

Burns looked as if he was preparing to give me a lecture on correct procedures for dealing with drug addicts, but we were disturbed by a loud scream. The nurse was having no luck in calming Will. The noise coming from his room made me want to cover my ears. It was the same bleak, insistent cry that animals make on their way to the abattoir.

When Angie arrived to take me back to the hotel, it was a relief, and for once she gave me some space. She kept quiet when we got into the car. The streets passed by without a single detail registering in my mind. Something was missing. Will couldn't have been involved in the killings, the idea was incomprehensible, but I would have to work fast to find out who was trying to implicate him. For a split second the idea that he was connected to it flew across my mind, but I shooed it away again, like an unwelcome fly.

Angie didn't bat an eyelid when I asked her to stop at the police station. She produced a key to the Benson archive as soon as we arrived.

'I won't join you,' she said, pressing a finger under her nose. 'Dust gets my sinuses going.'

I scanned the heaps of dirty manila folders and evidence files stacked in numbered boxes, before opening the first one my hand fell on. Dozens of witness reports were arranged by date, from neighbours and bystanders, relatives of the missing girls. It took a long time to plough through three of the files. One of them was full of pictures of the interior and exterior of the Bensons' hostel. Several shots showed the building being ripped apart, while the excavators hunted for bodies. There were dozens of photos of an ornate Victorian fireplace. Ray must have used his best DIY skills to dismantle it and make a cavity for two of the victims, then piece it together again.

Just as I was about to give up for the day something I recognised caught my eye. It was the picture of Suzanne Wilkes at the centre of a group that I had seen at her flat, except in this version she was part of a much bigger crowd. A large grey building loomed in the background, above a neglected garden. My heart turned over in my chest. Sixteen or seventeen people were standing in a circle. Marie Benson was at the back, giving the photographer her odd, gap-toothed grin.

But the face that kick-started my adrenalin rush was Will's. He was standing at the edge of the group, unsmiling, as though he couldn't quite believe he was there. Neither could I. The photo fell from my hands. How long had he spent in that hellhole, hiding from the world, while all those girls lost their lives? My thoughts raced. Surely Burns and Alvarez had seen the photo and knew that Will had spent time at the hostel? Or maybe he had given a false name, and escaped before the investigation began. The case had been closed for so long that Will was just another nameless vagrant, gathering dust in the archive room.

I was about to put the photo back in its plastic wallet when a key turned in the lock. Without asking myself why, I dropped the picture into my bag. Alvarez was standing in the doorway. He looked awkward, like I had caught him doing something questionable. The shadows under his eyes were even darker than before.

'You've been overdoing it,' I said.

'No choice.' He wiped his hand across his face. 'Or the next girl's going to turn up on our doorstep, covered in noughts and fucking crosses.'

'I keep thinking the answer's here somewhere. God knows why.'

'Me too.' Alvarez scanned the mountains of dusty paper, as if a clue might suddenly glitter and give itself away. 'And you want to help your brother, don't you?'

I looked back at him. He was the opposite of Sean, who was so confident that women loved him. Alvarez's shoulders were a little too bulky, mouth set in a permanent snarl, black eyes giving nothing away.

'You don't believe all that shit about Will, do you?' I asked.

For a second he didn't react, then he slowly shook his head. 'There's no way he's involved.'

At that moment I could happily have vaulted across the table and showered him in kisses.

26

'I thought I was going mad.'

Alvarez shook his head. 'It's Burns who's losing it. Everything has to be open and shut with him, no grey areas in between.'

His eyes were so dark it was like staring into a well, the water so far down that no light was ever reflected. He massaged the back of his neck hard, as if all his tiredness was stored there. 'The thing I can't figure out is who persuaded your brother to lend them his van.'

'That's the problem. Will never lets me meet his friends. I've seen people hanging around, druggies mainly, but he won't tell me their names.'

Alvarez scowled in frustration. 'We need him to recover, so he can tell us everything he knows.'

'Forget it. That could take months.'

His hand settled on my shoulder but I folded my arms. One crying jag was enough for the day. 'Don't be nice to me please. It's too much.'

'When can I see you?' he asked.

'You know where I am. Stuck in my ivory tower with hermetically sealed windows and shit food.'

'Tomorrow then,' he said. 'We'll have dinner.'

I rested my head on his chest for a second. He smelled of musk and citrus and it was a relief to feel his arms close round me. When the door creaked open we sprang apart like guilty teenagers. Angie was waiting in the doorway. When I glanced back Alvarez had already forgotten about me, sifting the evidence from the Benson case as though he was panning for gold.

It was seven o'clock by the time we got back to the hotel, and Angie handed me over to a middle-aged policewoman I hadn't met before. Mercifully she seemed happy to flick through a magazine and give me a minute on my own. I ate my grey hotel dinner from a tray in my bedroom, picking at a limp chicken Caesar salad. At least I had a view of the floodlit dome of St Paul's. I hadn't been to the Whispering Gallery since I was a kid, but I could still picture the visitors in the nave below, small as matchsticks, and the apostles' faces picked out in gold. They seemed to be eavesdropping on the sightseers' conversations. Each sentence reverberated for minutes afterwards, bouncing back and forth between the circular walls.

Before I could finish my meal the policewoman knocked on the door and announced that my visitor had arrived. Lola sprang into the room like an over-excited red setter, but I could tell from her expression that she wasn't having a good day.

'There you go.' She thrust the usual two bottles of red wine into my hands. 'Where's the corkscrew?'

I knew better than to ask what was wrong until she'd knocked back her first glass.

'Things aren't perfect in your world, are they, Lo?'

'Too fucking right.' She burst into theatrical sobs, then buried her face in her hands. 'It's Lars.'

'What's he done?'

'Fucked off back to Sweden.'

I put my arm round her shoulders. 'He's mad about you, that can't be right.'

'The police ran a check on him. He's conned loads of girls into giving him money to open a bar. One woman even remortgaged her house. I can't believe I was such a mug, Al. He's a confidence trickster, for fuck's sake.' Tears coursed down her cheek, forming a puddle on the bedspread.

'But did he ever ask you for money?'

She shook her head.

'There you go then. You were the exception, the one he fell for.'

She blew her nose loudly into a hotel napkin. 'Maybe he was just biding his time.'

'No way,' I protested. 'He was nuts about you.'

After two more glasses of red wine Lola was beginning to cheer up. 'At least I've experienced the best sex on the planet.'

'And that's worth something, isn't it?'

'God, yes,' she sighed.

'How did the audition go, anyway?'

She gaped at me in amazement. 'Didn't I tell you? They loved me. I'm starting Friday night.'

'That's brilliant. What's the part?'

'Chorus line in *Chicago*. It's only Equity basic, but it'll go on for months, and all that hoofing should shift some of this weight.' She looked down and inspected her imaginary spare tyre.

Lola stayed until after eleven. She lounged on the bed, in a nest of cushions stolen from the hotel chairs. By the time she left she'd given me an in-depth account of Lars's sexual skills, her costume fitting and her mother's ecstatic reaction when she found out her daughter was going to be in a West End show. It seemed to have slipped her mind that I was being held in captivity, in case someone decided to kill me.

'I'm staying on Craig's sofa. He's a darling, but I'd rather be with you. When are they letting you out anyway?'

'God alone knows.'

'We'll have a party when you get home.' She rose to her feet unsteadily. As usual she had downed three-quarters of the wine by herself. 'Better go. Big rehearsal tomorrow. And remember, steer clear of that Spanish bastard. Cross the street if you see him. He's a complete and total shit.'

'Will do.' I bit my lip. I was going to have to pick my moment to confess about my nights out with Alvarez.

Maybe it was the wine that made my mind race. When I turned the lights out ideas were bouncing off the walls like I was back at St Paul's, yelling my fears into the silence. If Will was innocent, why had both the murdered women spent time in his van? I pictured my mother wagging her finger, telling me I'd failed to keep him out of mischief. And Michelle kept reappearing too. It was hard to believe she'd only been twenty-seven. She could have been ten or fifteen years older, her drug habit sending the ageing process into overdrive.

Eventually I fell into an uneasy sleep, but I woke at six thirty, struggling for breath, desperate to be outside in the city air. It might be polluted, but at least it hadn't been recycled a hundred times. I fished in my bag for the photo I'd stolen from the Benson archive. Sooner or later I would have to tell Alvarez, or replace it when no one was looking. God knows why I'd taken it. Maybe it was my way of rescuing Will from the Bensons' orbit.

The faces of the residents had something in common; they were all outsiders. A group of misfits huddling together for comfort – badly dressed, acne-scarred, too fat or thin, too shy to look at the camera. All of them the butt of someone's joke. Will was pale and preoccupied, already more interested in the conversation inside his head than the ones going on around him. By contrast Morris Cley looked relaxed, hand fluttering in a jubilant wave. He must have felt at home for the first time in his life, surrounded by people who knew about loneliness. Suzanne Wilkes was beaming at the centre of the crowd. She seemed to have found her niche, shepherding lost souls, oblivious to the danger she was in.

Fortunately Angie was nowhere to be seen. I wasn't in the mood for non-stop chit-chat over breakfast, or being advised on how to spend my time. PC Meads was my bodyguard for the day, but it was hard to imagine he'd be much use if the chips were down. He had the anxious look of a boy about to start his first day at secondary school when he collected me from the hotel dining room.

'I've got some errands to run,' I told him.

Meads looked relieved. He always appreciated being told what to do, in case he made a mistake. I looked at the address I had scribbled down from the Benson archive. Burns would be incandescent if he knew who I was intending to see.

'I have to visit an old friend,' I said. 'It's not far.'

He scuttled off to get his car and before long we were heading east along the river. As we waited in the traffic on Bankside I watched a huge freighter loaded with containers pass under London Bridge, bound for America or the Caribbean. I closed my eyes and tried to imagine weeks on open water, with nothing to worry about except storm systems and tides. We headed deeper into Bermondsey, past housing estates still waiting to be gentrified, every tree tagged with graffiti, burned-out cars littering the car parks.

'You can wait here,' I told Meads.

He pulled up obediently in a side street off Jamaica Road. Net curtains twitched in the windows of run-down terraces, the whole neighbourhood wondering whose son or husband was in trouble again. I sauntered round the corner to Keeton's Road. It was a narrow street of 1970s low-rise flats, close to Bermondsey tube. A hundred metres away four lanes of traffic roared towards Elephant and Castle. The house had seen better days. The safety glass in the plastic front door was cracked, and frost had killed every plant in the tiny front garden, apart from a thicket of brambles that almost blocked the path. I clutched the aerosol in my pocket and felt my heart rate quicken as I pressed the bell. If he reacted badly I could always spray him in the face and make a dash for it. The door opened a few centimetres and a pair of misshapen grey eyes peered out warily.

'Hello, Morris.'

He scrabbled at the security chain. Morris Cley was still the opposite of God's gift to women. His grubby blue cardigan had seen better days and his mouth hung open in permanent amazement.

'Alice Quentin.' He said my name rapturously, as if he'd been expecting me for weeks.

'Can I come in?'

The first thing that hit me was an overpowering sweetness on the air, perfume or air freshener. A large bowl of potpourri was standing on the hall table, two more on the coffee table in the living room. His mother must have used them to disguise the smell of damp while she was alive. The place looked like an old lady still lived there, and she had just popped out to fetch her knitting. Crocheted arm covers adorned the sofa and chairs, lace doilies on the dining table. For some reason the old-fashioned clutter prevented me from feeling afraid. Cley was fidgeting on the edge of his chair.

'I'm sorry about the other night.' His voice was raw with tension, eyes lingering on my breasts rather than my face.

'That's okay, Morris. You didn't mean any harm.'

His shoulders lowered, as though he'd been given a reprieve.

'I wanted to ask you a few questions though. Is that okay?'

Cley nodded. This time his gaze swept down to my legs and I was grateful I'd worn trousers.

'You knew Ray and Marie Benson, didn't you?'

He nodded again. 'Neighbours.'

'Were they?'

'They lived across the way. Marie took Mum to bingo.' He sneaked a sidelong look at me.

I blinked. Bingo isn't the kind of leisure pursuit you expect mass murderers to indulge in. 'And you kept in touch after they moved to the hostel?'

'We got the bus up there for tea on Sundays. They let me help around the place. Ray did Mum's garden sometimes.' Cley smiled when he spoke about the Bensons. Maybe their killing spree had been too complex to take on board.

'I've got a photo here.' I placed it on the coffee table in front of him and watched him peer at it. He ran his finger across the row of faces, studying each one.

'Can you tell me their names?'

'Maybe.' For the first time his eyes made direct contact with mine. He surveyed my face, trying to work out how much the information was worth.

'I can't stay long, Morris. Are you going to help me or not?'

'If you give me something I will.'

'What?'

'A kiss.' He rubbed the flaking skin above his upper lip. 'Jeannie used to kiss me sometimes.'

I glanced at him. His frizz of grey hair radiated from his skull, cloudy eyes staring back at me. 'If you won't tell me, I'll leave. My friend's waiting outside.' I stood up and began to button my coat.

'All right, all right.' He held up his hands in defeat.

I shoved the photo back towards him. 'Tell me who you remember.'

Cley concentrated on the image again. He smiled as he identified Marie Benson, like she was his favourite auntie. 'Ray, Bill, Suzanne, Laura.' His finger hovered over Will's face and I saw him recoil.

'Did you know him, Morris?'

'No.' He shook his head vigorously.

'You didn't like him?'

Cley bit his lip. 'Gave me the creeps. Snooping about, watching people all the time.'

Suddenly Cley grabbed the photo and turned it over, weighting it with the palms of both hands. He pressed the faces into the grained wood of the table, and held them there for a long time, as though they were kittens he needed to drown.

27

'You will come back, won't you?' Morris Cley hovered over my chair, wringing his hands.

It was hard to tell if he was smiling or grimacing when he bared his discoloured teeth at me. Maybe he already knew that he'd never clap eyes on me again. I was like all the other social workers and probation officers, making their quick official visits, then vanishing into the ether. I led the way along the hall, anxious to avoid a rerun of our last meeting. My left hand clutched the aerosol in my pocket.

'I could give you the bus fare.' He fiddled with the buttons of his cardigan, a thick rime of dirt trapped under his nails. 'I gave Jeannie my benefits sometimes. She said it helped with the rent.'

The smile disappeared from his face when he thought about her. Part of me knew I had nothing to fear, but my fingers closed tightly around the handle of the front door.

'What happened the last time you saw Jeannie, Morris? You can tell me the truth you know, I won't mind.'

'Nothing.' The fidgeting started up again. He twisted the frayed collar of his shirt, as if it was too tight. 'I wanted to stay over, but she wouldn't let me. She said someone else was coming round.'

'What did you do when you left?'

'Kissed her goodbye, like this.' He lunged towards me, but I twisted away just in time. His lips left a cold trail of saliva across my cheek.

I jerked the door open and stepped out on to the path.

'And that was all you did?'

His silence went on for a beat too long, but I could guess what he'd done from his body language. The hand-wringing had stepped up a gear. One palm rubbing across the other, removing an invisible stain. My heart rate shot up as I took a hasty step backwards.

'Goodbye, Morris.'

When I glanced back, Cley's eyes were brimming. He was locked in a 1970s time warp, silhouetted against a background of orange flowers, the blue carpet swirling at his feet. It took half a dozen deep breaths to clear my lungs of the smell of potpourri, sexual frustration and despair. A dull headache pulsed behind my left eye.

All the visit had done was remind me that I was out of my depth. Some human rights lawyer had spent a lot of time and taxpayers' money liberating Cley from prison for a crime he had definitely committed. The expression on his face gave more than enough evidence. When Jeannie Anderson rejected him, he would have been unable to stop himself. The one woman who had ever let him touch her was turning him away, to be with another man. And he was stronger than he looked. It would have been easy for him to overpower her, hold a pillow over her face for as long as it took. God knows what he must have felt afterwards. Relief, probably. He couldn't have her, but neither could anyone else.

I walked to the end of Keeton's Road and sat down on a low wall to calm myself. If my instincts had been so wrong about Cley, what else had I missed? Maybe Burns was right about him being part of a group, intent on reconstructing the Bensons' crimes. Obviously he wasn't capable of carrying out a complex attack, but he could be valuable for other reasons. Maybe his friendship with Ray and Marie gave him a special kudos in their eyes. I could see the logic, but the idea of a gang didn't convince me. For some reason I felt sure the killer was acting alone, on his own obsessive mission.

I dragged in a final gasp of clean air and headed back to the car. I still had no idea why the sight of Will's face had scared Cley so much. All I could do was pray that Burns didn't get wind of my visit. If he did, he would stick me in a holding cell for weeks, on a diet of gruel.

Meads looked disappointed when I asked him to take me back to the hotel. Maybe he fancied an afternoon of free-wheeling, but he seemed happy enough once the TV was switched on. By the time I had made myself a cup of tea he had found the American wrestling channel, his eyes wide as saucers while huge men with glistening orange tans threw each other around the ring. I wanted to explain that the moves were choreographed, no one ever got hurt, but it would have spoiled his fun.

I lay down on my bed and closed my eyes. Through the door the wrestlers carried on shrieking in pretend agony. When I woke up, it was pitch dark outside. The guilt of allowing a whole afternoon to evaporate hit me as I sat up, but at least my headache had eased. A conversation was going on in the room next door, Meads' thin squeak blending with a familiar soft baritone. I inspected myself in the mirror, my eyes still puffy with sleep.

There was a knock on the door before I could finish combing my hair. Alvarez was wearing a dark grey tracksuit. He looked like a football manager, itching to get back on the field.

'I thought you might fancy a jog,' he said.

I suppressed a laugh. 'You hate running.'

'I said a jog, not a run. You won't be going at your normal Olympic pace.'

'Better than nothing.'

The door closed again and I got into my running gear. The prospect of escaping the hotel's stale air made me rush to lace up my shoes. Meads had disappeared by the time I came out, and Alvarez was lounging in the doorway, arms folded, like he'd been waiting for hours.

'Ready?'

I nodded. 'How was your day?'

'Don't ask,' he groaned. 'It's been non-stop since the crack of dawn.'

When we reached the street he set off at a slow pace, without looking back, heavy shoulders flexing with each stride. It looked as though he was conserving his energy, but I could easily have outpaced him if he turned on the speed. It took five minutes to reach the river path, the cold air chilling my mouth. A dredger fought its way upstream, its sides yellowed with rust, a barge clinging to its wake. We headed west towards Battersea and Alvarez shifted up a gear, from a jog to a run. Not enough to raise a sweat, but he looked steady, like he could keep going for days. Banks of ugly modern flats towered over us, fifteen or twenty storeys high, thrown together at the height of the last property boom. The endorphins were already kicking in. Maybe Alvarez felt invincible too, the smartest person in the world, ready for crusades. I sprinted past him and heard the heavy pounding of his feet as he battled to keep up.

'Let's see what you're made of,' I muttered.

Lambeth Bridge vanished behind us. I don't know how long we sprinted, but we raced until a stitch twisted in my side. There was no sign of Alvarez slowing down. The wealth of the Square Mile had disappeared by now, lines of laundry freezing on tiny balconies, ground-floor windows locked behind metal grilles. His hand closed around my wrist.

'You're killing me,' he gasped. 'I'm too old for this.'

'I don't think so. You could last longer than me, I reckon.'

'You're kidding.' His breathing was steadier now. He stood by the handrail, his eyes as black as the river. 'Come here,' he said.

The kiss was greedy and forceful, because he knew he wouldn't be refused. He grabbed my hand and pulled me down a set of stone steps I hadn't noticed before. The river lapped at our feet. In the dark the Thames looked like a torrent of oil, not water, reflecting light from the opposite bank in yellow flickering pools. The smell was overpowering: brine and waste, the sweetness of decaying fruit. Alvarez's hands tightened around my waist. He buried his face against my neck, pressing me against the cold wall, bricks icy against my back. Maybe it was the endorphins performing their magic, but I could have undressed for him there and then, taken a dip in the freezing water afterwards to cool off. But footsteps were rattling along the path. Someone laughed and then walked on again. Anyone could be watching us. Alvarez kissed me more urgently, his hand parting my legs. I let out a long breath.

'We can't,' I whispered.

'Why not?'

'Imagine the headlines if we got caught.' I held him at arm's length. 'Burns wouldn't be impressed.'

He pressed his mouth to my ear. 'I couldn't care less, but you love tormenting me, don't you?'

'The novelty's wearing off,' I laughed. 'Take me back to the hotel. Finish what you started.'

We jogged back more slowly, past a glitter of traffic on Waterloo Bridge, tail-lights sending red sparks across the river's surface like it was bonfire night.

The hotel foyer was bustling with tourists, waiting in a disgruntled queue to be checked in. Alvarez jogged beside me up the stairs, his hand on my shoulder blade. He kissed me again as I fumbled for the key to my room. All I wanted to do was lie back, watch him peel off his clothes. But someone was waiting for us on the other side of the door.

'Hi there,' Angie said breezily. 'I came early, boss. DCI Burns thought you might want an evening off.'

I didn't know whether to laugh or cry. There's a psychological syndrome that depressives suffer from, called delayed fulfilment. Everything gets put on hold. They make themselves wait for holidays, to change job or find a partner, because they don't believe that they deserve happiness. Alvarez moaned quietly, as if fulfilment had already been postponed for longer than he could bear.

28

By now Angie and I were starring in our own version of *Groundhog Day*. I had chosen my usual breakfast of fruit with Greek yogurt, and she was piling through a mound of fried bread, eggs and sausages.

'This'll set me up,' she said.

There was something irresistible about Angie. She did everything with gusto, from enjoying each mouthful, to the minute details of her job. I was lacklustre by comparison, and time had gone into slow motion, every action taking aeons to unfold.

The receptionist beckoned me as I crossed the foyer after breakfast.

'Some post for you, Dr Quentin.' She shunted the envelopes across the counter without making eye contact. Maybe she had chosen today to take a holiday from all forms of politeness.

Hari had forwarded my mail from work. Warwick University had sent me an invitation to speak to their students about clinical treatments for patients with a history of violence. And AstraZeneca were advertising a new generation of anti-anxiety drugs. No side effects, the leaflet announced smugly, as though worry would soon be a thing of the past. I almost missed the small white envelope at the back of the batch. This time I knew better than to open it, handling it gently, like a faulty grenade. Angie was by the entrance, chatting to

Alvarez. She loitered there when he walked over. Maybe she was hoping to win more brownie points from Burns. Alvarez looked more energetic than the day before. Either the run or the heavy-duty flirtation had done him good. I waved the envelope at him in greeting.

'The guy doesn't give up, does he?' he sighed.

We sat at a table in the empty dining hall. Everyone had finished their breakfast, apart from a straggle of tourists filling up on croissants before pounding the streets. When he opened the letter, the black writing was just as neat and controlled as before.

Dear Alice,

It's time for you to stop fighting. We need to be together. But when I came for you, you ran from me. I saw you jump from the balcony, but you won't always be able to escape. Any day now I'll catch you, and you'll tell me what you're really thinking, because pain makes people honest. Soon you'll be transparent, Alice. I'll see right through you.

'Jesus,' Alvarez whispered. His frown had reappeared, colour draining from his face, as if the threats were addressed to him. 'Thank God he doesn't know you're here.'

'Doesn't he?'

He waved the envelope at me. The letter had been forwarded from the clinic at Guy's.

'That's one good thing, I suppose.'

His eyes settled on my face, judging my reactions. 'You're going to have to settle here, Alice. You understand that, don't you? He's not making it easy. And you can't go home till he's caught.'

'Fuck that,' I muttered. Locked inside my immaculate beige hotel room, whole seasons could slip by without me noticing.

'Don't worry, I'll liberate you now and then.' For a second it looked like he might smile, but it was just a trick of the light. 'What is it that upsets you so much about being cooped up?'

'Everything. I should be at work, worrying about other people going mad. And my chances of a night on the town are less than zero.'

'We'll see about that.' He traced my cheekbone with his forefinger, then sealed the letter inside a plastic bag. 'Come on. You never know, your brother might feel like talking today.'

Miracles can happen, I thought, but on such a grey day they seemed unlikely. It began to hail as we got out of the car on Great Maze Pond. Hailstones stung the back of my neck as we raced across the quadrangle. They were big enough to hurt, thousands of tiny meteorites pelting us from on high. I must have looked like a drowned rat by the time we got inside. And the one person I hated seeing me in a mess was lurking in the corridor.

My mother surveyed my dripping hair and faded jeans with distaste. 'Alice, darling, why aren't you at work?'

My mother prided herself on never having missed a day at the library. It was her salvation. While she could stagger in and do her duty, normality reigned, and chaos was someone else's concern.

'I told you, Mum. The police want me out of things for the time being.'

Her attention had already shifted to Alvarez. Her pale eyes made a set of swift calculations. Apart from his dishevelled hair, he met her selection criteria perfectly. His coat was well cut and expensive, and his shoes were acceptable too, black leather Oxford brogues.

'And who might you be?' She held out her hand.

'Alvarez.' He held her hand for a few seconds longer than necessary. 'I'm really sorry about your son, Mrs Quentin.'

He had made a direct hit with my mother. Clearly she would have preferred to stand there making eyes at him, instead of dealing with the business in hand.

'Have you seen Will yet, Mum?' I asked.

Her attention drifted back slowly, as if I had spoiled a romantic moment. 'No, dear, someone called Dr Chadha is meeting me at ten o'clock.'

'Then you could have a long wait, I'm afraid. Hari's never on time.'

'Why not come with us, Mrs Quentin?' Alvarez was still on his best behaviour, inclining his shoulders towards my mother, like he was preparing to bow. 'It must be upsetting for you to see Will on your own.'

She gave a martyred smile. 'He's in so much pain. It's dreadful not being able to help your child.'

I resisted the urge to slap her. It was on the tip of my tongue to mention that my brother had been in pain for years, but she hadn't exactly dashed to the rescue.

Angie had arrived before us. She was perched on the chair by his bedside, alert as a pixie sitting on a toadstool, taking care not to miss anything. Her presence obviously hadn't disturbed Will. He was fast asleep, face whiter than the pillowslip, black hollows scored around his eyes. A nurse had removed his bedding to keep him cool. His left leg was trapped in plaster from ankle to thigh, the other exposed to the air, metal pins fusing the bones in place. The skin was shiny and taut, purple bruises blossoming under the surface. My mother's smile vanished instantly. For someone so squeamish it must have been horrifying to see so many wounds. I felt a flicker of sympathy for her. Some mornings before I went to school I'd see her standing by her bedroom mirror, undoing the buttons of her nightgown to inspect the previous night's damage, ripe bruises blossoming across her chest and shoulders. No wonder she couldn't stand the sight of someone else's injuries.

Alvarez pulled back the curtains and a shaft of light fell across Will's face. My brother blinked rapidly, and when his eyes opened fully he seemed to be coming round. He glanced from my mother's face to mine, then something startled him. Maybe it was the unexpected light, or Alvarez's hulking presence in the corner. His eyes snapped wide open, every muscle straining in his thin face, and then the screaming started. His arms flailed, as though he wanted to break anything within reach.

Angie looked up at Alvarez. 'Something set him off, boss. He's been quiet as a mouse till now.'

'Too many of us probably.' He stepped away from the bed.

'Calm down, darling,' my mother cooed.

She touched Will's arm but he shrugged her off. His screams had risen to a roar. I forced myself to wait, because sooner or later the hysteria would die down. A safety mechanism gets tripped and the level of cortisol falls, before rising again, panic surging through your system in waves.

'It's okay, sweetheart,' I said. 'You're safe, I promise.' I said it more to reassure myself than him, but maybe he heard. The yell thinned to a whimper, and he reached for my hand. He squeezed my fingers so hard that my knuckles throbbed. It was a relief when he let go.

'You don't know what I've seen,' he whispered.

'What did you see, Will?'

He whimpered to himself, eyes shut, as if he was afraid to remember.

'You can whisper, if you like,' I said.

After a few seconds he said something too quietly to be heard, but when I moved closer his mumbling became clearer.

'The devil,' he muttered, then his eyes turned towards the window. 'All the angels have disappeared.'

'It's just the drugs you've taken, darling. You're safe here, honestly.'

I stared out of the window. The low roof of the mortuary was almost hidden by trees. At that moment there was more chance of getting an explanation from the victims lying in the freezer than from Will. My mother was in the same position as before, frozen by the wall, her face even more mask-like than normal, smothered in make-up. She must have stood in her bathroom that morning, painting on a smile. Maybe I should have comforted her, but I couldn't muster the energy. Alvarez was nowhere to be seen. He must have gone to fetch a nurse when Will began to scream. Angie was keeping a low profile in the corner, and Will was ignoring us all, chattering to himself, hands cupping his eyes, as though he was playing hide and seek.

29

Hari arrived an hour late, but for once my mother kept her mouth shut. Only doctors and lawyers had that effect on her. She treated them with unquestioning respect, as if they were minor royalty.

'How are you?' Hari's chocolate-brown eyes studied me. I would have given anything to turn the clock back and sit in his office, eat a plateful of the sticky cakes he was addicted to.

'Bearing up, Hari. It's my brother I'm worried about.'

'That's why I'm here, to see what I can do.'

Alvarez loitered by the door. It seemed odd that he and Hari had become friends, hard to imagine them finding any common ground. But it was typical of Hari to reach out to someone in need of support, and his calmness seemed to slow Alvarez down. Certainly he had that effect on Will. He seemed more relaxed, but his eyes were still fixed on the open window, tracking spectres across the sky.

'Hello, young man,' Hari murmured. 'You're nice and quiet today. That's a good sign.'

'He was screaming his head off a minute ago,' I commented. 'Don't you think he needs chlorpromazine?'

'We can't rush him, Alice.' He leaned down to touch Will's forehead, chatting to him as though they were old friends. 'Come back at your own pace, young man. We'll start you on some valproate in a few days, see how that goes.'

'For God's sake,' Alvarez snapped. 'Don't you know this is urgent?'

Will reacted immediately to the anger in his voice, or maybe it was just a problem of scale. We must have looked like a family of giants, looming over him. He clapped his hands over his eyes again, and his chattering escalated to a loud whimper.

'Why don't we go outside?' Hari suggested.

Alvarez was ready to explode as soon as he got into the corridor. 'He's made no progress whatsoever.'

'Because he's very sick, Ben,' Hari said. 'He needs time to heal.'

Alvarez gave a curt nod. 'Healing's great, but without his story, we're fucked. He's part of a team, and another girl's gone missing.'

By now Hari's smile had been replaced by the expression he wore at department meetings, to warn us about budget cuts. 'The thing is, he's taken a whole cocktail of psychoactive drugs, on top of his illness. There's no antidote. We just have to bide our time.'

Alvarez nodded impatiently. 'You're telling me there's nothing you can do.'

'No. I'm saying you have to be patient. Right now Will thinks he's a caged bird. He's not going to snap out of it immediately, is he?'

A muscle ticked in Alvarez's cheek. 'You need to understand the urgency, that's all.'

'I do, and I'm sorry. We're doing everything we can.' Hari shot me an apologetic look, then he kissed my cheek. 'Everyone's missing you upstairs, Alice.'

He drifted along the corridor, back to the world I used to inhabit, full of appointments and prescriptions, things you could control.

Alvarez clasped his hands behind his neck. 'That's all well and good, isn't it? But it tells us fuck all about how two dead girls found their way into your brother's van.'

'There must be other ways to find out.'

His frown cut a valley between his eyebrows, deep enough for a river to run through. He insisted on walking me to Tooley Street, and when we got to the corner his gaze drifted to my mouth, like he intended to kiss me, in plain sight of Angie's car waiting across the road.

'Better not,' I advised.

He kicked at the hailstones still scattered on the ground. 'It's always better not with you, isn't it?'

'I'm just thinking of your job, that's all.'

'Maybe I'm sick of the fucking job.'

'Because you're working too hard, that's why.'

His mouth almost formed a smile. 'Someone's got to.'

'I'll call you tonight,' I said.

He walked away so slowly he seemed to be dragging an invisible weight.

Even the bitter cold had failed to reduce Angie's perkiness. Her elfin haircut made her look like a street urchin from *Oliver Twist*.

'The boss man's got a soft spot for you.' She monitored my reaction from the corner of her eye.

'Nonsense. He's just doing his job.'

'He's a heart-throb down at the station, you know.'

'You're joking.'

'Not that there's much competition. Most of the blokes make DCI Burns look like a lightweight. But you should hear the girls going on about Alvarez since his wife died.'

I wondered if Alvarez knew that he had a troop of obsessive fans. We were heading south along Southwark Bridge Road.

Within minutes the hotel walls would be folding around my ears again, like a piece of prizewinning origami.

'Go left at the next junction, can you, Angie?'

'Why?' She looked irritated. Unlike Meads she hated doing anything off plan.

'It won't take a minute, I promise.'

Angie tutted under her breath as we pulled into the cul-de-sac.

The memorial garden was easy to miss. There had been an article in the paper when it opened. Relatives hated it, and I could see why. They thought the artist hadn't done justice to the victims' lives. Certainly the garden was a tribute to minimalism. Circular flowerbeds and eight flat stones were scattered across a paved area, where the Bensons' hostel had stood before it was pulled down. The marble stones looked like huge coins, dull white under the overcast sky, like skin that hadn't seen the sun for decades. Angie peered at the list of victims' names. One of the memorial stones had already been tagged. It was only a matter of time before every stone was drenched in fluorescent graffiti.

When I closed my eyes I saw Michelle's permanently unfocused eyes, as though she couldn't picture a future for herself. With any luck nothing had happened to her. Maybe she was safe in another city, starting a new life. When I glanced back Angie's head was down, lips moving silently. It surprised me. Prayer didn't fit her streetwise image. Afterwards she looked embarrassed, as if I'd caught her with her hand in the biscuit jar.

'Come on then,' she said briskly. 'No point in hanging about.'

A bunch of carnations lay beside one of the stones, and I thought about the five girls who had never been found. There was nowhere for the relatives to lay their flowers when birthdays came around. But at least it was better than the prostitutes' cemetery. This was luxury, compared to the filthy, weed-strewn asphalt that sealed the hundreds of unmarked graves at Crossbones Yard.

The hotel's one saving grace was that it had wi-fi. If the worst came to the worst I could stare at pictures of empty landscapes, imagine myself running for hundreds of miles. When I logged into my work email the unanswered messages had risen to three hundred and ten. A vaguely familiar name appeared at the bottom of the first page. I decided to accept the invitation before I had finished reading it. In a few moments the phone call was made and we had arranged where to meet. Then I broke the bad news to Angie.

'I have to be in Brixton for six thirty,' I announced.

She carried on studying photos of bridal veils. 'I don't fancy the sound of that.'

'No, I didn't think you would.'

'It's harder keeping an eye on you outside.'

'I promise to move slowly at all times.'

'Brixton, for God's sake,' she moaned.

'We'll probably get kidnapped by yardies and sold as sex slaves.'

Angie's dark eyes fixed on me. 'You can laugh, Alice. But some psycho's out there, hunting for you.'

I took a deep breath. 'Believe it or not, that fact hadn't actually slipped my mind.'

She was still sulking when we left.

'I am grateful for what you're doing, you know,' I said quietly.

'Are you?' She stared at the chain of cars backing up from Lambeth Bridge.

'It's just that I'm used to being in charge, that's all. It's a shock to my system.'

Angie's good humour returned the minute I apologised, and the car swung south, joining the flood of commuters rushing towards leafier suburbs.

Brixton was the same as always. Rastas sporting red, green and gold, hanging around street corners despite the chill, selling weed to anyone who passed by. We parked outside a launderette. Two beautifully dressed African women were piling sheets into huge industrial cylinders. Evidently they were not prepared to sacrifice style for the sake of their careers.

We made our way towards Starbucks. I've always hated coffee chains. There's something disturbing about the way the lattes always taste exactly the same, dozens of identical leather chairs trying to look homely. But at least they're easy to find, round signs on every street corner, the same dirty green as a US dollar.

Angie seated herself at a table in the corner, within spying distance. Gareth Wright-Phillips was already halfway down his cappuccino. He was less relaxed than I remembered him being at Rampton. For some reason the prospect of our meeting seemed to worry him more than visiting the most prolific female serial killer in Britain.

'I hope it was okay to contact you.' He smiled cautiously.

'Of course. Anyone can be found these days, can't they?'

He seemed incapable of hiding his emotions. They travelled across his face like a weather system through an open tract of sky. I found myself admiring his turquoise-blue eyes again.

'So you don't just work at Rampton?' I asked.

'No. The prison service gets its pound of flesh.' He gave a wry smile. 'Two days at Wormwood Scrubs, then Rampton and Brixton for a day each, which leaves Fridays to finish my staggeringly original second novel.'

'I'm surprised you've got the energy after all that.'

He shrugged. 'The job's great for my writing; not many people get to hear killers tell their stories every day.' He seemed to be trying to decide whether he could speak freely. 'The thing is, Dr Quentin—'

'Alice.'

'The thing is, Alice, I don't know how to say this.'

His gaze jittered across the table, observing the mess of cups, spoons and spilled sugar.

'Take your time,' I said.

He drew in a breath. 'I've stolen something.'

He pulled a wad of papers from his briefcase. I glanced at the handwriting, the scrawled words eliding, as if the writer couldn't get their thoughts down fast enough.

'Who do those belong to?'

'Marie Benson.' He looked nervous. Maybe he expected to be arrested there and then. 'When she realised she was going blind, she started writing. I think she wanted to get everything out of her system while she had the chance.'

I glanced at the frantic scribble of drawings cascading down the margins of each page.

'And she doesn't know you have these?'

Wright-Phillips shook his head. 'I took them from her room a few weeks ago.'

'To use in your novel.'

He studied the dregs at the bottom of his cup.

'I don't blame you. Everyone wants to know what she's been hiding all this time.'

'It was a bit disappointing actually – some mawkish poems, and reams of self-pity.'

'Can I borrow this lot?'

'Of course, but there's one more thing.'

'Sorry, I'm rushing.' I perched on the edge of my seat. 'That's rude of me.'

'You won't tell her, will you?' he stuttered.

When I looked again I saw that his eyes were aquamarine, not turquoise, glassy with fear. Marie Benson might be half-blind and kept under lock and key, but he was still afraid that she would come after him, and exact her revenge in the middle of the night.

30

PC Meads was curled up on the settee when we got back, completely absorbed in the *Antiques Roadshow*. There was obviously more to him than met the eye. Maybe he was an expert on porcelain, and being a copper was just a sideline. The embarrassment of watching something so uncool was too much for him. His blush glowed salmon pink, as though he'd been caught checking out the porn channel.

Someone had cleaned my bedroom and folded my clothes into neat piles while I was out. Maid service is one of the things I've always hated about hotels. An army of underpaid women rummaging through your belongings, carrying out tasks you should do yourself.

I sifted through Marie Benson's notes. At first sight they were just a muddle of doodles and lists, panic trapped in the grain of the paper. She had tried to catalogue her whole past before the lights went out. One page held a description of a childhood Christmas, detailing every present, and the names of relatives who came to stay. At the bottom of the page there was a scribbled Christmas tree, with baubles hanging from its skewed branches. Wright-Phillips had been right about the self-pity. There were drafts of dozens of letters to politicians, pleading to be set free. It was a travesty, she said. Every day in prison compounded the miscarriage of justice.

Her drawings were more interesting, pictures of trees uprooting themselves and creatures with distorted faces. But one abstract pattern kept repeating itself, an irregular five-point star hovering above a rectangle. It appeared at the top of almost every page. Trawling through her dog-eared notes made me wish I had worn protective gloves, and it was a relief to stuff the paper back into the envelope.

Deciding what to do next was less easy. The choices weren't exactly dazzling. I could sleep, eat some more tasteless hotel food, or go for a run in the gym, without ever arriving anywhere.

My phone rang as I was pulling on my trainers.

'Lola. How are you?'

She sighed loudly into the receiver. 'Lars called me. The police picked him up as soon as he got to Stockholm.'

'I'm not surprised.' An image of Lars wearing only a charming smile floated into my mind. 'What did he have to say for himself?'

'He feels terrible about hurting me. I can hear it in his voice.'

'And I bet he's got a load of excuses. A bad childhood, loan sharks chasing him?'

'He loves me, Al,' Lola sobbed. 'I know he does. What am I going to do?'

'Nothing, sweetheart. You can't do anything.'

'I could get on a plane, couldn't I?'

'Don't decide now, Lo. You've got your show to think about. Why not come and have breakfast with me tomorrow?'

'The thing is, Al, I'm not like you.' There was a long pause while she struggled not to cry. 'I need him. I can't get by on my own.'

'You can, Lo, honestly. You're stronger than you think.'

She gulped down a sob. 'What time shall I come?'

'Nine?'

'Sorry I'm such a mess, Al.'

'Hang in there, kiddo. You can tell me about it tomorrow.'

The urge to exercise had evaporated. Lola's misery made the treadmill seem even more pointless, like a lab rat chasing its tail. I lay back and studied the ceiling, a flawless expanse of white, as though stains had been outlawed.

My phone buzzed again in the middle of the night. I must have been sound asleep, because I had to fight to remember where I was. The text was from Alvarez. I cursed him under my breath, then forced myself out of bed. Meads's regular snore drifted through the door while I got dressed. God knows what he dreamed about. Maybe wrestlers with Day-Glo tans hurling huge antique vases at each other, or perhaps he was too innocent for nightmares to enter his head. I tiptoed past without waking him. He wasn't exactly the ideal bodyguard – scared of everything, and oblivious to any kind of threat.

Alvarez looked even more stern than usual when I got to reception; something had neutralised his sense of humour. He turned on his heel without bothering to greet me. When we stepped outside I wished I had grabbed my scarf and gloves. Frost had already whitened every car and lamppost, powdery as a dusting of icing sugar. Alvarez strutted ahead, arms swinging, daring anyone to get in his way. But as soon as he was in the driver's seat, his self-control crumbled. He smashed his fist against the dashboard as if it had committed a crime.

'This fucking job,' he muttered. 'It wants everything you've got.'

I rubbed his shoulder and waited for him to calm down. The muscles were so tense my fingers didn't make an impression.

'Tell me what's happened.'

His head stayed bowed over the wheel. 'You'll see for yourself.'

The car raced along Southwark Street. For once the roads were completely clear, the Tate Modern's black silhouette menacing the houses at its feet, like a bully in the playground. Alvarez spun left, towards Waterloo. Sean would be fast asleep by now, a few hundred metres away, in his flat that always smelled of wine and spices. For some reason, it didn't occur to me to question Alvarez about where we were going. I just assumed he had good reasons for dragging me into the cold.

We parked in a narrow cul-de-sac called Nicholson Street. It was crammed with squad cars and an ambulance, almost blocking the thoroughfare. There was little to see, apart from an abandoned shop on the corner, lock-ups and small warehouses on either side of the road.

Burns was leaning against a telegraph pole. He didn't stir as I walked towards him. Maybe he had finally given up on the concept of movement.

'Thanks for coming, Alice.' Under the streetlight his round face was even whiter than usual. 'It's happened again, I'm afraid.'

I fought the impulse to yell I told you so. At least it proved that Will wasn't involved.

'You need a pathologist then, not a shrink.'

'But I think you know this one, Alice. We want you to identify her.'

My heart twisted uncomfortably in my chest as I followed him past the huddle of police cars. A white plastic tent had already been put up, beside a row of wheelie bins. The stench of rotting fruit hit me immediately, and something worse, like meat that's festered for too long in the fridge. I covered my mouth with the back of my hand. The familiar heap of black tarpaulin was lying a few metres away.

'Ready?' Burns asked.

'As I'll ever be.'

He pulled back the material gently, as though the girl might still be alive. Michelle's pale blue eyes stared up at me expectantly, like she had asked me a question weeks ago, and was still waiting for a reply.

'Oh God.' A store of words built up inside my mouth, curses jostling for space, making it hard to breathe.

'It's Michelle, isn't it?' Burns murmured. 'The lass you met on your run.' His Scottish accent had come back. Under pressure he always forgot to shorten his vowels.

I nodded, without meeting his eye. When I knelt on the pavement the cold hit me as frost melted through my jeans. I made myself look again. Her face had been destroyed. A deep cross cut between her eyebrows, as if she had joined a cult, her cheeks a mess of raw criss-crossed lines. The ragged wound in her throat was crusted with dried blood. All I could remember was her expression when she told me she had been offered a place at college. It was a mixture of amusement and fear. The idea that her life could improve was too hard to believe.

'Can I close her eyes?' I asked.

Burns hesitated. 'Forensics won't like it.'

Her eyelashes grazed the palm of my hand. It took two attempts to force her eyelids shut. She seemed determined to carry on looking at the world for as long as possible.

I sat on the kerb to get my breath back, fighting waves of nausea. My boots rested on a grate, strength draining through the soles of my feet, spilling into the city's sewers. As usual Alvarez was at the heart of things. Members of the forensics team buzzed around him, waiting for instructions.

It was an hour or more before Burns gave me a lift back to the hotel. There was a long silence. I assumed he was too tired to speak, until he drew a deep breath.

'I hear you've been seeing Ben,' he said.

'Who told you?'

'A little bird.' He tapped the side of his nose and laughed. 'Thank Christ something good's come out of this.'

I stared out of the window at the empty river. It was hard to imagine Alvarez marching into his boss's office to explain his relationships.

Burns looked unusually serious. 'My first reaction when I heard about it was, thank Christ for that. He's a tricky sod, but you'll sort him out.'

'So he's not in trouble?'

'Not if we keep it between ourselves,' Burns replied. 'When this is over, you'll go back to your day job, no questions asked.'

I thought Burns was going to congratulate me and kiss me on both cheeks, but he settled for escorting me inside. He made it up the first flight of steps, then ran out of breath, so we had to part company. When I waved goodbye his head was down, reluctant to face the cold, and the questions waiting for him at Nicholson Street.

I let myself into my suite as quietly as possible. Sure enough, Meads was still sleeping like a baby. I crept into my bedroom, wondering exactly how many days it would take him to notice if someone abducted me.

31

It was after 4 a.m. when I finally got to sleep. I couldn't bring myself to turn off the light, because whenever I closed my eyes Michelle was there, staring at me in amazement, struggling to believe how badly I'd let her down. The last five days of her life must have been unbearable – shivering in the dark, waiting for him to cut her again. A wave of nausea hit me. What kind of man would keep someone alive while he lacerated every inch of her skin? The attack had been even more obsessive than before. At least Suzanne Wilkes's face had been left untouched, but Michelle's had been ruined systematically. Maybe it was just as well she died. It was better than having to confront his handiwork whenever she cleaned her teeth. No skin graft could have covered wounds as deep as those.

I made it to the bathroom just in time, retching my room-service lasagne into the toilet bowl. Afterwards I felt hollow, like the dried-out bird bones you find on beaches, unbelievably light and empty. When I lay down again, sleep came easily, as if my memory banks had been wiped clean.

I must have dozed through the alarm, because it was ten to nine when I woke up. Remembering my breakfast date with Lola, I hauled myself into the shower. At least listening to her heartbreak would take me out of myself. For an hour it would be easy to forget about scars and death threats. Angie had replaced Meads by the time I was ready to go downstairs. Her normal perkiness had been diluted.

'I heard about last night,' she murmured. 'Are you okay?'

'Just about,' I nodded.

She gave a half-smile. 'You keep your cards close to your chest, don't you, Alice?'

'There's not much to say, is there? Another dead girl, and the letters keep coming. End of story.'

'I'd be jelly, if it was me. Do they train you to hide your feelings? I mean, shrinks can't start blubbing every time someone gives you a sob story, can you?'

'That must be it,' I agreed.

Angie seemed relieved to know that my heart was still beating. It would have taken too long to explain that concealment was just a trick I'd taught myself, and it wouldn't have comforted her.

It was nine twenty when we got down to the dining hall. I scanned the room for Lola's flame-red hair, expecting her to fling her arms round my neck at any minute, but she was nowhere to be seen. Maybe she had gone out last night to drown her sorrows, but that was unlikely. She had one more rehearsal this afternoon, then tomorrow was her first night at the Cambridge Theatre. She had invited me to sit with her family in the front row while she dazzled us with her high-kicks.

I collected a bowl of muesli, and Angie loaded a plate with toast. There was still no sign of Lola by the time we finished our second cups of coffee. And then the obvious fact hit me. She would be halfway to Stockholm by now, or maybe she was already in a taxi to Gothenburg prison, her bag stuffed with borrowed money to pay Lars's bail.

'Jesus,' I muttered. 'I think a friend of mine's about to do something unbelievably stupid.'

'For love?'

'Lust, more like.'

Angie smirked. 'You won't stop her then, it's a force of nature.'

'But I can try. If I don't, she'll only have a go at me when she sees sense.'

Lola's phone was switched off. No doubt she was busy pleading with a Swedish jailor.

'Don't do anything crazy, sweetheart,' I told her answering service. 'Call me when you get this.'

After breakfast I borrowed Angie's copy of the *Daily Mail*. SOUTHWARK RIPPER CLAIMS VICTIM NUMBER THREE, the front page shrieked. Someone had found a new picture of Michelle before her habit took hold, while her pale eyes were still calm, and her dark hair still had its gloss. She was beaming as though nothing could go wrong. Some hack had already planted the usual dramatic words in her mother's mouth. 'Let me kill the beast who stole my angel.' It reminded me why I hated newspapers. They either pedalled their political agendas or dumbed down each conflict to a battle between angels and devils, for the sake of good copy.

I kept texting Lola, but she didn't reply.

Angie rolled her eyes. 'No point. Just be there for her when it goes tits up.'

'I know,' I nodded. 'But at least I'm doing something.'

Meads began his shift at two o'clock, refreshed from his night of unbroken slumber. As usual he settled on the sofa with the remote control in his hand. This time he found a DIY programme. He looked on in open-mouthed wonder as an elderly man taught him how to hang a door. Inertia was his favourite state. Every TV programme received his undivided attention. I waited until the man had fixed the door safely to its hinges before making my request.

'Can we go for a drive?' I asked.

He sprang to attention immediately. 'Ready when you are.'

Life with Meads was delightfully easy. If I had told him we were going on a Himalayan expedition without sherpas, he wouldn't have batted an eye.

We drove past the Monument as soon as we left London Bridge. A few hardy tourists had braved the three-hundred-step climb to peer east from the viewing point to the warehouses at Limehouse. Before Canary Wharf obliterated the view, you could have seen past Greenwich and the Isle of Dogs to the hop fields of Kent. Our journey took us due north, dissecting the city as neatly as a cheese-wire. By Liverpool Street people were thronging outside the shops, but the money ran out when we crossed into the East End. Kingsland Road was a different story. The street names gave occasional reminders of the former wealth of the rag trade: Haberdashers Street, Curtain Road. No doubt you could still find sweatshops churning out parades of hand-stitched dresses, just like they did in Charles Dickens's day. The city grew affluent again as soon as we reached De Beauvoir Town. It was a cluster of Edwardian streets, each villa perfectly gentrified with a Farrow & Ball front door, and plenty of Montessori schools for the delightful middle-class children to attend.

Play Days Nursery was catering for the less moneyed end of the spectrum. Their clients were probably harassed single parents, earning just enough to keep their families afloat. Cheryl Martin was busy tidying up, brown curls swept back from her face with an Alice band, unwilling to let anything stop her concentrating on her job. The kids had been collected already, but the floor was a bombsite of Lego, building blocks and dolls. She was on her knees, scooping toys into brightly coloured crates. I thought she might have forgotten me, but after a second she rose to her feet.

'It's Don's friend, isn't it?' She gave a confused smile.

'I hope you don't mind me dropping in. I found Play Days on the Internet.'

She raised her eyebrows. 'But you haven't come to add your kid to our waiting list, have you?'

Her hands rested on her hips while she waited for an explanation. It took all my powers of persuasion to get her to talk. But when I told her about Michelle, she began to melt. The idea that she might be able to keep other women safe finally made her cave in.

'One last favour.' She frowned at me. 'Then that's it. If you or Don or anyone else ask me again, there's nothing doing. All right?'

I nodded. 'Understood. All you have to do is take a look at this photo.'

When I put it on the table I thought she might push it straight back at me, but she was as good as her word. She studied the faces so carefully that she could have been memorising them for an exam. Her sleeves were rolled up and I tried not to stare at the crosses on her forearms, narrow slashes of white scar tissue, with hardly any space in between.

'Recognise anyone?' I asked.

'All of them.' Her face had drained of emotion when she met my eye. 'Some of the names have gone, but I remember what they did round the place.'

'Can you tell me about them?'

Cheryl's finger hovered above Morris Cley's face. 'He was the best of the lot. Simple but sweet, desperate for a girlfriend. He popped in now and again, but he didn't live there.'

She picked out another woman, who was eyeballing the camera as though she had unfinished business with the photographer. 'I kept out of her way. Lisa, I think her name was. She'd be your best mate, then she'd hit the booze and be out for a fight.'

259

When she came to Will her reaction was almost the same as Cley's. Her body recoiled for a few seconds before she could look at his face again. 'That's the one I said about, last time.'

'Tell me what you remember, please.' My heart rate quickened. 'It could be important.'

'I told you. He was the gatekeeper. Hanging about in the garden, always having little chats with Ray, big eyes watching everything. Will, I remember his name now I see him.'

I swallowed a gulp of air and forced myself to focus. 'You're sure that Will and Ray were friends?'

She stared at me. 'They couldn't have been closer.' She buried her hands in the pockets of her jeans, as if they were cold. 'He got the best room in the place, and he was never short of fags. I reckon they were paying him too.'

She turned away abruptly and carried on with her task, dropping plastic trucks, Barbie dolls and horses into their separate boxes.

I muttered a quick thank you on my way out, but she didn't look up. Maybe she had already erased me from her memory, focused on what she had to do tomorrow to keep her flock of children out of harm's way.

32

Alvarez rang when I got back to the hotel, but there was no point in telling him what had happened. We would have to be face to face when I told him Cheryl Martin's story. His voice was so muffled that he sounded like he was calling from a thousand miles away.

'There's been some progress,' he said. 'A woman saw Michelle being dragged into a red Hyundai, not far from the pub where you talked to her.'

'Did she get a good look at the driver?'

He gave a deep sigh. 'Not really. She wasn't sure if there was one bloke in the car or two.'

'It's better than nothing.'

'Only just. Do you know how many Hyundais there are in London?'

'Not a clue.'

'Just over a million.'

I visualised a landscape full of red hatchbacks, as far as the eye could see. All I wanted to do was draw the curtains and lie down on the wide hotel bed with Alvarez for the rest of the afternoon.

'I wish I could see you,' he murmured, then a door slammed loudly in the background. 'But there's too much happening, Alice.'

'Don't worry about it,' I snapped.

'You realise I'm not doing this for fun, don't you?' He sounded aggrieved, as if the princess he was rescuing had escaped from the castle without his assistance.

I bit my lip. 'Sorry, it hasn't been a great day.'

His voice softened. 'The thing is, I can't stop thinking about you.'

'No?'

'Morning, noon and bloody night,' he whispered.

'You make it sound painful.'

'It is. God knows what you've done to me.'

There was still no message from Lola. No doubt she was avoiding me, in case I ranted and raved. I would have given a lot to share a bottle of wine with her and come clean about Alvarez. Ideas kept tumbling round my head, competing for space. If I stayed cooped up in the hotel for the rest of the evening, I was in danger of losing the plot. When I told Meads I needed to go out again he switched off the TV reluctantly. There was no end to his ability to absorb the plots of soap operas.

Sean was the first person I saw on Bermondsey Ward, walking along the corridor with a wad of notes under his arm.

'I've just seen your brother.' His eyes lingered on my face. 'At least his wounds are on the mend.'

'Great, except it's his mind I'm worried about, not his legs.'

'Sorry.' He gave an apologetic smile. 'You know me, strictly flesh and bone.'

'You've done what you can.' I touched his arm for a second. 'I'm grateful.'

Sean opened his mouth to say something else, then abruptly closed it again. I carried on down the corridor, but there were no footsteps behind me. I realised afterwards that he must have stood there for a long time, watching me walk away.

Will was asleep when I opened the door. The curtains were wide open, even though it was dark outside. I looked down at the lamp-lit quadrangle. Three nurses were racing for the car park at full pelt, clearly determined to be in the pub for happy hour. Will's arms twitched fitfully. I sat on the edge of the bed, but couldn't bring myself to touch him. His hair was damp with sweat, the toxins in his system flooding out of his pores.

'For fuck's sake, Will,' I muttered. 'Wake up and tell me what you've done.'

For a moment I thought he was following my instructions. His eyes fluttered open, and he seemed to recognise me. His gaze lingered on my face, then he slipped back into sleep. I kept on trying to process what Cheryl Martin had said. My chest ached, as though I had held my breath for too long. I wanted to yell into his face, force him to explain why he had allowed Ray Benson to recruit him.

When I woke up the next morning the first thing I remembered was that it was Lola's big day. She would have to fly back soon, to enjoy her first night. My phone sat on the bedside table, refusing to say anything, like a sulky child. Angie was preparing herself for another vast breakfast at the taxpayer's expense. She looked crestfallen when I told her I planned to go to the gym first.

The place was crowded with Chinese businessmen performing t'ai chi, each movement graceful and unhurried, as if they had all the time in the world. I ran for forty-five minutes, until a narrow band of sweat darkened my T-shirt down the centre of my ribcage. But for some reason the elation was missing. It was like drinking instant coffee after enjoying the real thing for years.

I let Angie finish her breakfast before breaking the bad news.

'I have to go into town to see someone.'

She scrutinised me over the top of her *Daily Mail*. 'Can't you get her to come here?'

'No,' I shook my head firmly. 'And it's a him not a her.'

Angie's curiosity got the better of her. So far she had been too polite to ask about my love life, even though she had given me every detail of her wedding plans. 'All right then, but if you give me the slip, I won't be best pleased.'

The phone rang while I was waiting for Angie to get her car. I answered immediately, without checking the caller's number.

'Lola, where the fuck are you?'

'Dreadful language, Alice.' My mother's voice was even chillier than normal, like she'd spent the last half-hour in a bath full of ice cubes.

'Sorry,' I murmured.

'At least I've got some good news.' Her tone of voice suggested that I should count myself lucky to be receiving it. 'Your brother said hello this morning, as soon as I saw him.'

'That's brilliant.'

'I know.' I could picture her, standing beside Will's bed in an immaculate little black dress and a rope of pearls.

'Can I speak to him?'

'Not now, dear. He's not that talkative, and he's about to have his breakfast.' Her voice was crisp with confidence, like she had never lost an argument in her life.

'Tell him I'll come by later, Mum.'

The line went dead immediately. No doubt she would tell her friends she had cured her son single-handedly, with the power of motherly love.

Angie's driving was a lot more cautious than Meads's. She paused at every junction, checking frantically for cyclists to give way to. Despite the grey skies, Soho was still managing to look colourful as we wove through the narrow back streets. Nineteen fifties neon signs flickered over the doorways of strip clubs, showing the hourglass figures of dancing girls. Some of the pedestrians had been there for decades too, old men tottering along in Columbo coats, as though they had only just survived a night of debauchery.

The flat I was visiting was over an adult bookshop. The titles in the window sounded educational, such as *How to be a Dominatrix*, but others were genuinely worrying: *Find Yourself a Schoolgirl*. Angie followed me up the narrow staircase, an appalled expression on her face, taking care not to touch the handrail. When I knocked on the door it took several minutes before a gruff voice instructed me to wait.

'Remember me? It's Alice,' I said when the door finally opened. 'Lola's friend, and this is Angie.'

Craig was wearing a pair of minute black underpants, remnants of glittery eye shadow still caked around his eyes.

'Of course, darling. Come on in.' His voice was croaky from last night's booze and cigarettes.

We followed him into his tiny living room. A scrawny tabby cat was perched on the back of the settee; it couldn't have eaten a decent meal in weeks. Actors' wages obviously didn't extend to pet food. Craig was equally skinny, or maybe it was a lifestyle choice because more parts came his way when he was elegantly emaciated.

'I wondered if you'd heard from Lola,' I said.

I watched in amazement as he pulled on my favourite electric-blue kimono, which Lola must have accidentally nicked when she left the flat.

'Madam's not in my good books at the moment.' He tossed his head irritably. His shoulder-length blond hair looked almost natural, apart from a few centimetres of dark brown roots. 'I'll tell you all about it, girls, but I need coffee if you want conversation at this hour.'

Craig flounced off to the kitchen, leaving us to admire his interior decor. It was a mix of Gothic and high camp. A picture of Mae West pouted at us from the wall above the fireplace, and a selection of sequinned drag queen outfits was draped across the chairs. Angie's mouth gaped, as she tried to take in a world she'd never imagined. After a few minutes Craig returned with three tiny coffee cups balanced on a tray.

'Espresso,' he sighed. 'God's gift to the hung over.'

I studied Craig's carefully plucked eyebrows and flawless skin. His beauty regime must have been a lot more rigorous than mine. 'So Lola's been misbehaving, has she?'

'You could say that.' Craig rolled his eyes dramatically. 'If you were being charitable.'

'When did you last see her?'

'Wednesday night. She was ranting on about that bastard she's been seeing.'

'Lars.'

'That's him. Anyway, she was in floods, so I poured her into a taxi. But when I got back, she'd vanished, taking my door key with her. The bloody locksmith cost me a week's wages.'

'She's left all her stuff, hasn't she?' A heap of bags was piled in the corner. 'Do you mind if I take a look?'

'Help yourself, sweetheart.' He took a long drag from his Marlboro. 'If she doesn't collect it soon, the binmen can have it.'

It looked as though Lola had brought all her worldly goods with her, stuffed into her battered red suitcase and the faded rucksack she hauled around Greece for a whole summer. If she was in Sweden, she was certainly travelling light.

Her passport fell into my hands as soon as I unzipped her backpack. I studied it for a minute or two, looking at the date stamps, unsure what to do next. Angie and Craig were busy sharing tips on skincare. I tried to steady my breathing, but it was impossible. All the air had been sucked out of the room.

33

'What was all that about?' Angie snapped. 'Why did you run out of there?'

'Lola,' I gasped, still trying to get my breath back.

'What do you mean?'

'He's got her,' I panted. 'I know he has.'

'That's not very likely, is it?' Angie looked exasperated. 'Your mate was pissed in that taxi, so she changed her mind, went to stay with someone else.' She pursed her lips. 'Her chum in there says she's always been flighty. She's just gone a bit far this time.'

'No way.' I shook my head firmly. 'That doesn't explain why she didn't call yesterday, or why she left Craig out in the cold.'

'She's done this before, he says. Always dashing from one party to the next.' Her voice was a bored sing-song that made me want to slap her.

'Bollocks. I've known Lola twenty years and she's never let me down. She's too thoughtful.'

Angie gave me a sceptical look then focused her attention on the road, like I was too naive for words.

My hands shook as I pulled my phone from my pocket and dialled directory enquiries. When they put me through to the Cambridge Theatre, a woman with a soft French accent answered almost immediately. I asked to speak to Lola, explaining that she was in the dance troupe, and she went to look for her. The line was silent for several minutes, and I pictured the receptionist searching the auditorium for clues, rummaging behind each chair. Her voice was quiet and apologetic when she returned. Lola had missed two rehearsals without letting the director know, so he had fired her, and given her dance kit to the girl who took her place.

'Jesus.' I gritted my teeth and stuffed my phone back in my pocket.

We were passing a construction site, two cranes hurrying to lay foundation stones, as though the city was crying out for another block of flats. Angie was immersed in dealing with the traffic, which was a blessing. If she had said one more word about Lola I would have gone down for GBH.

'Take me to the station,' I snarled.

I must have given the order with enough conviction, because for once she didn't argue.

Burns was ploughing through a stack of reports at least a foot thick when I found him. He rose from his chair by a few inches when he saw me. Maybe the original plan was to get to his feet, but it never happened. The invisible hydraulic system that shifted his bulk had finally broken down.

'I hear your brother's coming round,' he said. 'Ben's with him now.'

'I'm not here about Will.'

He listened coolly as I explained that Lola was in danger. I gave him all the evidence. Why would she jeopardise her dream job, leave a good friend locked out of his own flat, not even answer her phone?

His eyes narrowed. 'You do know her boyfriend's being done for fraud, don't you?'

'What's that got to do with it?'

'Quite a bit, I'd say.' Burns peered at me in disbelief. 'She doesn't make great choices, does she? Maybe she's followed his lead and done a midnight flit.'

'That's complete crap. She didn't have a clue what he was up to.'

Burns's eyebrows shot up. 'You're sure of that, are you?'

'You're not listening, Don.' It was a struggle not to shout. 'Lola would never treat anyone badly.'

He whistled between his teeth. 'I must have met a different girl. She was a right little madam when we arrested lover boy, called Ben every name under the sun.'

'So you won't even look for her.'

'I didn't say that.' Burns chose his words carefully, as if I might report him to the Police Council. 'Fill out a missing person's report and leave it with me.'

'And that'll do the trick, will it?'

Burns rested his hand on the tower of reports, clearly longing to get back to them. I stared at him until he had no choice but to meet my eye.

'I want it on record that Lola's been taken. That bastard's got her, and you've done nothing, except give me a fucking missing person's form.'

He didn't respond, but I knew what he was thinking. The strain was making me hysterical; leave it to Alvarez to calm me down. He picked up the next file from his stack and began to read, as though I had already left the room.

I don't know why I was so angry when I got back to the hotel, except that anger's always easier to deal with than fear. It's so powerful that it invigorates you, until it starts to eat you from the inside. I seethed for the rest of the day, snapping at Angie until she looked relieved to pass me over to Meads. He must have read the ferocious expression on my face because he didn't try to make conversation, just buried his head in his newspaper.

271

When I checked my phone there were two missed calls from Alvarez, and a garbled voicemail from Will. He was speaking so fast I had to listen to it twice before his words made sense.

'I'm scared, Al. He's here again, at the hospital. I see him every day. It's the devil, I'm sure it is. Help me, Al, please.' His voice petered out into a miserable whimper and I deleted the message immediately. Will's demons wouldn't go away until the drugs were out of his system, but at least he could string sentences together again.

I rubbed my forehead. My mind kept wandering back to what Will had done, my heart rate quickening. There was no getting away from the fact that he'd entertained two of the dead girls in his van, a prostitute and a charity worker. But what else had he done to them? I tried not to think about the knife he carried, with its razor-sharp blade. Ideas rushed at me, too quickly to filter. Maybe Will had told people about all the horrors he'd seen, and his words had inspired them to carry on killing. I gritted my teeth and forced myself to focus.

There was still no message from Lola.

For some reason I couldn't bring myself to sit down. All I wanted to do was run into the street and look for her: lift manhole covers, peer into garden sheds, check every cellar in London. I made more phone calls to try to find out who had seen her last. Then I forced myself to call her mother.

'Alice, how lovely to hear from you!' Tina's voice had exactly the same cadences as Lola's. I could picture her standing in her hall, a slightly heavier version of her daughter, with the same mile-wide smile, red curls faded to strawberry blonde. 'Are you excited about tonight?'

'Tonight?'

'Lola's show, darling. You haven't forgotten, have you? The

Tremaines will be filling the front two rows. I've got you a seat.'

'There's been some bad news, Tina, I'm sorry.'

I blurted out what had happened. There was a long silence at the end of the line when I explained that Lola was missing, and her boyfriend was in a Swedish jail.

'You don't think she's done something stupid, do you?' Tina's voice was dull with shock.

For the first time it occurred to me that I might be barking up the wrong tree. People sometimes make the decision in seconds, overwhelmed by the weight of despair. Often they don't even leave a note.

'No, of course not.' I kept my voice as calm as possible. 'I'm sure she's got her reasons.'

After I put down the phone, my mind spun with every possible reason why Lola would go missing. A road accident, memory loss, mental breakdown. Or maybe Lars's business dealings were darker than I knew, and one of the heavies he owed money to had come looking for her. But it was all distraction from the thing I didn't want to consider: that my pen-pal had got his hands on her. When I closed my eyes all I could see was her unblemished skin, dusted with copper and gold freckles.

By the time evening came the hotel walls were squeezing the breath out of me. Tina and I had called every one of Lola's friends, and all the London hospitals, but no one had clapped eyes on her. I perched on the edge of the bed, looking at the mud-brown sky. Not a single star in sight, only the moon's pale outline making brief appearances in the gaps between clouds.

I tried Alvarez, but he wasn't answering. He probably didn't even know about Lola. My complaint would be so low down Burns's agenda, he wouldn't have mentioned it.

Then I heard a familiar sound. It was only seven thirty,

but Meads's gentle snoring emanated through the door. And that's when I made my decision. I grabbed my coat and bag and tiptoed out of the bedroom. Meads was sprawled on the settee, the TV flickering. Exhaustion or a particularly boring episode of *Hollyoaks* had closed his eyes for him. It seemed odd to leave the hotel on my own. I felt like a wayward teenager, in danger of being grounded.

A taxi sailed nearer, its for hire sign lit up in gold. I took a deep breath and flagged it down.

34

The taxi pulled up on Kemerton Road just before eight o'clock. There were no lights on in the windows of Alvarez's house, and I wondered if he'd stopped at a pub after work, treated himself to a beer after a day of getting nowhere. I climbed the steps to his porch and rang the bell. His front door must have been crimson once, but it had faded to a dull rust, paint blistering from the wood. The prospect of another long taxi ride back to the overheated hotel didn't appeal to me. It was a relief to finally hear movement in the hall.

Alvarez's expression was a mixture of shock and pleasure. He was wearing faded jeans and a black shirt, and his feet were bare, wet hair slicked back from his face. He opened the door wide, without saying anything, then his arms closed around me. He smelled perfectly clean. I've always thought that the sexiest thing in the world is a man fresh from the shower, skin glistening, completely renewed. It was a struggle to stay focused on the reason why I'd come.

'I need your help, Ben.'

'Anything you like.' He lounged against the wall. 'But only if you have dinner with me first.'

Following him along the hall I could see why he'd neglected the exterior of the house. All his time, effort and cash had been spent on perfecting the rooms inside. It must have taken days to bring the old quarry tiles in the hall back to their original glory, and the walls had been painted a soft dove grey. A row of landscape paintings pulsed with colour. I paused to admire the casement of a grandfather clock, so tall it almost reached the ceiling.

'That was shipped over from Spain,' Alvarez called over his shoulder. 'Cost me an arm and a leg.'

He was already busy preparing the meal when I got to the kitchen. For some reason I didn't associate him with cooking. I thought he would be like Burns, subsisting on a diet of fast food and Mars Bars, waiting for the damage to hit. He chopped handfuls of fresh herbs deftly with a long-handled knife. The smell of garlic frying was already making me feel hungry.

'Can I do anything?' I asked.

He paused to drop a mound of linguine into a pan of boiling water. 'Choose some wine, if you like. Take a look in the cellar, it's the second door along the hall.'

It was a good excuse to snoop around. The living room was elegant and simple, a family of armchairs arranged around an Art Deco fireplace, delicate African sculptures lined up on the mantelpiece. I remembered Alvarez saying that his wife had trained as an interior designer. She certainly had a great eye for colour; the walls were the hot ochre of sunlight on a summer afternoon.

I paused by the door of the cellar. I've always gone out of my way to avoid them. The combination of confined space and no air always kick-starts a panic attack. But when the light flicked on, there was nothing to worry about. The space felt airy because the walls had been whitewashed, and an exercise bike, free weights and a bench press stood in the corner. That explained why Alvarez was fit enough to run, even though he claimed to be allergic to gyms. Two wine racks were leaning against the wall. I grabbed the first bottle that came to hand

and headed back upstairs. He inspected the label on the Rioja thoughtfully.

'Good choice. My father brought this over last summer. He's convinced there's nothing to drink in England.'

For a moment I thought he was going to smile, but it never materialised. It reminded me of a teenager I treated once who suffered from Moebius syndrome, which left him physically unable to smile. He had developed a brilliant deadpan sense of humour, but he still felt isolated, because other kids read his blank expression as coldness or hostility. I found a corkscrew and poured two glasses of wine.

'Your house is stunning,' I commented.

'I can't take any credit.' Alvarez kept his back to me as he tipped the pasta into a colander. 'Luisa chose everything in here. It was her obsession. She must have taped every episode of *Grand Designs*.'

I glanced at the earthenware bowls on the dresser, the antique ladder-backed chairs around the dining table, and tried to imagine how it would feel to wake up alone each morning, surrounded by beautiful relics.

Alvarez was too busy serving the meal to answer any more questions. He had made a crisp green salad to go with the garlic chicken and pasta. He watched me dig in, twirling pasta around my fork.

'So what do you need help with?' he asked.

When I told him about Lola he looked as sceptical as Burns had, but his expression changed as he heard all the details. I explained that I'd found her passport, so she couldn't be in Sweden, and none of her family or friends had heard from her since Craig poured her into a taxi in Soho. By the time I finished explaining we had polished off the wine, and Alvarez's frown had reappeared between his eyebrows.

'And Burns didn't do anything?' He looked amazed.

'It was like he had blinkers on. He just wasn't interested.'

Alvarez pushed back his chair from the table urgently. 'Look, Alice, I need to do something about this. I'll have to make some calls.'

I'm not sure why I felt like bursting into tears. Maybe it was simply relief because someone finally believed me.

He reached down and touched my cheek. 'It's okay, we'll find her. Look, it's going to take me a while. Why don't you take a look around? I know you're dying to.'

Alvarez picked up his phone and as usual when he was in work mode, he was instantly absorbed, everything else ceased to exist.

I wandered up the stairs, studying the drawings and watercolours lining the walls. The bathroom was immaculate, with stripped boards and a roll-top bath big enough to swim in. But if I'm completely honest it was the bedrooms I was most interested in. The first was much plainer than the rest of the house. The pale walls were blank, no mirrors or ornaments. It must have been Alvarez's room, because it smelled of him, and it looked lived in. Paperbacks and a radio were stacked on the bedside table, a clutter of shoes piled in the corner. The one space Luisa hadn't got round to decorating.

At first I thought the next room was locked. When I twisted the handle nothing happened. But when I tried again, the door finally creaked open. I switched on the light and blinked rapidly, not quite trusting my eyes. It had to be the room Alvarez had shared with his wife, but it looked like a museum piece. The bedding had been flung back, as though they had just got up. A woman's clothes were draped across an armchair, two bathrobes hanging behind the door, a vase of dead chrysanthemums gathering dust by the window. Maybe that was why the air smelled stale: the windows had been closed for months. He must have walked out of the room on the day she died and not gone back. No wonder the lock was stiff. I couldn't resist pulling open one of the wardrobe doors. It was still crammed with dresses, shoes and handbags. She was a size eight, even smaller than me. I pulled the door shut gently when I left the room, as if she was inside, taking a nap. For a second Morris Cley came into my mind, terrified of spending another night in his mother's house, surrounded by ghosts.

There's no word in the dictionary to describe jealousy of a dead person. I stood on the landing with my arms crossed, waiting for it to pass. Luisa was impossible to compete with, because she was perfectible. By now her memory had been airbrushed and polished; no faults would have survived.

Alvarez's voice drifted up the stairs, grave and insistent. I knew I should run back down and thank him for helping me search for Lola, but all I wanted was to escape to the simplicity of the hotel. A flight of stairs led up to another landing, but the urge to explore had vanished. I didn't want to uncover any more secrets, so I went downstairs and waited in the living room. The logs Alvarez had thrown on the fire were beginning to catch. When he finally joined me he was carrying another bottle of wine.

'That's all we can do for tonight,' he said. 'A team are working on it. It'll be on the news first thing tomorrow.'

I couldn't frame the words to thank him, so I reached over and kissed him instead. For some reason I wanted to confess about my foray upstairs, but when I told him about looking in the bedroom his body tensed, as though one of us had done something wrong.

'I'd feel the same,' I said quietly. 'I couldn't throw anything away.'

He stared at the fire. 'It's hard to start, that's all. I know I should have done something about it by now. I take off my wedding ring, but it always ends up back on my finger.'

I rested my hand on his chest, his heartbeat pulsing under my palm. When I looked down he was tugging at his wedding ring, sliding it from his finger. He placed it in the middle of the coffee table, a small chunk of metal, reflecting the yellow light from the fire.

'That's a start, I suppose,' he murmured.

'It is. But I hope you didn't do it for me.'

His eyes were as black and unreadable as ever, but the start of a smile twitched at the corners of his mouth. After he took off the ring it felt different when he held me, more relaxed, like a ghost had finally left the room.

We didn't make it upstairs, in fact, we didn't even try. The first time was incredibly quick – my fault, not his. He kept his eyes locked on to mine as he ran his hand along my thigh. I took a long in-drawn breath and watched him take off his shirt. His chest was a solid pack of muscle, no spare flesh in sight. Then he knelt in front of me, never taking his eyes from my face. He pushed my dress up around my waist, dipped his head down to kiss me. I came almost as soon as he was inside me. It must have been the tension, or the long wait, or the fact that I wanted him so badly.

'Sorry,' I murmured.

'Nothing to be sorry for.'

He brushed my hair back so he could see me again. His expression was impossible to understand. I thought I saw a spectrum of feelings there: desire, fear and pity, but that could have been imaginary. He carried on moving inside me. Normally I would have hated that, but this time it was different, a rollercoaster, rising and falling like panic. I don't know how many times I lost control. Pretty soon I stopped counting.

And then his breathing changed and his rhythm. I felt him start to let go and that's when I realised something was wrong. There was a look of disgust on his face, as if we had done something unforgivable.

35

I turned my head away to avoid seeing his distress. My own reaction was the opposite of his, a mixture of jubilation and relief. All I wanted to do was to curl up beside him, fall asleep in his arms.

When I woke up again, he'd disappeared. Maybe I should have climbed the stairs to search for him. He was probably sitting in his spartan room, head in his hands, punishing himself for cheating on his wife's ghost. But I couldn't face hearing him explain that it had happened too early, we couldn't see each other again. I kept on remembering his expression after we'd made love, completely blank until the shame set in. Sleeping with me certainly hadn't taught him how to smile. I pulled my dress back on and gathered my things, desperate to leave. If he didn't want me, there was no reason to stay. I lifted my coat from the hook in the hall. The house stayed silent as I left, holding its breath, and the front door seemed eager to shut behind me.

I stumbled down the steps, determined not to cry. I was hoping Alvarez would have a change of heart and come running after me, but there was no sign of him, even though I stopped to look back several times. It was 3 a.m. and Kemerton Road was still pitch dark, almost completely deserted. A lone car drove past, slowing to take a look at me before speeding on again. I was just about to call a taxi when my phone vibrated against my hip. The last thing I remember is a sense of relief. Maybe I had overreacted, and Alvarez was texting me, begging me to come back. My hand slipped into my pocket and then heat scorched the base of my skull. There was a shattering noise, like a plate landing on a stone floor, then all I remember is sound. A car door slamming and a squeal of tyres struggling to grip the icy road.

It was difficult to stay awake, even though it was freezing cold. I couldn't figure out what had happened. Maybe I'd found my way home, and now I was lying on the floor by an open window. When I came round, I was back in my usual nightmare, trapped in the dark, unable to move or breathe. There was nothing to navigate by, no landmarks except a solid wall of darkness. I tried all the usual tricks, counting to ten, reassuring myself that nothing bad could happen. But this time I didn't come rushing to the surface with a dry mouth, heart racing. This time the nightmare refused to stop. There was something wrong with my body. Perhaps I'd had a stroke. I couldn't see or move anything except my mind.

It was hard to decide where the pain was coming from. It was flowing through my body, affecting every joint. But it was worst at the base of my spine and the back of my head. It felt like I had fallen and bumped my way down a long flight of stairs. Even with my eyes open, I couldn't see anything. My eyelashes scratched against fabric. I was wide awake by now, struggling to breathe. My mouth was packed with something bitter that my tongue couldn't shift, dry and rough as straw.

And that's when I realised what had happened. I would be like the Crossbones girl. This time it would be someone else's turn to pull back the plastic sheet and count my scars. A wave of panic crashed over me, as tall as a house, pushing me under, no matter how hard I tried to stay afloat. All I could do was writhe like a line-caught fish.

My first reaction was rage. It was my own fault. I should have called a taxi from Alvarez's house, or forced him to drive me back to the hotel. God knows how long I'd been unconscious. Hours or days could have passed. I tried to sew the pieces together in my mind. Someone must have followed me to Alvarez's house. Maybe he hid in the shadows and saw us making love through the ground-floor window. He must have crept up behind me and knocked me out while I fumbled for my phone. Alvarez wouldn't have a clue what had happened. He was probably still wide awake, staring at the ceiling, trying to forgive himself.

My mind went into overdrive. For some reason it was Michelle's ruined face that loomed in front of me. I could see every incision, a latticework of neat cuts from a razor or a scalpel, blood congealing on her cheeks and forehead. And it would be my turn next. Suddenly it was impossible to breathe. The gag was blocking my airflow, bile filling my mouth. I kept listening for his footsteps, but the only sound was an impenetrable silence. He must have buried me somewhere deep underground. Maybe I would suffocate before he came back, deny him the pleasure of cutting me to pieces.

I lashed out in panic, but my ankles were bound together, and a rope had been tied around my wrists so tightly that it chafed my skin whenever I moved. If I swung my hands upwards they hit a solid wall of wood, locked or weighted in place. There was no give in it, no chance of shifting the lid, even if I kicked like a mule. I lay on my side and reached out again. My fingertips grazed another wall, rough and splintered like unsanded floorboards. I was locked in a wooden crate, two or three times as big as a coffin, and the only escape tool at my disposal was my mind. I tried to slow my ragged breathing but it was impossible. If I hyperventilated I would pass out, and that's how he would find me, unconscious and easy to hurt.

When you can't move or speak or see, everything is intensified, and time plays tricks on you too, shifting like the slide on a trombone. I don't know how long it took me to fall back into the past. Something kept dragging me there. The smell of stale air, dust and the chemical scent of fear.

Suddenly I was watching my father take his first drink of the day, as soon as he got home. He chose the worst booze he could find, cooking sherry or the cheapest wine, because the taste didn't matter. He wasn't drinking for pleasure. It was anaesthetic. Memories rushed at me from the corners of the box. My father's swagger when he was drunk. A small man, looking for someone smaller to punish. On Sundays he dragged us all to church, kept his head bowed through the service, wiping the slate clean. But the cycle started again as soon as we got home. And my mother became a monster too. She shrieked at him every morning, until it was his turn to yell. He chose my mother or me to empty his disgust on.

My brother was always his audience. That must have been why Will felt at home with the Bensons. It was more extreme, but he recognised the dynamic immediately. Two monsters destroying everything they saw. Cheryl Martin said that Will was the Bensons' right-hand man, so Christ knows what he'd seen. Until now I'd refused to imagine him leaning against the wall, watching the girls beg for mercy, calling for their mothers. Maybe he stood beside Marie afterwards, helping her to wrap their bodies in black polythene. A wave of nausea lurched in my stomach and I forced my mind back into the present.

My back throbbed, but at least my legs still worked. I pressed my feet against one of the wooden walls and pushed with all my might, but there was no movement. When I lay still, thoughts flew at me. There was no way to escape them. I realised that Lola must be dead. He had emptied the box to make room for me, so he had already killed her. Her body probably hadn't even been found. She would be lying on open ground somewhere, with nothing covering her wounds. Lola would have been glad about what happened next, because she always said that I needed to let go. After years without breaking down, I cried until my blindfold was soaked.

The footsteps came from a long distance away, slow and deliberate. He was making his way down a long corridor, and I began to understand what people meant when they talked about being paralysed with fear. My fingers were numb, a prickling feeling tingled across my lips as I struggled to breathe. My heart rate doubled, then tripled while he fiddled with the catches on the box. And then the lid slid back. I couldn't see much, but it must have been daytime. A blur of light filtered through the blindfold.

He grabbed my shoulders and jerked me upwards, the pain in my head so blinding that I almost passed out. I winced as he touched my face and pulled the gag from my mouth. His smell was the most frightening thing. There was nothing human about it, just an overpowering stink of ammonia, as if he'd bathed himself in bleach. My throat was so dry that I couldn't make a sound. Something hard touched my lips, clattering against my teeth. He was forcing me to drink. I managed to gulp down some of the water, but the rest spilled across my chest. He was in a hurry, pouring liquid into my mouth faster than I could swallow, panting, as if he'd overexerted himself. I twisted my face out of his hands.

'Slow down. Unless you want me to choke.'

His breathing changed. Maybe he was suppressing a laugh. He wasn't used to his victims telling him what to do. Then the footsteps again, and metal rattling against wood. When he lifted me I heard the fabric of my dress catch and tear on something. A cold rim of metal bit into my hip. I didn't understand at first, then I realised he had sat me on a bucket. He was moving around a few feet away, waiting for me to empty my bladder. Maybe he was tired of cleaning the box between each girl.

'You could say something, you know,' I muttered. 'What are you frightened of?'

The punch came out of nowhere. It landed on my jaw, hard enough to send me reeling. No time to put my arm out to soften my fall, my bound hands hanging in front of me like a dead weight. My blindfold rode up when I hit the floor. In the few seconds before he pulled the fabric tight again, I saw more than I wanted to. Black tiles on the floor and directly in front of my eyes, all his tools, laid out on a green towel. They were arranged by size, from the smallest scalpel to a butcher's saw, perfect for slicing through bone. He picked me up and dumped me on the bucket again. This time I was too terrified to argue.

After he replaced the gag, he hauled me back into the box, dropping me like a rag doll he'd grown tired of. My hip took the impact this time, as I landed on the bare wood. No wonder all his victims were covered in bruises. Bolts clicked into place above my head.

I tried to stop myself shaking, teeth chattering uncontrollably against my gag. If I listened hard, I might learn where he was keeping me. It was best not to think about his knives, arranged with an obsessive attention to detail.

Then the answer dawned on me, and there was so much evidence that it had to be true. I knew who he was. He had organised his instruments in the precise, methodical way that surgeons do before an operation. It had to be Sean. Of course it was. He cut people for a living, and he knew precisely how pain worked. It was his speciality. And it wouldn't have been hard to learn more about how the Bensons carried out their crimes. Something about their brutality must have excited him. Maybe he knew the surgeon who patched up Cheryl Martin's wounds and pumped him for information over a drink, pretending to be sympathetic.

Until he met me he was everyone's golden boy; handsome, talented, top in every exam. No one had ever refused him anything before. Rejection must have been more than he could take. I remembered the look in his eyes when I told him it was over. Disbelief mixed with fury, as if he couldn't decide whether to punch me or walk away. That was why he washed in bleach, to disguise his smell, so I wouldn't recognise him. I could still hear him, shuffling around, putting things straight in his empire. He must have hired a basement or a lock-up. Knowing Sean he would have been clever about it and found a remote location. Even if I managed to bite through my gag, it would be pointless to scream.

36

The next thing I heard was unexpected. A woman's voice, shrill with fear.

'No, please. Not again. Let me go.'

It was a weakened version of the original. Exhaustion and terror had knocked the music out of it, but the voice itself was unmistakable. It was definitely Lola. I shouted her name but nothing came out, just a dull squeal, deadened by my mouthful of rags. So I drummed my bare heels against the side of the box instead. At least she would know she wasn't alone.

'You fucking bastard, get your hands off me!'

Her yell was loud enough to penetrate the thick wood, and it was a relief to know she hadn't lost her fight. Then her voice fell silent. Maybe he was forcing her to drink, tipping icy water into her mouth quicker than she could swallow. After a few minutes I heard her speak again.

'Why don't you talk to me? Don't do that, please.'

Begging obviously didn't work, because after that her speech was muffled. He must have replaced the gag immediately. What I heard then was much worse than listening to her plead. Even the gag couldn't stifle it. A long-drawn-out wail, followed by a string of muffled cries. I clenched my fists. He was cutting her, and all I could do was pray that it wasn't her face. I pictured her pale cat-like eyes, and the mile-wide smile that sent men weak at the knees.

There was a scraping sound, then the thud of her body landing in the box next to mine. The lid slammed shut, and his slow footsteps grew fainter as he walked away. The whole process had taken minutes. He had forced water down our throats, like animals in a laboratory, and left his mark on Lola's skin. It made sense that Sean would act fast. He never slowed down – long hours at the hospital, then squash or football, out somewhere almost every night.

I thumped my bound hands against the wood three times and waited, but there was no sound. Maybe Lola was in too much pain to move. Her reply came back after what felt like hours, three soft taps. She knew we were lying side by side. Without the cages between us we would have been close enough to hold hands. I was still struggling to make sense of it. Maybe there were more of us. The room could be lined with outsized coffins, each one containing a woman, desperate to stay alive.

At least my claustrophobia had disappeared, because I had discovered worse things to worry about than confined spaces. It's amazing how terror puts a phobia in its place. Most claustrophobics would benefit from a few hours inside a sealed box, but I'm not sure the NHS would sign up to such a radical cure. It may sound strange, but before long I fell asleep. My mind was so busy keeping itself intact that I didn't even have nightmares. I dreamed of the best holiday I ever had, in Greece with Will and Lola when we finished university. In the dream I was diving from the side of the speedboat we hired for the day. Diving and surfacing, over and over, the sun blessing my face each time I came up for air. For a few seconds my body was at ease when I woke up, as if I'd spent the day sunbathing.

My waking thoughts were harder to cope with. The person I wanted most was Alvarez. By now he would be going mad with worry, his frown line getting deeper by the minute. I searched my mind for something comforting to latch on to, but there was nothing there. Memories flashed past my eyes like snapshots in a photo album. The first was of my father, when I was twelve years old. I thought I was the first person home, but a faint scratching noise came from the kitchen. I assumed the cat was pleading to be let in, but I found my father lying on the black and white tiles, still wearing his suit and highly polished shoes. His lips were moving, but no words came out; his eyes were wide, as though he had witnessed miracles. I must have been a well-trained child, because I dialled 999, but something prevented me from kneeling down to comfort him. I kept watch from the doorway until the ambulance arrived. Habit had taught me to keep my distance.

The next snapshot was of my mother, admiring herself in the hall mirror. Life got easier for her after my father's stroke. It silenced him permanently, and his pension from the tax office paid for a live-in carer. There was even a little left over, so she could indulge her passion for clothes. My father had only enough strength left to lift himself in and out of his wheelchair. And he couldn't even drink his way to oblivion, because my mother made sure the house was dry. His silence left her free to be as vicious as she liked. And it was my brother who suffered most, because he was the brilliant one.

The last picture was of Will, clutching an envelope, too scared to open it. My mother had chivvied and bullied him to the top of his class, but when his A-level results arrived he was paralysed. She grabbed the envelope from his hand. Maybe she believed his success was rightfully hers.

The box filled with anger. I held silent conversations with my dead father, asked him how he could forgive himself. I attacked my mother too, for the pressure she put on Will until he lost his way. But I kept most of the rage for myself. I had gone into relationships in bad faith, and the longer they lasted, the more damage was done. Maybe none of this would have happened if I'd steered clear of Sean. He had killed the girl at Crossbones just before we split up, but I'd been withdrawing from him for weeks. He'd seen the writing on the wall, decided to take out his rage on any woman who crossed his path. I was the reason why three women had died, and Lola was trapped in her makeshift coffin.

I should have been grateful that my anger finally came to the surface. It gave me the energy to work for hours on the ropes around my wrists, tugging at the knots with my teeth. They refused to come undone, but at least the ties loosened and my fingers could move again, the blood flowing more easily. I had more success with the blindfold, rubbing my head against the rough wood. At first all I got was a scalp full of splinters, but gradually it began to give. The material slid back from my eyes by a fraction and I could see light leaking through narrow cracks in the box. When the footsteps came again I knew what to expect. My whole body was trembling, but if I did nothing Lola and I would end up like Michelle, our skin slashed to ribbons.

I held my breath as he fiddled with the bolt above my head, imagining a river coursing through a valley, washing away cars and trees and houses, strong enough to clear every object from its path. Maybe he inhaled the stored-up rage when he opened the box. It weakened him for a moment, like a cloud of gas. When he leaned down to grab hold of my arm, I caught his bitter reek of ammonia. I thought of the Crossbones girl, so far from her own country, and Cheryl Martin wishing she had fought back when she had the chance. The trouble was, I had no idea how to begin, and I wasn't exactly a match for him, with my wrists tied. My bruised back thumped against the rim of the box.

When he'd settled me on the chair, I heard him moving around. I tried to guess how far I could jump with my ankles bound. He forced the metal cup against my lip. The water was warm this time, sour and slightly gritty. God knows what he'd doctored it with. Sedatives probably, stolen from the hospital supplies. The liquid ran from my mouth, just a few drops reaching my throat, and all I could hear was his laboured breathing as he forced my jaw open with his hand. My heart drummed painfully against my ribcage. Air stuck in my throat as I remembered the jagged wound on Suzanne Wilkes's neck as she gazed up from the pavement. I jerked my head free and managed to spit out a few words.

'I know it's you. The bleach doesn't work, I can still smell you.'

The idea that he had been recognised stopped him in his tracks for a second. And then he did exactly what I hoped. He lashed out. But this time I took my chance, knowing it could be my last. When his hand made contact with my face I bit down as hard as I could. My teeth locked on to bone, and my mouth flooded with the acrid taste of bleach. He gave an outraged moan, and tried to wrench his hand away, but I took a final deep bite and heard the snap of a bone breaking.

There was a moment's grace while he nursed his wound. It gave me time to push back my blindfold, jump away and grab a knife from his collection on the floor. When he came at me again, I raised my bound hands above my head then plunged them down with all my strength. I couldn't see properly with the blindfold falling back over my eyes, but I aimed at his face. Only his outline was clear, because he was wearing a balaclava, but I was lucky. The knife found its target. I forced it home and twisted the handle. His low inhuman moan was the sound that cattle make when they're being branded. He slumped to the floor, face first.

I don't know how long I stood there, doing nothing, watching the circle of blood grow wider, the knife still dangling from my hand.

And then I heard the tapping. I pushed my blindfold back, as far as it would go. In the dim light the boxes looked innocent enough. Four of them. Each one six feet long, less than three feet high. The type of rough wooden storage boxes you might use in your garden for storing logs or coal. My heart bumped unevenly as I opened the one next to mine. I didn't want to see what he'd done to Lola. When I prised the lid away, it was her back that I saw first, a raw mess of blood and bruises. But at least she was alive. Maybe I imagined it, but when she twisted around I saw the edges of her smile above the filthy gag he'd stuffed in her mouth. I tried to think of something comforting to say, but a mixture of shock and relief had stolen my breath.

Lola's skin was chalk white, with angry purple bruises all over her shoulders. But at least her face was intact, not a cut in sight. Sooner or later she would be able to answer questions, but in the meantime she was cold and naked, gibbering with shock. I picked up one of the small blades from the floor and began to cut the rope around her hands. Her wrists were raw where she had struggled to undo the knots, but as soon as I had freed her she was calm enough to return the favour. A bleach-stained towel was all I could find to drape around her shoulders. She still couldn't speak. She just slumped on the chair where he had made us sit, staring down at his body.

I peered under the lids of the other two boxes. Fortunately they were empty. He must have been planning a production line, but he ran out of time.

I was worried we might never get out, remembering Ray Benson's love of combination locks. It would be ironic if I had fought back, only to find there was no escape route. My heart battered against my ribs like a jackhammer, but I was still insulated by a thick layer of shock, numbing me as effectively as morphine. At that point it didn't register that I'd killed a man. I had no desire to check that it was Sean. I didn't want to pull back his balaclava and witness the damage to his ridiculously handsome face. All I had to focus on was finding a way out for Lola. It was my responsibility to get her to safety, but the door refused to open. It was like a scene from my favourite nightmare, every exit sealed, with no chance of breaking free.

I stared at the body lying on the floor. He was wearing plain blue overalls, and the keys must have been in his pocket, but I couldn't bring myself to go near him, let alone rifle through his pockets. So I tried the window instead. It was a standard wooden sash, filled with frosted glass, but it had been screwed shut. I looked around for something to smash it with, but the room was as empty and clinical as an operating theatre. Apart from the boxes and knives there was only a sink, two straight-backed wooden chairs, and the tin cup he made us drink from. I picked up one of the chairs and swung it at the window with all my strength. The shattering noise was satisfying. It would have been a pleasure to smash a dozen more while the adrenalin was still pumping.

For some reason I felt sure we were in a basement. If he was a true follower of the Bensons, he would have made a replica of the dungeon Ray spent months building. But when I stared out of the jagged hole in the glass, the drop was alarming. We were several storeys above ground. In the darkness it was hard to see exactly what lay below, but I could make out a drift of trees and a concrete path. There was no chance of lowering ourselves gently to the ground like Rapunzel without breaking our necks.

I was about to return my attention to the door, when I heard Lola say something.

'He's moving,' she muttered.

When I turned round the man's body was stirring. And then things went into fast-forward; he was crawling towards the knives, leaving a smear of blood on the black tiles.

'Get him!' Lola shouted.

But for some reason I couldn't move, still cosy in my bubble of shock, unable to react to danger.

Lola pushed me out of the way, just as his fingers closed on one of the largest knives in his collection, and then there was the sound of wood splintering. She brought the chair down on his head again, and he stopped moving. She was about to smash it down a third time, but I grabbed her arm.

'Who the fuck is he anyway?' Tears were coursing down her face.

Before I could stop her, she leaned down and pulled off his balaclava. I heard her gasp and then looked down. What I saw didn't make sense. The knife had sliced through his lower lip, dividing it neatly in two, exposing a line of perfect white teeth. Blood was still gushing from the wounds inside his mouth, and Lola had smashed his nose to a pulp. Between us we had made a mess of his matinée-idol face. But I knew that somewhere under the layer of blood I would find his familiar frown.

'It's the Spanish thug, isn't it?' Lola rasped.

'Ben.'

I heard myself repeat his name, then everything went quiet.

37

I was unconscious when the police battered down the door. When I came round I was lying on a stretcher, being carried down through Alvarez's house. It still looked immaculate, like a set of illustrations for *Ideal Home*. I caught a glimpse of the sofa in the living room and remembered the way he had looked at me when he took off his wedding ring. For a second my vision blurred. It was impossible to work out what was true and what was imaginary. But by the time we got outside Lola was beside me, looking indisputably real. When they put us in the ambulance she lay on her front, tears dripping from her eyes, as though someone had forgotten to turn off a tap. A paramedic was working on her back, swabbing away dirt and blood, surveying the damage. Three ragged crosses had been carved into her skin, at the base of her spine. I reached out and gripped her hand.

For some reason when we got to Guy's, I refused to be carried.

'Don't touch me,' I snapped at the man bending over me. 'Keep your fucking hands off me.'

'It's okay, love. You're safe now.' His face grew small then expanded again, like I was observing him through a broken telescope.

I don't remember much of what happened next, but I must have been taken for an X-ray, and someone sewed ten neat stitches at the base of my skull. The blood was washed from my matted hair. A neurologist I vaguely recognised shone a torch into my eyes and talked about concussion. He handled my head so gently when he examined me that I could have wept. After that my body shut down for a while. People kept on arriving and leaving, but I was too exhausted to keep my eyes open. Hari stole into my room to deposit a box of chocolates on my bedside table. He left me with one of his radiant smiles then tiptoed away again. Someone else must have visited too, because a vase of tiger lilies materialised on the windowsill.

Burns appeared just as I was waking up. His moon-like face hovered over me, the mattress tipping dangerously when he sat down. His skin was even greyer than normal, and I wanted to tell him to go home, take a beta blocker, wait for his blood pressure to come down, but he wouldn't meet my eye.

'I don't know what to say, Alice,' he stuttered. 'How can I apologise?' His small eyes were bright pink, still glossy with amazement. Maybe he'd spent the morning weeping in his office, behind a locked door. 'He never missed a day's work. Only Angie sussed it. She reckoned Ben was behaving strangely, and he was the one person you were in contact with the whole time.'

At least Angie would get the promotion she deserved. 'How did she know?'

'She saw you give him a letter at the hotel, but he never logged it as evidence. He must have binned it. And she clocked that your brother panicked every time Ben came into the room. It was the trips to Rampton that got her really worried.'

'What do you mean?' My voice sounded groggy and unfamiliar.

Burns took off his glasses and polished them against his shirt. 'When Angie phoned to book your visit with Marie, they asked if Ben would be dropping in again. Turns out he saw her at least once a month over the past year. Police business, he said.'

I closed my eyes. That explained Marie Benson's certainty that she would see Alvarez again, like a moth to a flame. I had watched her primping her hair, blindly flirting with him. A wave of nausea welled up in my throat. Hard to tell if it was the result of concussion or an overload of unwelcome thoughts.

'So it was him who sent the notes?' I asked.

Burns gave a miserable nod. 'We found scraps of paper at his house, little reminders, planning it all out. He knew Will was your brother from the start. He'd been keeping tabs on people who went through the hostel.' He kept his eyes fixed on the floor. 'For what it's worth, Alice, you were the only one he cared about. He could have taken you any time if he'd wanted to. Maybe he thought you could save him.' Burns's small mouth clamped shut, as though he'd lost faith in the power of speech.

'Except I didn't notice he needed saving.'

Burns studied his hands, clenched together in his lap.

'What's wrong?' I asked.

'It's my fault, Alice.' He took a minute to collect himself. 'He heard Ray Benson's confession, all that evil shit, all night long. Then Luisa died. I reckon that's when he snapped, but I didn't spot the signs. He'd been storing it up, all that time.'

I couldn't think of a way to comfort him so I rested my hand on his, gathering strength to ask the question that kept nagging at me.

'Is he alive?'

'Just.' Burns studied the floor. 'They couldn't save his tongue though.'

God knows why I chose that moment to break down, after everything that had happened. Maybe it was the thought that

Alvarez had lost his baritone voice, or that I had been incredibly stupid.

It was a surprise when Burns put his arm round me. I cried until my throat felt raw, and when he stood up to say goodbye there was a large wet patch on the lapel of his jacket. Hauling himself to a vertical position required even more of Burns's strength than usual, and I wondered who he would find to do his legwork now.

After he left I gazed out of the window. The sky was completely blank, no sign of cloud or vapour trails. I kept thinking about Lola. She would need a skin graft, but, knowing her, she would turn the experience into a triumph. As soon as the director knew what had happened she would get her job back. The headlines would describe her as the plucky heroine who overcame an evil madman, high-kicking her way to stardom.

When I woke up, new thoughts kept arriving unannounced, so I hauled myself to the window to look for distractions. It must have been early morning. A couple of nurses were standing on the frosty grass, grabbing a sly fag before going on duty. Then I spotted Sean crossing the quadrangle with his hands in his pockets, striding briskly towards the operating theatre. Maybe it was the familiarity of his walk that made me feel so guilty, or the fact that I knew exactly how he would spend his day: mending people and stitching them together again. I pressed my hand against the window's cold glass for a second then turned away.

The pain in my head throbbed dangerously as I put on my torn dress. I had to sit down, resting unsteadily on the edge of the bed. The objects in the room floated for a few seconds before settling back into place. When I leaned down to find my white hospital slippers the tiled floor rocked up to greet me.

A nurse appeared just as I was making my escape, her grey hair twisted into an unforgiving bun. She had a sour expression. Disapproval seemed to be the only emotion in her repertoire.

'What on earth are you doing? That's a serious head wound, young lady. You should be in bed.' I didn't bother to answer as I stumbled away, but her shrill voice pursued me along the corridor. 'You can't discharge yourself, you're under observation.'

For once it was a relief to get into the lift. At least the metal doors silenced her.

The foyer was packed with people when I arrived, and for some reason I had become weightless. My limbs were light and uncontrollable, like I was wading through a swimming pool. Standing on the corner of Great Maze Pond, I realised that I didn't have a penny to my name. My purse must be lying somewhere in Alvarez's house. The winter air drained the last of my strength. I slumped on the kerb and let my head rest on my knees to stop myself from fainting. When I opened my eyes again a taxi had pulled up beside me. I caught a glimpse of myself in its dark windows. A street urchin in a filthy dress, my forehead a mass of raw bruises. I looked like a poster girl for domestic abuse.

'Are you all right, love?' the taxi driver asked.

'No,' I snapped. The pain at the base of my skull was sharper than ever.

The man didn't bat an eyelid when I confessed to having no money. He lifted me into the back of his cab, because my legs had stopped working. And when we got to Providence Square he didn't just dump me on the pavement, he put his arm round my waist and hauled me up three flights of stairs.

'You deserve a medal,' I told him.

'Karma,' he said. 'Someone'll do the same for me one day.' He jogged back down the stairs, ponytail bouncing. My luck seemed to be changing. The city's one and only Buddhist cabbie had rescued me.

It's hard to describe how it felt to come home. I didn't care that the place was a junkyard, or that the police had ransacked every cupboard. Plates, cups and saucers littered the kitchen table and work surfaces, as though someone had thrown a giant tea party in my absence. But I couldn't begin the marathon task of cleaning up, because someone had turned the room into a fairground ride, the floor tipping from side to side whenever I turned my head. Messages blinked on my answer-machine, and for some reason I propped myself against the wall to listen to them. My mother's voice was cold with rage, informing me that I had missed our fortnightly breakfast meeting, then there were three calls from a persistent double-glazing company. My finger hovered over the delete button when the next message cut in. The familiarity of the deep male voice made me catch my breath.

'Alice, it's Ben. Call me please, when you get this. I need to know you're safe.'

I pressed the repeat button. There it was again, that imitation of genuine concern, like he was the only person who wanted to keep me alive. God knows why he'd called me, when he knew I was at the hotel. He must have been covering his tracks. I should have deleted it, but couldn't bring myself to. Maybe it was because I knew he would never speak again.

A pool of winter sunlight had collected on the settee. I lay down and hugged my knees against my chest, trying not to think about Alvarez. The disbelief still hadn't worn off. It seemed possible that he would appear at any minute, to apologise for his mistakes. But the image of his face when Lola pulled back the balaclava was inescapable. I pictured him alone in his prison cell, unlikely ever to be released. Even with my eyes shut, tears forced themselves between my closed eyelids.

It occurred to me that people sometimes die from unsupervised concussion, but at that point I couldn't have cared less. My brother kept appearing in my mind, unable to move or make sense of all my questions. I stayed awake for as long as possible, but I was lucky. There were no dreams at all. When I woke up, the sun was in a different position. It was midday, and when I checked my phone a whole day had passed. The pain in my head pulsed as I sat up, but it was weaker than before. It no longer felt like an ice pick driving through my skull. I made myself drink a glass of orange juice then phoned for a taxi.

My mother was emerging from Will's room when I arrived at Bermondsey Ward, but I ducked into a doorway just in time to avoid her. She looked the same as always, a paragon of maternal duty, immaculately coiffured and groomed.

Will was wide awake when I opened the door. Apart from his injuries, he looked better than he had in weeks. Someone had washed his tow-coloured hair and the hollows under his cheekbones were less pronounced. There was only a slight tremor in his arm when he stretched out his hand. I perched on the edge of the bed and held on to it without saying anything.

'I'm sorry, Al.' His voice was a dull croak. 'I tried to warn you on the phone.'

'I know you did, sweetheart.'

'He recognised my face.' Will's gaze flickered towards the window. 'I liked him at first, but he kept coming to the van almost every night, asking questions about the hostel.'

'And he gave you the knife?'

Will nodded. 'He borrowed my van one time, then made me go upstairs at his house. I saw the room with the boxes.' He closed his eyes.

'And he told you what he did?'

'Everything.' Will turned his face away. 'He wanted me to help him.'

'And that's why you jumped?'

'Partly. And I think he put something in my drink. I saw angels outside the window . . .' His voice petered out. 'I thought they might save me.'

I squeezed his hand. That must have been why Alvarez screwed the window shut afterwards, to avoid any further accidents. I still couldn't work out why he'd bothered to deliver Will to a place where he would be found. He must have gone into a blind panic when his plan backfired. I studied Will's face. Despite the pain he was in, he was calm for the first time in months. I took a deep breath and prepared my question.

'What happened when you were at the hostel, Will?'

He shifted uncomfortably on the bed. If he could have thrown back the covers and made a dash for it he would have done. 'It's not what you think.'

'No?'

'They treated me like a son at first, gave me my own room.' His face twitched into a smile. 'Marie said I could be part of their family. But after a few months, they wanted more. I saw things there, Al. Stuff you wouldn't believe.'

I pressed his hand between mine, then looked him directly in the eyes. 'Did they make you get involved?'

He shook his head vehemently. 'I had to keep watch, that's all. They wanted to know if anyone at the hostel started talking. Ray said he'd kill me if I ran away.'

I wanted to ask how he'd got sucked into something so evil, but the answer was obvious. It was because he was desperate

306

for a home, and he didn't believe he deserved any better. His illness blurred the boundaries between nightmares and reality. My brother's clutch on my hand loosened, but his gaze remained fixed to the window. Maybe angels were still hovering outside, white feathers fluttering against the glass.

I sat on the chair by his bed, watching him fall asleep, exhausted by so many questions. And then the pieces began to slot into place. My long night of sleep had shifted fragments of information into the correct position. Marie Benson's face appeared in my mind, with its leering, Cheshire cat grin, and I remembered the pattern she had drawn. A five-point star above a rectangle, doodled on every page of the notes her writing tutor had stolen. It reminded me of a poorly drawn compass mark, like the ones I'd seen scribbled in the corners of early maps in the British Museum, the cartographer racing to note down every hill and inlet.

I realised that Marie had been drawing her own map. The reason for the Bensons' kindness to Morris Cley's mother made sense at last. Those dull trips to bingo had a purpose, and the afternoons when Marie drank endless cups of tea in her kitchen while Ray toiled in the garden on Keeton's Road. I pulled my phone from my pocket and Burns answered in seconds.

'Alice, how are you doing?' His accent was veering towards Bermondsey that day, as though he'd finally cut his Scottish roots.

'Never mind that,' I cut in. 'I know where Ray and Marie buried the last five girls.'

'Sorry?'

'Get over to Morris Cley's house and start digging.'

Burns's pen scratched noisily across a piece of paper as I explained where to look. God knows why I hadn't worked it out before. Marie Benson's doodle was a burial map, drawn again and again, before she lost her sight. The rectangle was the Cleys' house, and the five-point star showed the location of each girl's body in the grounds. Ray must have spent hours in the garden, digging his shallow graves. Burns rang off before I could say goodbye, eager to start immediately. A team would start clearing Morris Cley's garden that afternoon. It would take weeks for the ground to be excavated, but at least the girls' parents would get their daughters back. Each of them would get a proper burial.

I glanced across at Will. He was out for the count, his broken body grabbing the energy required to heal itself. I relaxed back into the chair and was drifting into a relieved sleep when the door swung open. The outraged nurse who had tried to stop me leaving had finally caught up with me. Maybe she had spent the last twenty-four hours sprinting from corridor to corridor. Her expression was so sour she must have existed on a diet of grapefruit.

'There you are,' she barked. 'You're coming with me, young lady.'

She marched me back to my room and I was too weak to argue. I let her tuck me into bed, tutting under her breath, but the urge to sleep had passed. I lay there for the whole afternoon, doing my best to keep my mind as empty as the blank winter sky.

EPILOGUE

Lola is waiting for me at Borough tube station. She flings her arms round me as usual, but her mile-wide grin travels across her face a fraction more slowly than before.

'Are you ready for this?' I ask.

'Ready as I'll ever be.'

She looks beautiful today, in a long green dress two shades darker than her eyes. It's April, but the sun's so warm it could almost be summer. We cross the road and retrace the route I took in January, past shop fronts blackened by decades of polluted air.

'Hang on.' Lola stops outside a florist's. Through the glass I watch her chatting to the assistant, deliberating over which flowers to buy. She emerges with two huge bunches of gypsophila, blossoms white and frothy as whipped cream. She hands me one of the bouquets and we make our way to Crossbones Yard. The gates look just the same as when I found the first girl there, wrapped in her plastic shroud, hundreds of tributes tied to the bars. A man in a blue uniform is waiting for us, jangling a heavy set of keys.

He gives us a stern look. 'Ten minutes, ladies, and that's your lot.'

When the gates swing open we walk to the centre of the site. It's thirty metres square, weeds flourishing in every crevice, scraps of newspaper shifting in the wind. I bend down and touch the warm tarmac with the flat of my hand. It's easy to imagine a thousand women lying just below the surface, face up, longing to be released. My breath snags in my throat. When I turn round Lola has made herself comfortable, sitting cross-legged beside her pile of flowers. The man from London Underground stands by the entrance, tapping his foot.

'Ignore him,' Lola says. 'I'd love to see him try to chuck me out.'

'I wouldn't.'

Lola looks about fifteen with the sun on her face, waiting for someone to explain what to do next. 'Do you think we should say a prayer?'

'We can't, Lo. We're not religious.'

She looks disappointed. 'A minute's silence then?'

'That's better.'

She takes off her watch and places it between us. I close my eyes and listen to the city's heartbeat, planes buzzing overhead, reggae drifting from an open window. Lola opens her eyes, as if she's woken from a long sleep.

'Let's go home,' she says. 'The miserable sod can lock up again.' She links her arm through mine and I glance back at the gift we're leaving behind. A cloud of flowers, pale and blameless, fluttering in the breeze.

ACKNOWLEDGEMENTS

I would like to thank the following people, all of whom have given me excellent support and advice: Teresa Chris, Ruth Tross, Hope Dellon, Dave Pescod, Miranda Landgraf, Martin Simmonds, Julian Earwaker, Shirley De Marco, Andrew Burton, Clare Crossman, Helen Johnson, Elizabeth Foy, Jessica Penrose, Melanie Taylor, Digby Beaumont, Andrew Taylor, Manda Scott, Joy Magezis, Bob Biderman, Joanna and Ted Kraus, Mandy Green, Honor Rhodes, David Levy, Sarah Shaw.

You've turned the last page.

But it doesn't have to end there . . .

If you're looking for more first-class, action-packed, nail-biting suspense, join us at **Facebook.com/ MulhollandUncovered** for news, competitions, and behind-the-scenes access to Mulholland Books.

For regular updates about our books and authors as well as what's going on in the world of crime and thrillers, follow us on **Twitter@MulhollandUK**.

There are many more twists to come.

MULHOLLAND:
You never know what's coming around the curve.